THE SMUGGLER'S SPY

Michael Aye

THE SMUGGLER'S SPY

MICHAEL AYE

BITINGDUCK PRESS
ALTADENA, CA

Published by Boson Books
An imprint of Bitingduck Press
ISBN 978-1-68553-022-8
eISBN 978-1-68553-023-5
© 2023 Michael Fowler
For information contact
Bitingduck Press, LLC
Altadena, California
notifications@bitingduckpress.com
http://www.bitingduckpress.com
Cover art by Mike Benton

Author's note
This book is a work of fiction with a historical backdrop. I have taken liberties with historical figures, ships and time frames to blend in with my story. Therefore, this book is not a reflection of actual historical events.

BOOKS BY MICHAEL AYE

THE FIGHTING ANTHONYS SERIES

The Reaper, Book One

H.M.S. SeaWolf, Book Two

Barracuda, Book Three

SeaHorse, Book Four

Peregrine, Book Five

Trident, Book Six

Leopard, Book Seven

Ares, Book Eight

Andalucia, Book Nine

WAR 1812 TRILOGY

War 1812, Remember the Raisin, Book One

War 1812, Battle at Horseshoe Bend, Book Two

War 1812, Battle of New Orleans, Book Three

PYRATE TRILOGY

Pyrate, The Rise of Cooper Cain, Book One

Pyrate, Letter of Marque, Book Two

SMUGGLERS

The Smugglers of Deal, Book One

WESTERNS

The Rise of the Gray Ghost

DEDICATION

To my writing partner and my partner in life. Without you there wouldn't be a manuscript!

To all the loyal readers whose great reviews keep the stories and contracts coming, thank you.

To my writing partner and my partner in life. Without you there wouldn't be a manuscript!

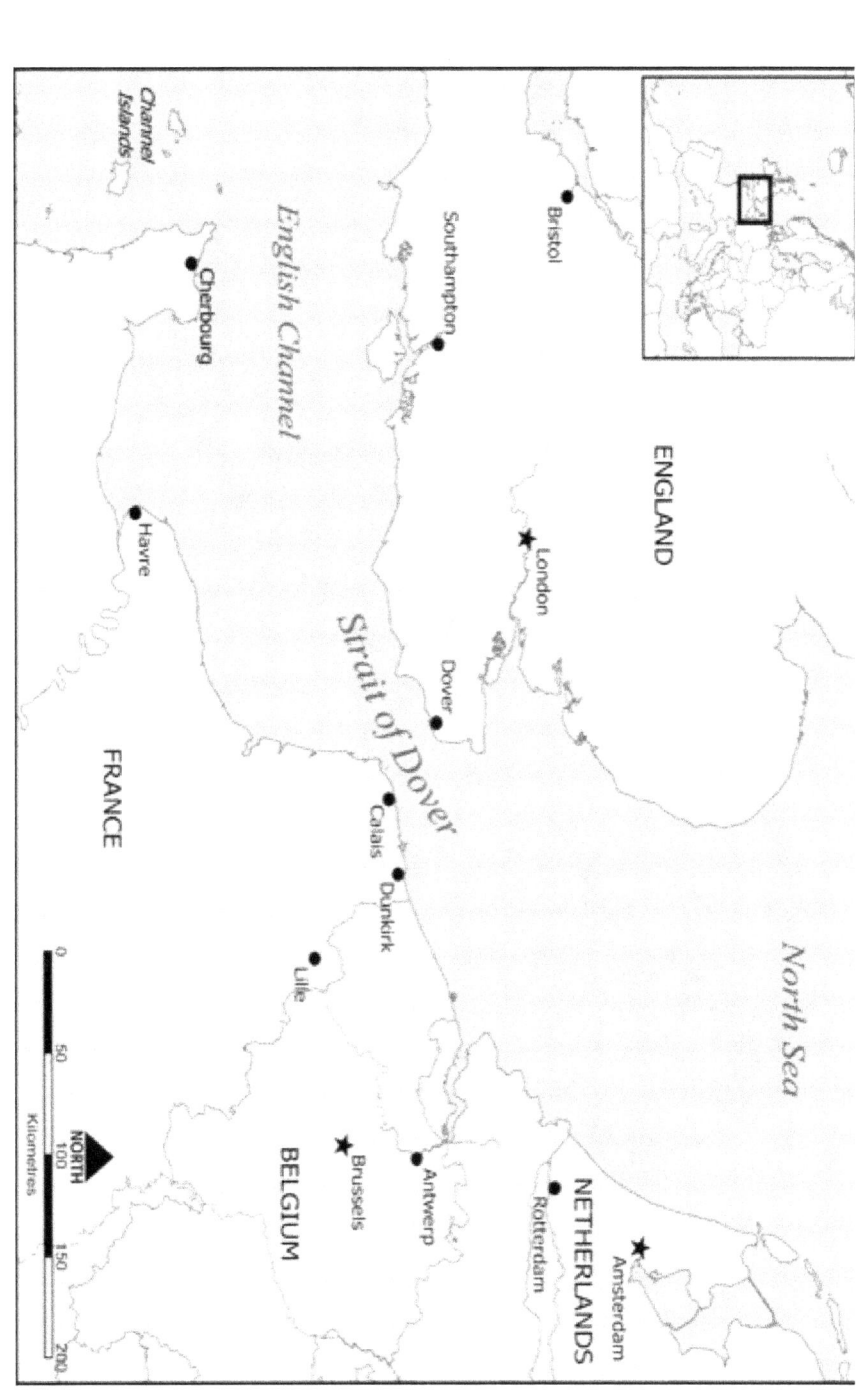

The Smuggler
Captain

The captain calls his mate
Get our spies ready
They'll transfer to a boat
Before we reach the jetty.

The government made a promise
And they gladly pay
If the smuggler hauls their agents
They'd keep the duty men away.

But pray the spies don't talk
If by chance they're taken
The smugglers' lives then forfeit
Madame Guillotine could be waiting.

But what goods a promise
If French cannons sink the ship
Who cares for the women at home
With babies on their hip.

Michael Aye

PROLOGUE

T HE KETCH'S CAPTAIN WAS NERVOUS. *They were to have gotten underway an hour ago. People along the dock at Calais knew that the supplies had been loaded. So why was the ship still tied up alongside the dock? There was no need for it. The captain was not following the standard protocol.*

It was not unusual for the smugglers to cross the channel at night. It was easier to avoid the revenue cutters and Navy ships that sailed the English Channel, especially along the Strait of Dover where the distance between England and France was a little over twenty miles. You could stand on one side and see the other side on a clear day. Since war existed between the two countries now, the job of avoiding the British patrols made it much more difficult. This was known to everyone on the dock. People would soon start to talk and it wouldn't be long before something was said to the soldiers.

A French caporal finally walked over to Captain Edus Clark of the ketch, Dragon Fly. Clark had always had some little gift for the man. "Trouble?" the caporal asked.

"Oui—yes," Clark responded. "Ah, a belle femme—a beautiful woman. My mate, he is amour," Clark said, using his hand to make frustrated gestures.

The caporal smiled. "Bonsoir—good evening."

"When..." Clark let out a sigh. He'd been crazy to agree to bring the passenger, but the gold was hard to turn down. He'd been approached one morning as he walked from his cottage.

The man had called him Captain Clark. He said that he knew Clark was a smuggler, a renowned smuggler. Clark had made several trips in the Dragon Fly. His days as a smuggler were about over. Were he to agree to give passage now and then, he'd never have to worry about the revenue cutters or the duty men. To sweeten the pot, a small sack of gold would be paid by the passenger for each trip. The passenger would always identify himself as a friend of Mary McGregor. He would give the date of sailing also. All Clark had to do was arrange a cargo. With the money he made, plus the gold for passage, obtaining a cargo should not present a problem. It had not been, until tonight.

The passenger was never gone more than an hour from the time they tied up at the dock. It had already been three hours tonight. An hour since the cargo had been loaded. Glancing at his timepiece, Clark realized another quarter of an hour had passed. He'd give him fifteen more minutes and then they'd set sail. All the gold in the world was not worth getting shot or being put in some French prison for some spy from the Foreign Office's Secret Department. He'd never been told who the man was who hired him, but he knew. No one else could make the promises he did. Was he the only smuggler to provide transportation for spies? He was sure that he wasn't. He didn't know any names but he knew that they would never trust the spy network to just one smuggler.

***

JOHN WATSON WATCHED THE DOCK. Where he sat was hot, wedged between two stacks of crates. He was hot, sweating, and he was also bleeding. He looked back behind him. He could see several drops of blood on the planks along the boardwalk. He'd met his man, Henry de LeFleur, who had been the Maitre d'Armes or fencing master until the French Revolution killed all those whose sons would have attended a Salle d'Armes. Henry now passed on as much information as he could obtain, but at some point he had grown careless or maybe trusted the wrong person. They were waiting and when Henry had started his summary the police had entered. How they gloated. And while John didn't catch their every word, he did pick up 'Fouche' would certainly love the arrest. The name struck fear in Henry. He pulled a sword quicker than John would have given the man credit for. Henry ran his blade through two men before they knew what was happening. The third man attacked Henry but John pulled the first of his two pistols and shot him. The police capitaine then shot John in the back. Henry ran his blade through the capitaine's throat, but not before he got off another shot, mortally wounding the old master.

Outside, people had heard the shots. The police capitaine had fallen against the door. His body had to be pushed aside. This gave John time to escape out a rear door. He'd grabbed Henry's cloak and hat to attract less attention. He could hear the crowd now. Were they following his blood trail? If not, they soon would be. It was that obvious. He had to move. He felt the bulge in his coat pocket. He had a small pistol, but was it loaded? Had he even shot it? He cocked the pistol and aimed at a warehouse window just in front of the crowd. He then looked at the Dragon Fly. The captain had just stepped on board and they were leaving the dock.

John aimed at the window just as the crowd came even with it. Bang...Crash.... The crowd stopped with their attention on the shattered glass. John then threw the pistol in the water and took off. He was running as hard as he could but his wound and blood loss had zapped a lot of his strength. The loss of blood made his head swim. He was now at the edge of the dock, and he leaped, giving it all that he could. A shot was fired then. John landed on the deck almost on a man sitting there.

"Grab the tiller," Clark shouted.

The crewman who'd had the tiller was dead, shot in the back. Clark had to make a quick decision. If he didn't come about he'd never be able to return. If he kept going, a guard boat would catch him and he'd spend the rest of his days rotting in a French prison or shot.

The spy started to get up, and Clark ordered, "Stay still. Jones, take his bloody cape off and tie it around Wood's shoulders. Pass his hat over now. Fields, stay down, but when I come about pass our passenger over the side. Run a length of rope through the scupper so he will have something to hold on too. Jones, check Woods' pockets. I don't want anything left there to identify his family. Pass the word."

"Remember Woods had gone to see his chérie," Clark hissed. As the *Dragon Fly* maneuvered up against the dock a sous-lieutenant was there with the caporal. A squad of French infantry was with them, and a crowd was behind the soldiers. Everyone was trying to speak.

The caporal turned and shouted, "Silence." He shouted it again before the crowd quietened down.

The sous-lieutenant spoke to Clark, "Who is that man, Capitaine?"

"He's part of my crew, Lieutenant. Why did you shoot him?"

Disturbed by the capitaine's anger, the lieutenant turned to the corporal. "Non—no." The sous—lieutenant spoke to the crowd in broken English. "Who shot this man?" There was no response, so he asked again. Finally someone said, "He is a spy."

"Fool," the caporal returned. "I've known him for years."

"He was running," someone in the crowd said.

"He'd been to see his chérie," the caporal snapped.

"Was she your daughter?" the sous-lieutenant asked.

"Non—no."

"He shot at us," the crowd said.

Captain Clark shook his head. "He doesn't own a gun."

The caporal stepped on board the ketch and searched Woods, removing everything from his pockets. "No weapon," he said to his officer.

"Where did you last see your spy?" the sous-lieutenant asked.

The crowd was quiet for a minute. "We didn't actually see the spy, but the police officers are dead and Henry de LeFleur is dead with them."

"So, you saw a man running and shot him?" the sous-lieutenant asked. "These men have been coming here for years with the blessings of our country. You have now killed a man running to catch his ship. Mon Colonel will be most unhappy."

The rain had started to come down in huge drops and was splattering the boards. Hopefully, Clark thought if there was any blood on the planks it would be washed away quickly.

"You…you and you," the officer said, pointing out men. "Follow the caporal so he can take your names and where you live."

"Comrade Capitaine," the French officer said, trying to endure himself to Clark. "It is a most unfortunate mistake. Should you wish to make a complaint, you may follow me and tomorrow Mon Colonel will be glad to hear it."

Thunder was heard and the rain was picking up. "This weather will help us slip through the patrol, otherwise I would stay and speak to the colonel," Captain Clark said. "I unfortunately have people waiting on this cargo." You know this already, Clark thought to himself. "I would like for something to be given to the man's family."

"Oui, I will see to that myself."

You'll keep half or more, Clark thought but replied, "Merci –thank you. Bonsoir, Lieutenant."

"Bonsoir, Capitaine."

Once they were away from the docks the spy was pulled back on board the ketch. He'd only been in the water thirty minutes, but he was shaking with the cold. He was taken below and given a full cup of brandy.

"The wound, it's bad, isn't it, Captain?"

"I'm afraid so,"

John nodded, "When my contact comes to check on me, tell him what happened. Tell him that the police came in on us as I was leaving. Tell him also that Henry is dead. Fouche has his men checking on informers. Let him know that Napoleon's contacts and his abilities are rising and he is expected to become the ruler of France." The spy paused and took another swallow of the brandy and then leaned over the small table.

When he didn't move Clark checked the man's pulse. There wasn't one. The spy known as John Watson had run out of luck. It was a dangerous job, the smuggler thought, himself a man who lived with danger.

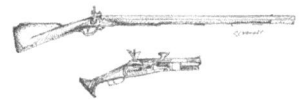

CHAPTER ONE

ORD BICKFORD'S COACH SAT JUST off the waterfront while the army offloaded their cargo from the transport ships in the harbour. Several boat loads of the soldiers had made it ashore. Letters had come to Belcastle some six weeks ago stating that the 10th Royal Hussars, also called Prince of Wales Own Regiment, was expected to return to England. The exact date had not been given as no man can predict the elements.

Catherine and Anne, however, were pleased to wait in Portsmouth until the ships arrived. Lieutenant Cole Buckley and Major Samuel Huntington would be on one of those ships. Major Huntington was Lord Bickford's son-in-law. He was married to the Lord's daughter, Catherine. Lieutenant Cole Buckley was the Lord's ward, and he'd grown up as a brother to his children, Catherine and Phillip.

Phillip had left as a midshipman on board HMS *Diamond*, a thirty-eight gun frigate. He was now acting third lieutenant. One of the ship's lieutenants and two midshipmen had been killed in ship-to-ship battle with a forty-four gun French frigate. The day had ended with twenty-two dead and twice that number wounded, and the French ship sunk. Phillip was now a seasoned officer. He would soon sit for the lieutenant's exam.

The Prince of Wales Regiment had been sent to the Caribbean in 1794, and other than a few minor skirmishes they had not been tested at all. Cole was able to purchase a lieutenant's commission as one of the lieutenants in the regiment had died of the fever.

Anne, Cole's wife, was only too glad that he'd not been in real battle. She knew her husband and if a battle had raged, he'd have been in front of his unit leading his men.

A band started playing and cheer broke out. Someone shouted, "Bakers Light Bobs." Catherine and Anne looked at each other. Smiles creased their faces and they began to clap their hands. Bakers Light Bobs was a nickname for the 10th Regiment. The crowd parted and a colonel riding a magnificent bay horse rode into view. He was flanked by a lieutenant colonel on one side and a regimental flag carrier on the other side. Several officers rode behind him.

"There's Sam," Catherine shouted. "There's Sam."

The next group was captains and then the officers with their own companies.

"Look, there's Cole."

Cole rode just in front of his company. Even though he heard his name shouted, he continued to look forward. He did give a salute with his sword letting Anne know that he heard and saw her.

"What now?" Catherine asked her father.

Lord Bickford was the Earl of Belcastle. The general in charge of the regiment was a friend of the Earl. He had said that the regiment would hold muster before they rode on to London. That would be the time for the earl to speak to the colonel. The general had not traveled to the Caribbean with the regiment.

True to the general's word, once away from the waterfront and nearly outside of town, the regiment stopped at an area of vacant lots. This had undoubtedly been planned as the grass and weeds had been cut and a large awning had been setup.

Once the regiment had reined in and got into formation, the colonel announced, "Officers' call, majors and above in thirty minutes."

Once he rode away, the order to dismount was given. Sergeants took muster and gave it to the lieutenants, who reported to the captains, who then reported to the majors. The majors would give the report to a lieutenant colonel, who was the man who actually ran the regiment.

Cole put his men at ease, and put the sergeant in charge. He then quickly walked to where Lord Bickford's coach was parked. He shook Lord Bickford's hand and gave Catherine a quick kiss on the forehead. He then ran around the coach to his wife.

"Damn I've missed you," Anne hissed after they broke from the kiss.

"I have to hurry," Cole said. Looking at his wife, he spoke as he rushed back to his company. "I love you, darling."

It was a full hour before Major Samuel Huntington could walk to the coach. "I've only a minute," he said. "We will ride to London and tomorrow most of us will be granted leave. I've been told that the colonel would welcome a minute with you, Lord Bickford."

Sam then took Catherine in his arms. After they embraced, Sam escorted Lord Bickford to the colonel.

Colonel John Biddulph stood as Bickford walked up. "Charles... my Lord. God man, it has been years."

Lord Bickford smiled, "Yes, it has."

"Major, would you believe that Lord Bickford was once a daring young captain, with nerves of steel. I was his lieutenant back then."

"You are now a colonel of the Prince's own," Bickford said.

"They had to find some place for an old warrior, my Lord."

"You're not that old, John, and I can still see the steel in your eyes," Bickford replied.

"Thank you for that, my Lord," Colonel Biddulph said. He called to his servant and he poured two glasses of brandy, and then as an afterthought, he poured a third.

"What brings you out, my Lord?" the colonel asked.

"Major Huntington is my son-in-law, Colonel, and Lieutenant Buckley is my ward, more like my son really. His mother raised my children after my wife died."

"Major, why was I not made aware of this?"

Before Sam could speak, Lord Bickford spoke again, "I'd asked the major not to bring it up, Colonel. General Murray was aware of it, as you realize, I'm sure. But I wanted Cole, Lieutenant Buckley, to make it on his own merits."

"I admire you, Lord Bickford. There are too many who use the army to rid themselves of a problem child."

"I can assure you that Cole is far from a problem child. He took it upon himself to ride down a man who'd killed several individuals and made an attempt on his father-in-law, Sir William Brabham, the magistrate of Deal."

"A man who is not afraid to act," the colonel responded. "The major and I will keep our eye on Buckley for you, my Lord."

"Thank you, Colonel, but no special favors."

"Of course not, my Lord," the colonel replied.

Other officers had walked up, so Lord Bickford bid his farewell and departed. The unit soon saddled back up and started to London. As it was over sixty miles the thought was that they'd make camp about halfway and then finish the trip the next day.

THE EARL'S LONDON HOUSE WAS on the west end, where not only many aristocratic landowners lived in sophisticated architecture, but the shops were the most grand that Catherine and Anne had ever visited. Did the earl know what he was doing giving the girls a blank check, along with the coach and a footman, to pick out new gowns for the reception the Prince was giving to welcome home his regiment?

The rumor, circulating at the time, was that George IV would ask his cousin, the Princess Caroline of Brunswick, to marry him. This didn't raise even one eyebrow. The aspect, being so rampant in rumor, was would she allow George IV to keep his mistress, Lady Jersey, in her household. Anne and Catherine wondered if Lady Jersey would be at the reception Friday night. Both girls wanted to see this grandmother who meant so much to the prince. For a moment, Anne thought of the widow, Linda, who had bedded Cole on numerous occasions before he'd married. If she was anything like Linda, she'd turn the heads of more than a few.

A smile creased Anne's face. Wasn't it unusual for a man's former lover to be friends with his wife? Maybe, but Linda had actually written Anne a letter. It was the letter that put them back together.

Catherine picked out a ruby colored gown and Anne one that was sapphire blue. After the gowns were picked out, the lady of the shop said, "I understand your husbands have just returned to England, yes?"

The girls nodded their heads up and down in reply. The shop owner continued, "While these gowns will turn every man's head at the party, I have a few items left that I imported from France before the war."

Anne thought to herself, *Or from a smuggler recently.*

Stepping into an area behind a wall, which had ladies accessories, were the latest French gowns made for the bedchamber. The gowns were made from translucent muslin. The fabric would cling to the body revealing what was beneath.

"It's almost like a chemise," Catherine said, holding a gown to her.

Some of the gowns were cut low with a red lace ribbon around the borders. This was made in such a way that the entire breasts were exposed. Another gown came up to the neck but everything beneath it was exposed. Some of the gowns were floor length, while others only came down to the thigh. Many of the gowns, though, made of the same see through material were of various colors, black, red, peach, and white. All of them with silk ribbons to accent certain areas.

Anne liked a short white gown that had black and red ribbons, while Catherine went for a black long gown with red ribbon and a slit up one side to further expose a leg.

"Do you feel naughty looking at these, Anne?" Catherine whispered.

"Yes, delightfully so." Anne then said, "I saw a picture of a prostitute in a penny novel wearing one where the entire backside was exposed." Cole had said maybe it was so that she could have a relationship and not take off her gown if it was a busy night. She didn't repeat that but shuddered at the thought.

After picking out the surprises for their husbands, Catherine and Anne each decided on three pairs of the new drawers that seemed to be in fashion. These were made of white linen and trimmed in lace. The saleslady had a girl wrap up the drawers and negligées. The gowns would be ready Friday morning. When the lady added up the total, Catherine and Anne almost gasped. The cost of the gowns were only a little more than the drawers and negligées.

Outside the shop, Catherine said, "Damn, that's a lot of money to dress up like some French courtesan to please our husbands."

Anne smiled, "I believe that we could gain the same excitement with our bare arses."

Catherine laughed, "But won't it be fun?"

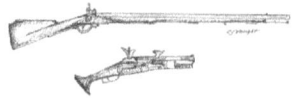

CHAPTER TWO

THE WELCOME-HOME RECEPTION WAS THE grandest thing Anne had ever attended. She made mental notes to tell her mother. Catherine did not seem amazed as Anne, but of course, she'd been raised around royal gatherings. Once the officers of the Royal Hussars arrived, however, all thoughts of who wore what and who was with whom lost their importance. Other than a few brief periods in the past week, Anne had not been with her husband in nearly two years. He was what mattered now...the only thought that mattered. Anne and Catherine weren't the only ones who thought so. The reception hall was full of women who, if given their druthers, would have taken their men and bid the prince and his mistress a fond farewell.

The officers walked in with the colonel leading the way with the British flag and the Regimental colors only a step behind him. A man announced each of the officers by rank. Cole was near the end but was the first lieutenant announced. They gathered in formation and stood while the prince gave a short speech. Then the general said a few words, followed by the colonel. Biddulph kept his words to a minimum, basically telling the officers that they would have a month off before having to report in. They would have to make sure that the company sergeants knew where to reach them should the need arise. He ended his speech saying the Prince was looking for a campaign for the regiment so that they could show all of Britain how the 10th Royal Hussars fought.

Cole thought to himself that the only honorable thing that they'd accomplished, so far, was to return to England with their mounts. The few skirmishes they'd been involved in did little to bring recognition to the regiment.

The formation was dismissed and the officers, their wives, and distinguished guests mingled for nearly an hour. Lord Bickford spent time with his group before a lieutenant colonel came over stating that General Murray would consider it a privilege if the earl would attend him and George. George being George IV, the Prince of Wales.

Lord Bickford kissed Catherine and Anne, and shook Cole and Sam's hand. "We came with two coaches, so feel free to take one and leave when you can."

The dinner that night was the biggest spread any of their group had ever seen. There were soups, oysters and mussels with a white wine; beef, lamb and pork with a red wine; and every vegetable that Cole could think of. The breads were hot and a generous portion of butter or olive oil was offered. Then, there were the desserts, which were too numerous to even try a small portion of each.

"My God," Anne whispered to Cole. "The scraps and leftovers could feed the poor people of Deal for a month."

The royal toast was made by the junior officer present. When they all stood for the toast, Cole could see that the earl was seated at the right hand of the prince.

"What an honor," Anne whispered.

"He probably intends to hit the earl up for a contribution for the regiment," Cole whispered back. I understand that the prince is in debt up to his eyeballs."

"My goodness, and such a feast," Anne replied.

Cole's eyes were feasting on his wife's cleavage. Anne noticed but didn't say anything. Her man, at least, was looking at her unlike some of the officers with their wives. The one colonel was undressing the ladies across from him with his eyes, while his wife, still an attractive woman for her age, had half the men at the table staring at her. Her gown was cut so low that Anne expected a breast to pop out at any second. No wonder the men were looking. Anne thought to herself, *Cole can look at me all he wants to.*

The dinner was finally over and the junior officers were making their departures. Sam came over with Catherine, "Give me fifteen minutes. Field grade officers are expected to say goodnight to the colonel." He looked at Catherine, "It will be much cooler outside if you want to wait at the coach with Cole and Anne."

Catherine winked at Anne, "I'll play the dutiful wife another fifteen minutes."

Cole and Anne departed for the coach. Once they were inside, their lips met. After they broke apart, Anne asked, "Do you like this gown?"

"Of course, but I like what's inside of it even more," Cole replied,

Anne smiled at him, "Wait until you see what I have for you at home."

They kissed again and broke apart when Catherine spoke to the driver in a voice loud enough to warn Cole and Anne that she was about to enter the coach. Cole took his hand from beneath Anne's gown where he'd been holding her leg.

"I'll tell you one thing, Anne Buckley, you smell and feel much better that my horse."

"So, you are comparing me with a nag?"

"No, darling, a beautiful Calvary steed," Cole said.

"I'm glad to know it wasn't just any old nag."

Anne had left instructions with the night maid to have water heated for a bath when they returned. The water was ready and so was Cole. It was all that Anne could do to keep him from ravishing her body in the time they took off their clothes to bathe, driving home her thoughts that her bare butt was all that was needed to entice her man.

She rinsed off and with a towel around her, went behind her dressing screen. Cole finished his bath and dried off. The lantern by the bed was turned down just enough to light up the immediate area.

Cole was lying propped up on two pillows when Anne stepped out. He sat straight up. "Damn," he said and then gave a low whistle.

"You like?" Anne asked, but knew the answer before he spoke. His wedding tackle had answered before he could.

"I've never seen a more beautiful woman. You remind me of a painting of a nymph." He was standing next to Anne now. "No, you are more beautiful than a nymph, you are a goddess."

Cole's hand couldn't help but explore Anne's body beneath the transparent fabric. Their mouths came together, a kiss of burning desire. His lips then went to her neck as his hands caressed her breasts through the thin material. Their first coupling was wild, a frenzy of uncontrolled desires. A burning flame that could only be quenched one way.

After they made love the first time, the negligée came off at some point. Anne didn't count the times their bodies became one, but once they were sated and spent from their passion, they fell into an exhausted sleep.

The sun was high when nature called and they had to get up. Once they were dressed, Cole kissed Anne and asked, "How many of those little ...ah... "

"Negligées," Anne supplied the term for him. "I only bought the one. The cost of that little beauty could feed a poor person for a week."

Cole was surprised. He gave a sigh and said, "It was well worth it."

Once they were downstairs, it was obvious that Sam and Catherine had had a busy night as well. A note had been left by Lord Bickford stating that he expected to be back by noon. If the group wanted to attend the theatre that evening, they could and then leave for Canterbury the next morning. If they didn't desire to go to a play or other event, they could travel halfway that afternoon and stay at a good coaching inn. The earl had a particular one that he stayed at, which was owned by a widow. Cole and Phillip had always felt that the widow provided more than just a room for the earl. Anne had never been to the theatre, but she didn't seem to be overly interested. They'd leave it up to the earl, they decided.

Pastries and a choice of coffee, tea, or cocoa were offered for breakfast. The cook said that the earl had already ordered cold meats, cheeses, and bread for lunch. There were more and more people following Lord Sandwich's route of putting meat and slices of cheese between two pieces of bread. It was even called a sandwich. The earl preferred roast beef to salt beef. He also was likely to apply a little horseradish sauce to his sandwich.

CHAPTER THREE

OLE WOKE UP AND GLANCED over at his wife. They had been home a week and it had been good to see his mother and father. They spent most of the first day looking at horses and new colts. The second day he and Anne rode over most of the estate. Cole had ridden his horse, Apollo. Anne had named the stallion, which had been a gift from his father and the Earl on his eighteenth birthday. Anne was riding an Arabian mare. When the ride was over, Peter and Margaret, Cole's mother and father, and Lord Bickford were at the stable.

"How do you like the mare?" Peter asked.

"She's an absolute joy to ride," Anne replied.

"I'm glad that you like her, seeing how she is now yours," Lord Bickford threw out. "Yes, dear, we knew how much you and Cole liked to ride."

Anne was off the horse and hugging Cole's mother, and then she kissed Cole's dad and Lord Bickford. Lord Bickford flushed as she kissed him. All three of them were smiling at Anne's surprise and her joy.

Anne said, "Outside of Cole, she's the best present that I've ever gotten."

"Me...a present," Cole said.

"Yes...from God," Anne responded.

They wanted to ride to Deal that afternoon. Cole was ready to see how long the trip would take riding horses and not be encumbered with a wagon or coach. He penned a quick note to his sergeant stating they would be in Deal for a week and gave the regiment Anne's parents' address.

***

THE RIDE TO DEAL HAD been pleasant so far. As they reached the oaks that were a resting place for many who traveled in wagons, Cole found himself thinking back on the first time he'd made the trip with his Uncle Angus MacFadyn. It was the beginning of his education about smugglers. He wondered what Sir William, Anne's father and the Magistrate of Deal, would say if he knew that his son-in-law had participated in hauling smuggled goods a few times. He'd never hear it from him though.

"Do you want to rest a bit?" Cole asked Anne.

"No, my mind was on last night," Anne replied.

A report had come in that unfortunately told of the British being defeated in another battle with the French. So far, not a single major battle had been won by Great Britain and her allies. The war news would have been even bleaker, were it not for the Royal Navy. The Navy had done a wonderful job taking or sinking French ships.

Lord Bickford had been adamant in his beliefs that buying commissions for the army was the cause for so many losses. A navy captain for the most part has to prove himself to be the captain of a ship. The true professionals in the army were rarely able to rise above the rank of captain, and only a very few men were promoted to major. Whereas, the upper ranks were filled by men of means, but who didn't have a clue when it came to strategy and deployment of men and assets.

"If we're ever going to win the war, we've got to recognize capable men and put them in leadership roles," Lord Bickford swore. "I'd venture to say that Cole has a better aptitude at soldiering than all of the colonels in the Prince's Regiment."

"Sam knows his job," Cole said.

"There is no doubt that our good major could teach a few soldiers," Lord Bickford agreed.

"I hate to think of you going to war with some old bumbling idiot being in charge," Anne said. Cole reached over and took his wife's hand and held it.

***

SIDNEY WAS OUT FRONT OF the Cock and Bull when Cole and Anne rode up. He gave Anne a hand as she dismounted and then shook Cole's hand.

"It's good to see you again," Sidney said enthusiastically. "Shall I tie the horses out front or put them in the paddock?"

Cole looked at Anne letting her decide. She said, "Put them in the paddock, I've ridden far enough today."

Cole's uncle, hearing the voices, came outside. Seeing Cole, Angus bellowed out, "Florence, be leaving the scullery and come greet yer nephew and his bride. Aye, a beautiful lass she be. Is it home ye be now?" he asked.

"I'm just on leave," Cole responded.

Angus leaned in and whispered, "There's naught been the excitement since ye left, lad. But there is something in the air, I can see it."

Cole knew his uncle meant a landing for the smugglers. Anne had stated in a couple of letters that she'd written to him that there'd been a great deal of bloodshed closer to Dover between the smugglers and duty men. She had even said that her father suspected an alliance between Sir George, who was thought to be the money man behind much of the smuggling, and young Dalton Stephenson. It had been Cole who had killed, or at least caused the death of, Dalton's father.

Joe had written Cole, or at least he'd had Mary Stuart, his fiancée, to write the letter. He stated that Dalton had no ill feelings over the death of his father. Joe, or rather Mary, had said that Dalton had matured and seemed to flourish in his role as head of the house. Cole had to smile at that information. It had to have been Mary who wrote that sentence. He could never see Joe using the word 'flourish'.

Anne had said in a letter that Belinda, Dalton's sister and Anne's friend, was much happier since her father's death. Anne related how Belinda had grown tired of seeing women or young girls debauched. When her father was drunk he was loud and never closed a door, so frequently their carrying on was in full view for Belinda to see. Dalton had told his father that he needed to take his sordid behavior elsewhere. Belinda had said that she cried herself to sleep many a night while her brother held her. Cole was glad that Dalton and his sister no longer had to suffer through such ordeals.

Florence had their cook lay on a fine spread for the evening meal. Afterwards Anne and Florence walked over to Dan Thompson's shop. Angus would be having a birthday in a week so Florence wanted to pick something out of the usual for him.

While the women were away, Cole went out to the front of the tavern with his uncle to restock his cigars and pipe tobacco.

"I see Agnes still rolls a fine cigar," Cole said.

"Aye, her eyes are starting to dim but she rolls more by feel than sight," Angus replied.

The conversation went from one topic to another, how did Cole like the Caribbean, was it fun being in the Army, being a junior officer did Cole get stuck with a lot of foolish details and so on. When Cole told his uncle that he was now a lieutenant and he was no longer the most junior officer, Angus beamed.

"When will ye be making colonel?" Angus asked.

Cole laughed, "I don't know that I ever will."

As they finished up with the cigars and tobacco the evening crowd started coming in. Several of them stopped and spoke to Cole. Back into the tavern itself, Cole started helping Betsy and Chloe. They had come in the back door and both of them gave Cole a big hug.

Betsy's dress was cut so low that it was hard not to see her nipples. "'Tis disgraceful," Chloe said when she caught Cole looking.

"It's why I get double the tips that you do," Betsy responded to Chloe's comments.

"She's near as bad as Peg was," Angus declared. "She does draw a crowd, though."

When it was just the two of them behind the bar, Chloe leaned over Cole in a soft voice, "Have you heard from Phillip lately?"

"It's been a while," Cole admitted. "He was at a place called Gibraltar at the time."

"I think of him often," Chloe said.

"I'm sure that he thinks of you, as well," Cole responded. Phillip probably did think of Chloe, Cole thought, but doubted that it was in the same manner in which she thought of him. His Lordship would have a stroke if Phillip brought home a tavern wench for a bride.

Cole and Anne had talked in detail about Phillip and Chloe, with Anne driving home the point that Chloe was no trollop to be used and cast aside. They were both sure that Phillip and Chloe had sex, but while it was just lust for Phillip, it was love for Chloe. Anne had said that Chloe was going to be heartbroken when she realizes that there will never be a 'them.'

Belinda Stephenson told Anne that one of the young maids who her father dallied with had become pregnant. Stephenson laughed at her when she brought up marriage, so she went out and hanged herself.

"We'll not let Chloe harm herself," Cole said.

Anne looked at him and replied, "You think she'll come tell us her plans, do you?"

Anne's statement hit Cole hard. It was something that he promised himself to discuss with Phillip when next they were together.

Joe came in the tavern at nine that evening. "I heard Angus was having such a hard time bringing in help that he'd hired a poor soldier."

"It would take the training of a good soldier to handle the likes of you," Cole returned as he came from behind the bar. The two friends gave each other a big hug.

They had just sat down at a table when Dalton Stephenson came in. "The whole town is talking about the prodigal son who has returned to his family and friends." The two men shook hands vigorously. *If there were any hard feelings in regards to his father's death, he is damn good at hiding it,* Cole thought.

It proved to be a good homecoming and Cole was in good spirits when he made it to their room. "You've waited on your husband, have you?"

Anne smiled, "I was about to put on my little French outfit and go to the taproom to see if I could draw you away from your friends."

"Nay! Your father would have me up on murder charges. I'd have shot or run through every sod who looked upon you, my dear lady."

Cole had called her negligée her *little French outfit*. "The next time we are in London, buy a dozen of those," he had said.

"Do you remember how much they cost," she had countered.

"Does it matter?" Cole responded. "There's only the two of us right now."

"You really like it, don't you, Cole?"

"Come here, wench, and I'll show you."

Later, Anne whispered to him, "If actions are louder than words, I'd say you liked it."

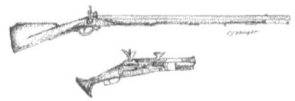

CHAPTER FOUR

SIR WILLIAM, ANNE'S FATHER, HAD reserved a room at the Blue Post Inn as a welcome home dinner for Cole. Captain Letchworth had just come in but before he sat down, he whispered in Sir William's ear. Sir William looked at the captain and shook his head.

After the meal, when the men went outside the inn to smoke, Sir William walked over to Cole. "Captain Letchworth says that a man from the Foreign Office desires you to call upon him at the noon hour, at Deal Castle, upon the morrow."

Cole didn't know what to say. That he was surprised was an understatement. "I've heard the term Foreign Office, but I don't know that I know anything about them," he said.

Anne's father sighed, "I know enough about it to know I don't like it. The secret section is part of the Foreign Office and the way this has come about, I get the feeling that they are involved."

If Sir William Brabham, Magistrate of Deal, didn't like the Foreign Office calling on Cole, then he damned sure didn't like it.

The thoughts of the Foreign Office were still on his mind as he and Anne lay in bed, later that night.

"I've decided on a name… do you hear me Cole?" Anne asked.

"I'm sorry, Anne, what did you say?"

"I said that I've decided on a name."

"A name for what?" Cole asked.

"You haven't paid me a bit of attention," Anne said.

"I'm sorry, love. Please tell me again."

Anne took a breath and gave a sigh. "I've decided on a name for the mare."

Her birthday gift from Cole's parents and Lord Bickford had not been named as of yet. Anne had said that she'd name the horse when the perfect name came to her, something that fit the horse in every way.

Anne had decided that night. "I'm going to name her Pandora." Pandora meant 'all gifts', and was the first mortal woman. Each or all of the Gods gave her something of themselves, both good and bad. So far, the only bad that they'd discovered with the mare was when you put on her saddle blanket, and you were not quick with the saddle, she'd shake it off.

Anne realized that something was on her husband's mind. It was on her father's as well. "What's bothering you?" she asked.

Cole told her about his summons to Deal Castle.

"I wonder what it's all about," Anne said.

"That's two of us…no three of us and by this time it's probably four of us. I'm sure your mother is questioning your father," Cole replied.

✳✳✳

THE RIDE TO DEAL CASTLE was an enjoyable outing. Cole puffed on one of his Uncle Angus' new cigars. It was a thinner cigar and seven inches long compared to Angus' other cigars that were four to five inches long and thicker. It was called a cheroot or China cigar and much different than those from the West Indies.

As Cole neared Deal Castle he was surprised at the changes since he'd last been there. The government had devoted a great amount of men and resources to lessen the coast's vulnerability to a French invasion. New and larger guns sat upon the bastions, ready to use against enemy ships. Cole saw men everywhere and quickly concluded that these were local volunteers.

He spotted Sergeant Duncannon as he drew rein on his horse. Since Cole was in uniform the sergeant came to attention and saluted. The sergeant then shook Cole's hand and said, "It's a fine figure of an officer you now be, lad...er, sir."

Cole smiled, taking no offense at the sergeant's gaffe. "Is Captain Letchworth about, Sergeant?"

The big Irishman stood at attention with a big smile again, fairly beaming with pleasure. "It's captain no longer. Word came in today, it's Major Letchworth ye be seeking. I'll take you to him personally."

Cole followed the sergeant into an office. The captain...now major was holding his new rank badge in his hand. "Congratulations, Major."

"Thank you, Cole. This was my father's, but I dare say it's a bit worse for wear. I think that I'll have to buy new uniforms." Letchworth then winked, "I doubt any British officers' uniforms have been smuggled across the channel."

Cole had to laugh, "I'm sure it could be obtained, given time."

Major Letchworth then got down to business. "There's a gentleman here to see you, Cole. This meeting is to be held in strict confidentiality. You understand?"

"Yes, sir," Cole answered in military fashion, realizing the friendly banter was at an end.

"Follow me then, Lieutenant."

Letchworth led Cole to his quarters. A gentleman in a dark coat was seated there at a table. He appeared to be about forty as his dark hair was starting to turn gray. He was seated so Cole couldn't tell how tall he was...nor did the man rise to greet Cole. The man nodded at Major Letchworth, who turned and left the room. He still had not introduced himself nor put Cole at ease.

"It is my understanding that you are a bright young man with knowledge of the smuggling operation in Deal, and that you, in fact, made a trip to France in one of their craft."

Cole didn't answer as the man had his facts down. There was little use to confirm or deny them.

"I'm well aware of your actions against an assassin before you were commissioned. You are the kind of man that I'm looking for, young and fit. You are more than a capable shot and you can think for yourself."

Cole still had not spoken, and the man continued, "Aren't you curious as to how I came across this information?"

Cole spoke then, "Most of its common knowledge in Deal. The rest is an opinion that you've formed by putting the facts together."

The man smiled and said, "Have a seat, Lieutenant. My name... the name by which you will know me is James Atkins. What conclusion do you make from that comment?"

Cole paused for a moment. "For the sake of secrecy your real name is withheld, possibly to protect your family and because you have more than one person answering to you. These people might know each other but for some reason they are not to know that they report to the same person. This might prove beneficial should they become captured or even to prevent them from comparing notes, as it were."

Atkins smiled, "I was told that you were bright...bright and loyal enough to protect a lady when doing so risked your happiness."

Cole did wonder now who Atkins had been talking to, but again, that incident was common knowledge as well.

"Some would have said that I've acted rather foolishly on occasion, risking my life and my status. In regards to the lady," Cole responded, "any man who wouldn't come forward is a man I would hold in contempt as a man without honor. As for putting my life in danger, I hold my family's lives for more dearly than I do my own."

"The man that was killed was the father to a friend," Atkins said. "Had you known that in advance, would it have made any difference?"

"No, my friend couldn't help who his father was," Cole replied.

Atkins didn't speak for a while. When he did it surprised Cole somewhat. "Do you know we are on the verge of losing this war?"

Cole responded, "I know that things are not great."

Atkins paused again. "I need you, Lieutenant. I need you to help England win this war. Your regiment will not be sent anywhere until we can put the right men in the right positions of leadership."

"How do you know that we aren't going to be sent to France?" Cole asked.

"It would be demoralizing and an embarrassment for the Prince's own to get their arses kicked, that's why I know."

Cole could understand that. "What would you have me do?" Cole asked Atkins.

"We have agents in the field who are much more adept at subterfuge than you, Lieutenant. Your job is to meet with these agents, some of which are men, and the others are women. You will gather their information and return with it to Deal, or wherever we decide, for a rendezvous. At times, you may be sent to bring an agent out and bring them home. In fairness, you need to know the previous agent was shot and killed. Frankly, Cole, I'd much rather be shot and killed than tortured by Johnny Crapaud."

The use of his first name let Cole know that there was a personal side to James Atkins and he was honest. "People get killed in war, but I will endeavor to stay alive to the best of my ability," Cole said.

Atkins smiled, "One last thing. When a secret is shared with someone, it's no longer a secret. We will come up with a story for your family to cover your absences...your regiment will be aware that you've been given an assignment but nothing specific. One last thing. You will be promoted just as you would if you were still with your regiment. Any questions?"

Cole thought for a minute. "How long do you expect this assignment to last?"

Atkins replied, "A year at most." Cole nodded his head. What Atkins didn't say was that he'd not had an agent live more than a year.

"We will be in touch with you, Cole. One more thing. Get rid of the uniform. People need to get used to seeing you as they did before the war began."

"One last question," Cole said. "How will I be contacted?"

"One of two ways," Atkins replied. "Saul, the widow's man, or by Dalton. Neither one knows of the other."

Cole nodded in response. This could play hell with his marriage. He'd have to find a way around that. The only positive thought he had was, *At least Linda will be compensated for her work. God knows she could use the money.*

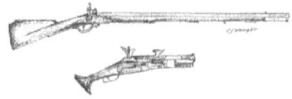

CHAPTER FIVE

OLE WAITED ON THE FAMILY to gather at the evening meal to tell them of his new assignment. What he was going to tell them was not entirely the truth but it rang true. Sir William actually brought the subject up.

"Were you surprised at the changes to Deal Castle, Cole?"

Cole smiled and said, "Yes, sir. There appears to be a great amount of money spent by the government to make the old place look the part of a coastal defense. The volunteers, though, would likely run if a French ship decided to bombard the place."

Sir William smiled at Cole's response. "I thought as much but it gives the home folks a sense of security."

"I met the government official," Cole said, thinking official sounded less hostile than agent. "It seems I will be seconded to the Foreign Office for a year. I will be acting as somewhat of a courier for the office. It seems my knowledge of the area makes me the right candidate."

"You will be home more, then," Anne said excitedly.

"Yes, but when called upon I may have sudden absences with little warning."

"For how long?" Anne asked, not nearly as enthusiastic as she'd been a moment ago.

"I wasn't told that," Cole replied, "but I imagine that it wouldn't be for no more than a few days at a time."

Anne's mother put a spin on things that lightened up the moment. "Just think, dear, except for when Cole is doing his work, he will be right here at home with us every night instead of in London or worse France, or some other faraway place."

Anne was smiling again, "That is wonderful, mother, isn't it?"

Cole was quick to notice that Sir William had said nothing. Had he picked up on Cole's tale as just that, a tale to cover his real activities.

***

SAINT LEONARD WAS PACKED. THE vicar, who was over eighty, still performed the services but the church had sent a younger man to help with some of the vicar's activities. The old vicar still had a good voice, and when he got into a subject that stirred him, it would boom out.

Today's message seemed to be that even though the country was at war, God still reigned above them all. At one point, he used himself as an example. Were it not for God's goodness, he'd hardly have been able to serve the church. It was a moving service and gave Cole reason to think more about heaven and the afterlife than he'd thought on it before. It comes with responsibility he decided.

Once outside the church, Cole saw Saul, Linda's man of all trades. He was in conversation with Sir William's driver, Henry. Seeing Cole, Saul walked over and smiled. He then whispered, "Tomorrow at two o'clock in the afternoon."

Saul, seeing Anne, put on a big smile. "Mrs. Anne, you get more beautiful every time I see you."

Anne smiled back. "How's Ms. Linda?"

Saul answered as he walked on, "She's well, and busy helping Ms. Stuart plan her wedding."

Anne turned to Cole. "Joe's really going to settle down. Do you believe it?"

Cole smiled as well. "Joe's and Mary's ideas of settling down might be two different things."

Sir William smiled. He could have added a thought to the conversation but decided to stay out of it.

After church, Anne and Cole had a leisurely afternoon riding. As an afterthought, they decided to ride by the Stephenson home. Neither Dalton nor Belinda was at the service that morning. Cole had never been to the Stephenson home, but knowing the family's wealth he was not surprised to see such an expansive home.

Dalton and Belinda had just gotten down from the family coach when Anne and Cole drew up at the front of the house. Belinda, seeing her friend, ran over to see Anne.

"We've just returned from Portsmouth, and who do you think I met? Mr. Midshipman Phillip Bickford," Belinda said. Cole was now all ears.

"Yes, Cole's brother, I believe," Dalton said finally. "The *Diamond* has been in battle with a larger French vessel, and though victorious, it requires an overhaul. It appears that Captain Best was severely wounded and lost a leg. Phillip asked us to tell you that he is doing well. It appears his First Lieutenant Atwater fought the ship after Captain Best was wounded."

A groomsman came and took Cole and Anne's horses. Dalton touched Cole's arm, holding him back as the women walked up to the house.

"We need to have words," Dalton said.

Cole immediately felt a difference in his friend. The boy was now a man...a man in charge of the Stephensons' vast holdings.

"First, I hold no ill will toward you, Cole, for what happened to my father. His richness led to his demise. After mother died, he realized that his wealth gave him anything he wanted, until it didn't. Had mother lived, I doubt that he'd have done what he did." Dalton took a deep breath and exhaled. "No doubt Sir William has told you that I'm the money man for a smuggling operation. That is true, but only to add to my front with the French. I understand that we are both employed by the same agency. A time may come where we have to rely on one another or die. Such is this dangerous game that we play for our country. That's why you had to know...you had to hear it from me, Cole. We were friends and, as far as I'm concerned, we still are friends." Dalton, saying this, held out his hand.

Cole took the offered hand, "Friends," he said.

***

ON THE RIDE HOME, ANNE went on and on about Belinda meeting Phillip and how brave he was. "She talked about how much a gentleman he was."

This caused Cole to laugh. "Phillip was laying it on in hopes of getting into her drawers," Cole said.

"I've no doubt that she wouldn't have welcomed him," Anne said, recalling times that she and Cole had come close to going all the way.

Cole's mind, however, was on Chloe. Belinda would be considered an agreeable match while, with Chloe it could never be. No matter how in love the girl was. *Damn*, all these society and social standings. Well, it was not something that he could fix right now, or ever fix if he was honest with himself.

"What weighs on your mind, Cole?"

"Nothing," he said.

Anne reached over and touched his arm. "You don't frown like that when there's nothing on your mind."

Cole gave a sigh. "I was just thinking of Chloe."

Anne pulled up on her horse. "It is sad, isn't it?"

Cole nodded, "What if your father had forbidden me from seeing you?"

"I'd have left home."

Cole smiled, "Not if six shillings a week were the most that we could hope for."

Anne's hand went to her heart. She didn't say anything, but the point was taken.

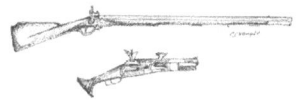

CHAPTER SIX

OLE HAD MIXED FEELINGS ABOUT seeing Linda again. He had thoroughly enjoyed their lovemaking, plus he truly liked the woman. Had Anne not been in the picture, he could have been happy spending his life with her, even though she was ten years older than him. It had been Linda who had put Anne and him back together, after Anne had become aware of his affair with Linda. Something that Sir William knew and encouraged. He'd encouraged the affair to keep Anne 'pure' until marriage. The affair had come to an abrupt end when it was thought that she might have been hiding a murderer when it was, in fact, Cole.

Cole had protected her by telling the truth, not realizing that Anne was within hearing distance. She had broken up with Cole until Linda had written her a letter. Cole and Anne got back together because of the letter and, as strange as it may seem, the two women had become friends.

As fate would have it now, Cole and Linda were being put together again in a clandestine manner. Were it not a secret, Cole would have told Anne upfront. And he still might if it looked like his marriage was being placed in jeopardy.

***

COLE PASSED SEVERAL PEOPLE ON the road going to meet Linda, but few recognized him in his garb and riding a different horse than Apollo. He had told Anne that he didn't want to be conspicuous wearing his uniform, and everyone would recognize Apollo. She had frowned but said nothing.

Once he turned off the main road, he paused to see if he was being followed. What was it the agent, James Atkins, had said. Take nothing at face value. Always be cautious even among people you think you know and lastly, always check your back trail to see if you are being followed. Failure to do so has cost a few agents their lives.

When Cole felt assured that he was alone, he rode on to Linda's house. Saul was in the yard talking to a man who appeared to be the driver of a small coach. Another man had just entered Linda's house. Cole was hesitant to dismount but realized that he was told to be there at a certain time for a reason. The message had specified a time. There was nothing that had been alluded to, that would point out that it would be just Cole and Linda alone.

Cole dismounted and Saul took the horse's reins and said, "Go on in."

Walking in the side door briefly stirred old memories in Cole. Linda came forward and gave him a friendly hug, her nearness making the memories more real. *Damn,* Cole thought. *Would those feelings ever go away?* He'd never cheat on his wife, but this job may prove harder than he expected.

Linda had spoken to him but his mind had been on a memory and so he missed what she had said.

"I'm sorry," Cole said. "I'm a bit stuffy today and didn't hear what you said."

Linda smiled, and he wondered if the memories affected her also. "I said that it's good to see you back from the Indies."

"Yes, it's good to be back," Cole replied.

When they moved into the sitting room, Cole realized the person that he'd seen and thought a man was actually a woman in men's clothing.

"Cole, this is Lois Breeding," Linda said.

Breeding, that's a German name. Was it her maiden name or a husband's? Cole wondered.

Lois was of medium height. Was that due to her knee-high riding boots, or was she that tall? Her eyes were a beautiful green and her hair was shoulder length and blonde. Up close, she'd never be thought to be anything but what she was…a beautiful woman. Her breasts caused the loose, ill-fitting shirt to stand out. From a distance, an untrained eye might think of her as a man, or if one only had a glimpse of her. Lois Breeding, otherwise, was a woman… all woman.

"Our agent in charge wanted you to meet Lois," Linda said. "The two of you will be going to Calais on Wednesday, aboard the lugger, *Blue Pearl*. You will meet here at eight p.m. and Saul will lead you to the cove where the lugger will wait on you for fifteen minutes. Saul has all the signals down. Cole, once you are at Calais, you will escort Lois to Sir George's wife's mother's residence. Her son, Henri, still lives at the Boche home. You will introduce Henri to Lois and, at certain times, you will meet her there. On the nights that you are to meet Lois, there will be a candle lit in the side window and one on in her bedroom. If there's only one candle burning it's not safe to enter. If you ever see three candles burning, Lois' life is at stake and you're to use any means available to save her. Behind the house is a stable with a lean-to for the carriage, and behind that is a small boat shed. Henri and the senior Monsieur Boche both like boating. There's an old skiff in the shed that they used when traveling the Loire. Lois will always try to meet you at the boat shed if there's danger. If she's not there you will have to act as you see fit, Cole. Here is a list of phrases with replies. If at any time either of you gives an incorrect phrase or reply, abort. Just in case the candles can't be lit, the phrase by Lois to alert you is 'It's a beautiful night out tonight.' Cole you will always initiate the phrase, and Lois will only reply to your phrase."

Linda walked over to a book then and took out a sheet for both Cole and Lois. "Memorize the phrases and replies. Cole, if you know anyone to help you improve your French, do so. Learn the first three phrases and replies first."

"Who would you suggest that I ask to help me?" Cole asked.

"Andrea, Sir George's wife, or Dalton if he is in town," Linda replied.

"It was nice meeting you, Cole," Lois said.

"You, as well," he replied and then added, "I don't say this to be rude. If you are to pass yourself off as a man, I would have someone bind you up."

Linda laughed and said, "We discussed that just before you came in. I told Lois if anyone would notice your…"

"Attributes," Cole said, supplying the word.

Linda finished her sentence, "If anyone would notice your attributes it would be Cole."

***

THE RIDE BACK TO ANNE'S parents' house was taken slowly. There was so much on Cole's mind, not the least of which was that he could lose his wife by going to Linda's house without her knowing. He'd come close to it before. He'd not risk it again. Atkins, the agent, said a year. Cole's service was expected to last a year. There was no way in the world that he could go to Linda's on several occasions that word would not get back to Anne, or Sir William, or both.

He could deal with Sir William if the situation arose. Anne was another thing, though. No, when he got home he'd get her alone and talk to her. Anne had never been one to run her mouth or gossip. If the agent didn't like that, to hell with him. Having made up his mind, Cole picked up the pace. When he arrived at the house, Anne was on the front porch with Joe. She got up and rushed to Cole, giving him a kiss and then taking his arm.

"Joe has some exciting news," Anne said.

Joe reached out and took Cole's hand. "I've come to ask that you be my best man."

"I'd be delighted as long as you understand that my new duties are subject to change without warning."

Joe shook his head, "If that should happen, then I'll stand alone."

The two men shook hands, and Joe said, "We see the vicar this Wednesday."

Anne was delighted. A wedding meant women things. It also meant a change from the boring routine.

When Joe left, Cole took Anne's hand and said, "Let's go for a walk."

Anne was suddenly aware of a change in Cole's voice and demeanor. This frightened her but she steeled herself so that Cole would not see her emotions.

"You know that I've been given a special assignment as a courier." Cole could not bring himself to use the term agent. Anne nodded her head. Cole continued, "What I'm about to tell you, Anne, is a secret. I'm not even supposed to tell you."

Anne felt her heart pounding in her chest at Cole's words.

"I have found out, Anne, that one of the people the government has decided to use as an intermediary—a person whom I get messages and instructions from—is Linda."

Anne looked at Cole and said, "So!"

"So...I will have to be going to Linda's house at different times, and without you," Cole replied.

Anne burst out laughing. Cole stood there, looking at her puzzled.

Seeing her husband's look, Anne took his face and pulled it to her, kissing him upon the lips. Smiling, she said, "I laughed because I was so relieved. I thought that you were being sent to France to assassinate someone, Napoleon, maybe. To know you'll only be going to Linda's for messages is a relief."

"You're not upset that I'll be going to Linda's at odd hours?"

"Should I be?" she asked.

Cole looked at his wife. "No, but I didn't want somebody to see me and get word back to you. I didn't want you to think the worst."

"Cole, I trust Linda. She put us back together. She had to know that had she said nothing, you may still be sharing her bed and not mine. But, more than that, Cole Buckley, I trust you."

Cole smiled now and pulled his wife to him. "You must keep this secret, my love. Only you shall know the truth. If this got out, it could well cost Linda...and yours truly, our lives."

Anne frowned at this and Cole explained, "You know smuggling is still going on even with the war. Do you not think that the French have not filled the purse of a few men to report anything they feel might be important? As easy as our smugglers make the run, do you think it would not be just as easy for the French to send an assassin. Possibly even on one of our craft."

Anne held her hand to her face. "I shall not breathe a word, my dear."

"I know you won't," Cole said. "You also must know if I get up and leave at odd hours it must not be discussed even with your parents."

"If they ask what shall I say?" Anne asked.

"Just one word…work. He had work and you will not say another word," Cole replied.

"Oh, Cole, you are scaring me."

"No need to be frightened, Anne. I believe that I'm in far less danger than I would be if I were in France and had a regiment of Frenchmen shooting after me."

"Cole."

"Yes."

"Hold me, hold me tight."

Cole held his wife, and Anne said, "Let's go back to the house."

"Why? It's nice here," Cole said.

"I don't want dirt and grass on my bare arse as you make love to me," Anne replied. Cole just smiled.

Anne's mother heard the two of them as they walked past the sitting room. She walked to the hall as Anne's door shut. She heard the lock when it was set. She smiled to herself then, envious of their youth and their love.

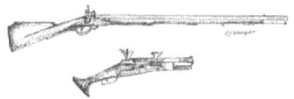

CHAPTER SEVEN

HE *BLUE PEARL* WAS A fairly new lugger. Her captain was a man named Kevin Lunn. While the *Blue Pearl* was new, Lunn had been the captain of a smuggler for years. He'd started out with the senior Stephenson. He'd had a fishing yawl that was no longer seaworthy. Stephenson had offered him the lugger *Wren* and a job running goods. Lunn had wondered when he got the news that Stephenson had been killed if his job as over, but Dalton had met with him. He now had the *Blue Pearl*, as fast a lugger as crossed the Channel.

He still ran the Channel fairly often but he also took legitimate cargo up to some of the markets in northern England and even to Edinburgh via the Firth of Forth. He'd been no further than the estuary, but he thought that one day he'd like to sail into the North Sea In a larger ship, of course.

Kevin was crossing the Channel tonight. He was to pick up a load of cargo at Calais but he knew that was a front, and that it would be sold and a nice profit made as with all smuggled goods. The passengers below were the reason for the trip this time. The man he knew, as did most of Deal. He was Angus MacFadyn's nephew and if the rumors were true, he was the man who had killed the senior Stephenson. However, the younger Stephenson, Dalton, from outward appearances, at least, had no ill will toward the man. Kevin had seen the two men sharing a wet and having a laugh at the Cock and Bull.

Who was the woman with the man? Yes...woman. She was dressed as a man and had spoken very little, but a boot that small was a woman's.

A boat was to be waiting a mile out to take them off. The man beneath his cloak was dressed in seaman's garb. He was to return to the ship at the dock. If he was not there, Lunn was to wait no more than half an hour, and then set sail. For thirty minutes he could dally, finding something to draw his attention. Were it nothing more than having a glass with the agent there and listening to him complain about his fat wife or something. He could maybe even talk of finding some mademoiselle, who might prove willing to entertain him for a few minutes. Since he was not married that seemed to be the best course. His mate saw to the cargo so that he would not have to worry on that end. He'd plant the seed tonight. The thought 'plant the seed' seemed to have a double meaning.

The lights of Calais were visible when the boat was spotted. It was far less than a mile offshore, a half mile at the most. The woman and man came on deck and the password was given along with the correct reply. The agents went into the boat and Lunn saw a fishing net being pulled over them as they departed. He didn't think the woman would appreciate the stench from the net. However, the stench was only a lesser evil if she were caught as a spy.

Lunn had already heard how some of the captured women were reportedly raped and sodomized by French soldiers. Since the

Revolution, very few of the army's surviving officers held a high sense of honor. In fact, they were often the first among the rapists.

✦✦✦

COLE AND LOIS WERE LYING close together out of necessity. They were so close that their faces were almost touching. Lois tried to move her cramped arm from under her. She jostled against Cole, putting an elbow into his chest.

"I'm sorry," she whispered. It hurt, but Cole managed a smile. "Linda has told me about you," she continued, still whispering.

"I hope it was all good," he replied.

"She told me enough that while I don't feel safe, I feel safer having you with me."

"If you are speaking of danger, be assured that I will do my utmost to see you home safe and sound," Cole said.

"I will undoubtedly benefit, if you are near," she replied.

Lois smiled to herself. Linda had also said that Cole would never admit to his chivalry, but rest assured it was there. It grew quiet as Cole didn't speak and Lois couldn't think of anything to say since she didn't know the man that well.

The man, what a way to think of him…yes, the man. It came to her then; it had been a long time since she'd been this close to a man. The last one had been her husband…her husband and her life. He was gone now. When he died part of her had died too. Perhaps that was why she had agreed to do this. If she were killed it would be no great loss to anyone. Also, if one believed, as she did, she'd be reunited with her love that much quicker. But for now, she was close to this man, so close that she could feel his heartbeat against her chest. She could also feel him breathe. She could feel the warm air as he breathed on the side of her face. His arm was actually beneath her shoulders and neck, a cushion against the hard planks of the boat. Her one leg lay between his two legs. They were so close and yet it was a necessity. Did he realize how close their bodies were entwined? *If he didn't, he was not a man*, Lois thought to herself. He was, at least, being a gentleman about it.

One of the Frenchmen said something. She felt the net being lifted off her head and then the boat scrubbed on the sand. Cole rose up a bit and rubbed his eyes. *Damn*, Lois thought. *I'm lying here thinking thoughts of how close our bodies were and wondering if he felt excitement about it, and he was asleep. How could a man sleep at a time like that?* She looked up at him and saw that he was smiling. He hadn't been asleep. Did his thoughts mirror hers? She damn well wasn't about to ask the rogue. *Huh*...she thought to herself. In her mind, he'd gone from a gentleman to a rogue and he hadn't even uttered a word. Had he been asleep, after all, and was smiling now because he'd been caught sleeping? Oh, the devil with it. At least, he took her hand as she got out of the boat. The tide came in lifting the boat. He lifted her and sat her on a rock so that her boots wouldn't get wet. *He is a gentleman.*

The Frenchmen pulled the boat up in the rocks, turning it upside down and throwing some brush over it. They then led them up a path and to a road. They stayed off the road walking parallel to it. At one point, the sound of horses was heard and they ducked down behind some bushes and rocks. A troop of cavalry rode by headed away from town. They'd not gone far when Cole recognized the intersection where they had turned left to go to the Boche home. When they were coming back, he'd turn right and it was but a short distance to the waterfront.

They had moved along at a fast pace. Cole could tell that Lois was starting to tire. They'd come between three and four miles with a mile left.

"Do you need to take a break?" Cole asked Lois.

"Non," a Frenchman said. "We must hurry."

"I'll be all right," Lois said.

They continued on but Cole could tell that Lois was limping. She saw Cole looking and said, "I think that I've developed blisters."

Cole paused and then said, "Get on my back. I'm sure that your father let you ride on his back as a child."

Lois went to protest but Cole continued, "On my back or over my shoulder. You've got britches on." Cole thought that might be her concern.

"*Nous devons nous dépêcher.*"

Lois got on Cole's back. "He says that we must hurry."

She weighed less than Cole imagined, so it was no problem to match pace with their guides. When they got to the entrance to the Boche home they stopped.

"Au revoir, good-by," their guides said, and were gone before Cole or Lois could reply.

"We are to go to the rear door," Lois said.

She followed Cole, as he'd been there previously. Before they could knock, Henri opened the door.

"Monsieur Cole," Henri said.

Lois stepped to the front. That was not the password. Was there trouble or did Henri just recognize Cole?

"Est-ce que Calais est par ici?" Lois said, asking *is Calais this way?*

"Oui, Madame." The reply was correct. Had he used mademoiselle, it would have meant danger, and she would have replied, "Merci." Merci meant thank you, and they would have left, had they been able to.

Henri and Cole shook hands and then Cole introduced Lois. Cole took a quick glass of wine and hurriedly set out to Calais. By the time that he was on the *Blue Pearl* and they'd made their way out and into the Channel, Cole was thankful that he was in the Dragoons and not the Infantry. His feet were killing him.

Once they'd landed outside of Deal, Cole walked up the cliffs expecting a horse to be waiting…one was, and it was Apollo, with Joe standing by.

"A good trip," Joe asked.

Cole didn't answer the question. "How did you happen to be here?"

Joe smiled, "Who better than someone you trust."

"None," Cole replied and grasped his friend's hand.

"You can thank Linda for my part," Joe said and then he added, "No one knows but you, me, and Linda. Everyone is used to seeing me at the landings so I'm the one person that would not raise suspicions."

"True," Cole agreed.

"Cole, you're the only one outside of Linda who knows my part. I meant that when I told you. I don't want my family to know."

"Know what?" Cole asked.

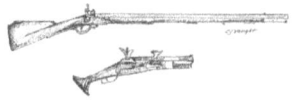

CHAPTER EIGHT

I<small>T HAD BEEN ALMOST TWO</small> weeks when Cole got his next message. This time it was from Dalton Stephenson. He was to return to Deal Castle the next morning by seven a.m. He was told to bring clothes for a few days. He thanked Dalton's messenger and went in the house to tell Anne that he'd be gone a few days.

They'd had Sunday dinner and Kimberly Jordan was there. Cole drew near the sewing room and he heard Anne's voice, "We have done nothing to keep from having a child. While I do want children at some point, I'm glad that I'm not in that way now. Cole and I are both still young. He was away for over a year. I'm lucky that he has this new job and we are together for more than if he was with the Regiment in London. I had expected, of course, to live at Lord Bickford's house to be with Cole, but that would have meant leaving mother and father."

Kimberly smiled and remembered that Mary had said she was fully expecting Anne to leave when Cole returned. As a mother, she was most happy to have her daughter at home as long as possible.

When the conversation was at a lull, Cole deliberately made a noise as he approached the door. He paused in the doorway.

"My, my, I believe the three most beautiful ladies in all of England have gathered in one room." Smiles broke out as Cole knew that it would. "Do you still desire to go for a walk this evening?" Cole asked Anne.

In truth, there had been no mention of walk but Anne rose up. "I'm sorry, Cole. The time completely slipped away from me."

"Go ahead," Anne's mother said. "It's beautiful outside."

Once the two of them were away from the house, Cole said, "I have to report to Major Letchworth tomorrow morning at seven a.m. I was told to bring enough clothes for three days."

Anne nodded, but didn't speak. Later that night, they made love and afterwards she wondered if it would change their lives if she got pregnant. She had heard that it did, because the baby suddenly became a woman's focus. She didn't want anything to take her focus on Cole away. However, they were at war. She realized that Cole could be killed right away. She didn't want to lose Cole without first giving him a child…a son.

She wiped her tears and snuggled closer to her man, feeling his hand come to rest on her breasts. She loved that feeling and hoped that she would feel his hand there for the rest of her life.

❋❋❋

THE WOMAN WAS SHORT, JUST barely over five feet tall, Cole imagined. Her hair was black, *as black as ravens,* Cole thought. Her long eyelashes and eyebrows were black also. Once she looked directly at Cole, causing an involuntary shudder.

Major Letchworth introduced her as Josephine Rousseau. "Mademoiselle has vital information that must reach London. You must guard her with your life, Lieutenant Buckley."

"Yes sir," Cole replied.

"I don't see any weapons," Major Letchworth said.

"My pistols are in my bag and my sword is on my saddle."

"Good. The sergeant will take care of your horse and place your bag in the coach. You're wondering why a coach," Letchworth said.

"It did cross my mind," Cole admitted.

"We have reason to believe that our boat was followed. There is a strong possibility Mademoiselle Rousseau's life is in jeopardy. This was only decided last evening. By traveling in a coach, the likelihood of being shot from an ambush is lessened. By the time a coach is stopped, hopefully you will be ready to defend yourselves. I understand that the coach will be slower and necessitate a layover. You will only get one room. Modesty and privacy must not be as important as your safety."

The woman spoke for the first time. "I understand that the lieutenant is a gentleman."

The sky was darker than usual when Cole had arrived at seven a.m. It was nearly eight a.m. and the sky was still dark. When Cole helped Josephine into the coach, the first drops of rain started, splattering down on the coach's roof.

Cole hadn't asked any questions but he felt the coach give on its spring as first one man and then another climbed up in the driver's box. He didn't say anything but Letchworth was sending along a guard. A movement caught Cole's eye as a corporal passed up a blunderbuss. He recalled shooting a highwayman with one of those and almost tearing the man in half.

The coach gave a big heave as they pulled out, throwing Josephine onto Cole. He caught her, getting a handful of breasts as he did so. His first thought was *she's got a set of catheads to otherwise be so small.*

"It may be best if we sit on the same seat," Josephine said.

Cole swallowed and scooted over closer to a window. "My apologies, Mademoiselle, I didn't mean to grasp you so."

Josephine waved away his apology and then said, "It would not have been bad had it been intentional." Cole didn't reply, and the woman added, "I've made you blush, Lieutenant, but I shan't apologize."

After the second change of horses, the guard asked if they needed to 'get down and refresh,' as he put it.

"Yes, I believe that I do," Josephine said. She followed the guard and Cole walked behind.

Inside the inn, the guard spoke with the proprietor who led them to a small room that contained the water closet. The room smelled, but that was to be expected. It probably didn't get cleaned until after the inn was closed for the night. It was a step above a chamber pot, at least.

Josephine sounded a bit unladylike when she announced, "I'm glad all I had to do is pee."

There was a community bucket of water where a person could wash their hands. After one look, Josephine declared, "I'd rather wash in the horse's water trough."

Cole smiled; he could hear Anne saying the same thing.

As they left the inn, the rain that had all but stopped started again.

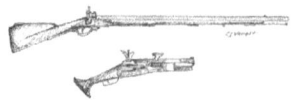

CHAPTER NINE

THEY HAD TRAVELED ALMOST THREE hours since the last stop when the coach slowed. The guard leaned over and said, "The next inn will be the best we come to before it gets too dark. The rain is making it harder for the horses. The driver thinks that we should layover there for the night."

Josephine sat forward to look out her window. As she did so, a shot rang out. "Oh," she cried as she slumped back.

Cole saw the rider and fired a pistol. The sound of the blunderbuss followed right behind the sound of the pistol. Cole saw a man grab his shoulder when he fired but he was knocked off his horse by the blunderbuss. The driver was using his whip on the tired horses.

"Are you hit bad?" Cole asked Josephine.

"I don't know," she replied. She took a deep breath and said, "I'm hit in the chest, but it doesn't seem to affect my breathing other than it hurts like hell. I shouldn't have looked out the window. It was stupid of me."

It was near dark in the coach. Cole was afraid to light the lantern. He touched Josephine's front and felt the wetness. She was bleeding profusely. Cole took off his coat and, folding it up, he pushed it against her chest.

"Hold this tight against your chest," he instructed. He took off his sword belt and put it around Josephine's chest to hold the coat tightly against her, hoping it would help stop the bleeding.

It seemed like forever before they got to the inn. They pulled up in front and the driver got down. "We have a wounded lady out here, and she needs a bed quickly and a doctor."

"Damnable highwaymen," the owner, of the inn, cussed. "They plague this road still."

Since the man used the term highwaymen, Cole didn't correct him. Let him think that. It would be better than saying it was a French assassin.

"We need two rooms," Cole said. When the owner looked at him questioningly, Cole added, "One for us and one for my men."

"I only have one left," the innkeeper said.

"We'll put down a blanket by the fireplace," the driver said.

The innkeeper said then, "I'll send for the doctor but he's usually drunk by this time."

"I'll get your bags," the driver said.

"Good," Cole replied. He turned to the innkeeper again, "Do you have any bandage material?"

"I'll ask my wife."

"Do it quickly," Cole said. "I'll pay for it."

Josephine, who had been listening to it all, moaned loudly, "Cole, darling, I hurt badly."

"Follow me," the owner said, calling over his shoulder to a girl to get a bucket of clean water and heat it up.

Once in the room, Josephine was placed on the bed. "I'll get a chair and be outside the door," the guard advised.

"Thank you, Claude," Josephine said. It was the first time that Cole had heard the man's name.

Once the door was closed, Cole spoke to Josephine, "I need to look at your wound."

She nodded but didn't speak. Cole untied the belt and removed the coat. The blood only penetrated one layer. *Good*, he thought. Josephine's top buttoned in the back. Cole, thinking it was ruined anyway, took his knife and slit the top up the middle. Beneath the top, there was a chemise. Cole slit it open as well. Her breasts were now fully exposed, causing more pain as they wanted to pull to the side.

"I didn't mean to hurt you," Cole said.

Josephine gave a pain-filled smile. "Is it bad?"

"I don't know yet," he said. "Your breasts are covering up the wound." He carefully lifted one breast and then the other. He smiled when he saw the wound.

"Are you enjoying yourself, Cole?" she asked.

"I'm pleased," he replied.

"I'm glad. I'd hate to think a man was playing with my tits and wasn't pleased."

"I'm pleased at your wound, the way it looks," Cole said.

"So, my tits have nothing to do with your smile," she questioned Cole.

Cole didn't know what to say. He'd heard Anne use the word before but nobody else.

"You're blushing again," Josephine said, seemingly enjoying herself at making Cole ill at ease.

A knock was heard at the door. Cole covered Josephine and said, "Yes!"

"It's the lady with the bandages and hot water," Claude said.

"Let her in," Cole responded.

"I'm Mercy," the girl said.

"That's a good name," Cole said.

"It's probably not in the way that you are thinking. It's Mercy, as in God have mercy on me, it's another girl."

Cole and Josephine both laughed, with Josephine wincing as she did so.

Mercy came over and looked as Cole showed her the wound. "Another inch or more and your husband would be a widower."

Josephine said, "Thank you. He seems more interested in my breasts than my wound."

"Ain't you the funny one," the girl said. "I can see 'concern' all over his face. Let's be getting her top off," Mercy suggested.

Cole held Josephine up as Mercy took off the top and chemise. The water still had vapors rising from it, but Mercy dipped a cloth, waved it about to cool it off some and then she laid it across the wound. "That will loosen up the clots a bit and then we can clean the wound."

Cole held up Josephine's breasts as Mercy worked to diligently clean the wound. Once it was clean, Mercy applied an ointment made of sulphur, glycerin, and hog lard. A clean, new chemise was cut to form a bandage and tie to hold the bandage in place.

"That looks new," Cole said as he helped Josephine up into a sitting position."

"It was, but it also was the best that I had to make a bandage."

"Cole," Josephine called.

"Yes."

"I have two chemises in my bag. Bring it to me."

Cole thought that he was used to seeing Josephine's nude top, but as he got her bag and turned, he realized what a perfect set of breasts she had. In any other circumstance, he'd have been aroused, or maybe *more aroused* would have been a better statement. How could a man look, touch, and feel those perfect melons and not feel something?

He handed the bag to Josephine and she dug into it until she came out with two chemise tops. One was of the usual cotton material, while the other one was a new silk top. She handed the silk one to Mercy.

"It should fit," Josephine said.

"Oh, I couldn't take this," Mercy replied back.

"You can, and you shall. My man will buy me another one," Josephine responded.

As Cole and Mercy put the cotton chemise on Josephine, she stretched just a bit, holding her arms up.

"It felt real good until then," Josephine said.

Mercy smiled, "I will come back in the morning. Husbands are no good at these things." She said this with a smile and then left.

"Can I get you a brandy or anything to help you rest?" Cole asked.

"Send Claude down for a bottle and two glasses."

"Are you hungry?"

"Yes, I believe that I am," Josephine replied.

Cole went to the door and gave Claude his instructions. He locked the door then and took a seat in the only chair in the room.

"Come sit by me," Josephine said. "I feel safer with you near."

Cole came and sat on the bed, and Josephine said, "I'm sorry."

"For what," he asked.

"For the way that I've deviled you with my forward comments," Josephine answered back. Cole smiled, and she continued, "Has anyone been as forward as me?"

He smiled again and then said, "My wife and a...special friend."

"A lover," Josephine returned. "I knew that you were too damned good-looking to have only one woman."

Cole looked at her and responded, "My wife is all that I have."

"What about your lover?"

"She and my wife are the best of friends," he said.

"If I was your wife, I wouldn't share you with anyone," Josephine said.

"That's how my wife feels also," Cole replied.

"So you are true to her?"

"Yes, I am."

"I like you all the more then, Lieutenant Cole Buckley. Most men could not have done what you did without wanting to go further."

"Who said that I didn't? You are too beautiful a woman to not want you. I could feel my heart pounding when you were sitting up."

"You wouldn't touch me, though."

"Never!"

"Well, I could eat you alive but not only do I like you more by the minute, I respect your feelings. I will say that I'd love to meet this wife of yours. She must be something."

"I think she is. I'm going to lie back, I feel very tired. Wake me when the food gets here if I fall asleep."

Josephine made her way over to the other side of the bed. "Feel free to share my bed," she said...after a pause, she added, "I promise not to seduce you."

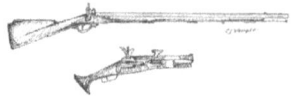

CHAPTER TEN

OLE'S EYES OPENED. WHAT WAS that sound? Was it a thump? He reached over to the chair that he'd pulled over next to the bed. He picked up each of his pistols as he rose up to a sitting position. He'd taken Josephine's invitation and shared her bed, only he was fully dressed and slept on top of the covers.

His stirring woke Josephine and she asked, "What's wrong?"

Cole put his finger to his lips to silence her. "Can you move over against the far wall?" he asked.

Josephine moved without answering. Cole took two pillows and placed them under the cover to appear like a sleeping person. It was not perfect but was good enough for what he wanted. The door lever was moving and it squeaked. The movement paused then.

Cole took three large steps to put him across the room from the bed. The door suddenly burst open then. The intruder, tired of the stealth, kicked the door open. Seeing the shapes on the bed, he fired a pistol into where a person's back or chest would be. Cole raised his pistol and, in a deliberate manner, he shot the man in the head. As the man fell back, he knocked a second man into the hall wall.

Cole stepped forward and, seeing a pistol in this man's hand, he shot him in the chest. The rogue's pistol fired into the floor as death gripped him. Cole stepped over to Claude. He had fallen asleep in a chair outside the door. It would be his last mistake. He'd been struck so hard it cracked his skull.

People were coming up the steps to see what the commotion and gunshots were all about. The first one was the coach driver, followed by the innkeeper and Mercy.

"You must be carrying something valuable," the innkeeper said. "We've never had them come into the inn before."

"That's just it, we have nothing beyond a few pounds to travel on," Cole said.

"Revenge," Mercy said. "You killed one of their own, back along the road. They were out for revenge."

"Let's drag them out," the innkeeper said.

"Wait!" Cole looked at the driver. "Search their clothes."

After the search was completed, a sum of eighteen pounds had been found. A paper with a name on it was also found. DuFort! It had no meaning to Cole, but he stuck it in his pocket. He gave the innkeeper ten pounds of the money and the other eight pounds to Mercy.

"When we stop by this way again, I expect to see the beautiful things that you purchased with this," Cole said. He had no idea if they would be stopping back this way, but said what he did so that the innkeeper wouldn't try to take Mercy's money.

Across the room, Josephine was looking pale. The innkeeper had brought a lantern up the stairs with him, so Cole said, "Bring the lantern over here so that I can check on my wife."

The lie rolled off Cole's tongue easily. There had been nothing said about him still being dressed but if asked, his concern over his wife was why he'd not undressed.

Josephine was sliding down the wall when Cole reached her. He picked her up and took her back to the bed.

"Give me the lantern and leave," Mercy said to the innkeeper. "We must check her wound."

When the men had left the room, Cole held the chemise up while Mercy checked the bandage. "There's no new bleeding," she said. "The excitement was just too much for her."

Tugging the chemise down over Josephine's breasts, he felt her hand over his. "Both of you are so gentle," she said.

Mercy smiled, "You are a lucky man to have such a beautiful wife."

"Thank you," was all Cole could think of to say. He followed Mercy to the door and took the chair Claude had been sitting in and propped it against what was left of the door lock. He then re-loaded his pistol and sat them back in the chair by the bed.

Looking at Josephine, Cole saw that she was watching him. "Would you mind carrying out this deception a bit further, husband?"

"In what way?" Cole asked.

"Lie down and hold me," Josephine replied. "I strangely feel very safe with you near me."

Cole lay down on the bed, letting Josephine nestle into his arms. Feeling a bit moved by her little girl demeanor, he kissed her on the forehead. Josephine, her eyes closed but not asleep, did feel very safe in this man's arms. He was a strong and gentle man. One who didn't hesitate to protect her when it was needed. Why hadn't she met someone like Cole before marrying Rousseau, the now dead gambler?

LONDON WAS BUSTLING. THERE WERE carriages and coaches passing each other going in separate directions. A pie man yelled out a curse as a carriage splashed water on his cart. Cole could feel the wheels slide over the wet cobblestones, as the coach turned on a side street.

Clerks, shopkeepers, and domestic servants rushed up and down the street. A peddler whose cart was full of vegetables had several women gathered around it. A constable was easily identified as he walked along the street tapping one hand with his truncheon as he kept his eye on a gang of street urchins.

The driver stopped soon outside a very plain -looking building. He came to the coach window and said, "I'll check to see if the building is open yet."

They had awakened early with Mercy knocking on the door. "I would like to change the bandage before I get busy in the scullery," she said.

Cole helped change the dressing and was glad to see that there was only minimal inflammation. *Mercy should be a doctor*, he decided. They'd had a quick breakfast and were on the road by six a.m. The innkeeper said that it was only nineteen miles to London. However, after only four hours, they made it to the outskirts of London and by 10:30 they were at the Foreign Office's Secret Division building. The driver undoubtedly had been here before as there were no signs on many of the streets and none on the building.

Cole, sitting back next to Josephine, said, "Maybe they will have a place for you so that you can relax now."

She smiled, "Last night was the first time that I've relaxed in years. If you were not a married man, I'd have made love to you in such a way that you'd never forget me." It was a gentle moment.

"I don't think that I will ever forget you anyway," Cole responded. "You are a beautiful woman. If I was not married, I'd take you in my arms and never let go."

Josephine reached out and touched Cole's arm. "Believe it or not, I believe you."

"You should," Cole said.

"Do you believe in premonitions, Cole?"

"Yes," Cole replied.

"I've had a premonition that I will not live to see the end of the war. I know too much and certain men will not rest until I am either dead or they are. I can go to my grave now knowing that I've been touched and held by an honest man. Do you know the name 'Joseph Fouché,' Cole?"

"No," Cole responded.

"He's head of the secret police in France, and a very powerful man. He is also a deadly man, and a deadly enemy. I was the mistress of his main lieutenant. It was not a pleasant duty. He was a cruel man in his own right. He liked to use the end of his cigar to burn people to make them talk. He captured a friend of mine and put the burning end of his cigar to her nipples, trying to find out who her informant was. It was me. He had her tied down and was burning the second nipple when I got close enough to blow his brains out. I went to the door and locked it before the guards came in. They were used to gunshots, screams, the smell of burning flesh, but he didn't like to have the men in the room when he was torturing his prisoner. He did like for me to be there, to see what would happen to me if I betrayed him. I cut Andrea's bonds and gave her a dress to slip on and we ran. We made it out of Paris, but before we got to Andrea's contact, she developed an infection where she'd been burned. She knew that she was slowing me down, so while I was asleep she slit her wrist. I made it to Deal, but as you see Fouché is still after me. DuFort was…is…the next in line. He is probably the one Fouché assigned to kill me."

Cole was holding Josephine's hand when the sound of footsteps reached his hearing. He turned, pistol in hand. It was James Atkins, and he said, "Come quickly." Cole helped Josephine out of the coach and they entered the building.

Atkins said, "I understand that you've been wounded."

"It's nothing," Josephine replied, but her pale skin said differently.

Atkins motioned for a man to come near. "Take her to the surgeon."

"Yes, sir."

Josephine paused, as they headed downstairs, "Lieutenant Buckley, I thank you for everything. I've never been treated so well or felt so safe as I have with you." She then followed the man downstairs, not giving Cole a chance to reply.

"It seems that you've made a favorable impression, Cole. She's known as a lady of steel," Atkins said.

"You'd be surprised at how close people become when they've gone through the fire together," Cole responded.

Atkins was silent for a moment. It surprised Cole when he did speak. "Our head agent wants to speak with you, Lieutenant."

Cole sat outside an office with only one visible door. The upper half of the door was glass, leaving Cole to ponder what kind of business used to occupy the building. The area where he waited was very dull. The fading paint was peeling around the window sill. A stick was atop the lower window so that it couldn't be raised. Cole thought that raising it would certainly help with the stale odor of the room. He was about to doze off when he heard a voice.

"Mr. Buckley."

Instantly awake, Cole stood up, "Sir."

"Be at ease, young sir. This is not the army," the speaker said this with a smile. "I'm Randy Skalla, and the head of this little service. I've been talking to Miss Rousseau."

Cole was quick to note the use of Miss, instead of Mademoiselle. Was he trying to limit the French connection?

Skalla looked at Cole and said, "The dear lady, were it not for your quick actions, would be dead and we would not have been informed of her information. She also said that you have a piece of paper taken from the pockets of the men you shot. Did you read it?"

Cole pulled out the paper from a vest pocket. "It only has one word."

Skalla took the paper and saw that it had one visible word on it. "You'd be surprised what we can ascertain from a seemingly blank sheet of paper," he told Cole. "Would you prefer to go back to Deal with the coach? It will head back tomorrow, or would you like to go back today? We have a horse that you could use."

"I'll take the horse." Skalla nodded his head. "May I say goodbye to Josephine?"

"Unfortunately, she is being moved to a safe house. One that is difficult to find," Skalla replied.

Cole nodded and then had a thought. *They found her quickly enough on the way to London. Who's to say that they would not find the safe house and finish their deadly task? No, she needs some place that they would not expect.* Cole said, "She could be taken to Canterbury. We have empty tenant houses that would never be expected."

Skalla stood looking at Cole. "For a moment, I had forgotten that you are Lord Bickford's ward, or should I say second son. We may take you up on that," Skalla said. "I've known Charles for years."

Using Lord Bickford's first name let Cole know that Skalla was more than just an agent. He was likely an Earl.

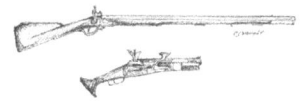

CHAPTER ELEVEN

OLE STOOD AT JOE'S SIDE. The wedding was held at the church, but because both Joe and Mary had so many friends, it was held on the steps instead of inside. Belinda Stephenson was Mary's bridesmaid. Upon looking up the duties of the best man, Cole found that in the sixteenth century the best man was usually the best swordsman as he frequently had to steal the bride from a neighboring community.

Cole looked around as thoughts came to him. Thoughts that hadn't entered his mind at his own wedding. They had stood before God to make these vows. The vows were so important that they did it before their family and friends so that all could share in their joy and happiness. They swore they'd never love anyone else but each other. But that wasn't really true. Cole loved Anne with all his heart...she'd always be first. If they'd not met he could have loved...did love, Linda but not to the point that she'd take Anne's place. What about Josephine? Something told him that she'd do her utmost to make him love her if he wasn't already taken. *Am I dishonoring Anne with these thoughts, or is it just admitting that I am aware of things?* he thought. It was a knowledge that a prudent man kept to himself. *Anne will always be my love…my main love, but does God expect one to have no other if a spouse is taken from this life? Why am I even having these thoughts? Is it to acknowledge that the same thoughts might pass through Anne's mind?* He stood a much greater chance of losing his life suddenly than Anne. There was little doubt that he was Anne's first and only love.

Joe was Mary's first and only love. Joe, however, was much like Cole and played a dangerous game. Death loomed large for both men, with Anne and Mary being aware of this.

"The ring…" Cole was suddenly brought out of his reverie by the comment. He fished it out of his uniform coat pocket and handed it to Joe. Taking the ring, Joe placed it on Mary's finger. They were both so happy and had the brightest smiles on their face. Everyone could see how much they loved each other. The ceremony had finished and the reception began.

Table after table had been set up and covered with sheets until the two had become one. The tables were full of all sorts of food. The one that perked Cole's interest was the dessert table. He'd helped Anne and her mother set it up. Kimberly Jordan's chef had contributed, as did the baker. There was enough to feed the village, which was a good thing as most of Deal had turned out. Sir William, Anne's father and the magistrate, was seen talking to Sir George Aylward, the money man for the largest smuggling operation around.

Cole was not sure of the exact circumstances, but Joe had bought one hundred acres from Sir George. The land bordered John Stuart's land. Putting the two parcels together meant that Joe and Mary's father now had the second largest holding in Deal. While the Stephenson family had more land, it was scattered about.

A small cottage sat on Joe's land next to a brook. The sound of the water cascading over the stones in the brook provided a very relaxing sound, and it was always cool. A larger house would have to be built, at some point. The cottage, however, was just right for Mary and Joe, for now.

After Joe kissed Mary, Cole took her hand. "You are absolutely radiant," he said. "I'm so proud for you." He kissed Mary on the cheek.

Mary took Cole's hand in hers. "I'm so glad that you could be Joe's best man. It meant a lot to us." She then surprised Cole somewhat. "Joe said you were the only man he ever loved, and that you were the best friend a man could have."

Cole could feel emotions swelling up inside of him. He gathered himself together. "I'm your friend as well, Mary."

She wiped a tear and responded, "I know that."

Others were crowding in to wish the couple their congratulations, so Cole kissed the back of Mary's hand and walked off. Dalton was standing close by, so Cole struck up a conversation with him.

A few hours later, Cole drove the two newlyweds to the cottage. As he drove off, Joe was toting Mary across the threshold.

✳✳✳

ANNE HAD GONE HOME WITH her parents but was waiting when Cole returned. She had on a little shift but nothing else.

"A long day," she said.

"It was," Cole replied.

Anne said, "At one point, you seemed to have your mind on something else."

"It was, to a degree," Cole responded. "I was thinking about when we were wed," he fibbed. "I hope Joe and Mary are as happy as we have been."

Anne had been sitting on the side of the bed. She leaned back and lay across the bed. She laid there a moment and then rose up on her elbows. "What?" she said.

Cole was looking at her upper legs and thighs. "Damn woman," he said. "I thought that I'd had all the dessert a man could stand in one day, but looking at those luscious legs of yours is stirring my appetite."

Anne smiled, "You're not too tired?"

"No!" Cole replied.

"There's nothing that says you can't have a midnight snack."

Cole lay down by his wife. "I want more that a snack."

She smiled and said, "What are you waiting for then, husband?"

Cole's lips met Anne's and when they broke apart, he asked, "When was the last time that I ravished your body?"

"This morning, I think."

"That's been too long ago." He lips went to her neck, and his hand slid under her shift, raising it up until his hand rested on her breast. "Mmmm, I love to feel your breast."

Anne rose up and in a quick motion the shift was off and on the floor. "It's hard to make love with your uniform on."

"Let's see what we can do about that," Cole replied.

He woke up and looked out the bedroom window. The sun was high in the sky. He'd slept long and hard. Anne had already gotten up. Cole washed off in the basin, dressed quickly and went out.

"Do you want breakfast?" Anne asked.

"I don't think so," Cole said, "but coffee or tea will be good."

Mary, Anne's mother, called to Cole, "There's an envelope on the table for you."

Cole opened the envelope. The note inside was short. 'Cock and Bull, one p.m., no uniform.'

CHAPTER TWELVE

ALTON WAS HAVING A BIT of meat and cheese while drinking from a tankard. Cole noticed that he'd gotten a bit thick around the middle lately. *Good living*, Cole thought.

"Have a tankard," Dalton offered.

Chloe was working and, whether she heard Dalton or not, she recognized Cole well enough that she drew a tankard for him. They spoke as she sat the tankard down and then left.

"I'd marry her in a heartbeat, but she hardly recognizes me," Dalton said.

"I'll speak to my uncle," Cole replied.

"No, Cole. She's the most beautiful woman I know, but she's got her cap set for another man."

Cole knew that Chloe was hoping for his brother, Phillip. Hopefully, Dalton didn't know that. Dalton said nothing about the reason for meeting until he finished eating and they were at the carriage.

Cole paused before boarding the carriage and ducked back in the Cock and Bull. He took a handful of the new cheroots and showed them to Chloe, before he laid his money down on the counter. If his uncle had been present, he would not have let Cole pay for the cheroots. He offered one to Dalton as he was climbing into the carriage.

Dalton turned down the offer, "I could never understand what people see in 'the devil's weed'. You buy a rolled up weed and then set it on fire."

Cole laughed and said, "It's no different than drinking spirits."

"I beg to differ. Everyone knows that water is bad for you, so you have to drink what isn't. No, Jesus turned the water into wine for a reason. I intend to follow his teachings in that regard."

Hence the thick middle, Cole thought but kept it to himself.

Cole's cigar was still unlit when Dalton spoke, "While I do not smoke, I don't mind you doing so. In fact, I enjoy the smell of good tobacco."

Cole got his cigar lit and had a nice plume of smoke going when Dalton said, "We are going to meet our handler in Dover. I imagine that we will be given an assignment."

Hopefully it's escorting another agent, Cole thought to himself.

It was about eight miles between Deal and Dover. The coach pulled up to a pub on the outskirts of Dover called The Cliffs. *If this isn't a smugglers hangout I'll eat my hat*, Cole thought. When Dalton didn't move to open the door, Cole sat still as well. The two hour trip had been pleasant, with the conversation going from the weather, taxes, what was wrong with the army, and inevitably to women.

While Dalton didn't approve of the sex parties his father had thrown at their home, more so because of his sister, Belinda's presence for some of it, his father had been a blade of some renown. That was the only thing that Cole had ever heard Dalton say about his father in which he actually sounded prideful. *It's something at least*, Cole thought.

The coach driver returned and sticking his head in the window, he nodded and stepped back. Entering the pub, Cole saw that James Atkins was sitting at the first table. Cole and Dalton sat down across from him. A girl brought them each a tankard.

"I have assignments for both of you," he said, handing an envelope to each of them. "You can read them later. I could have sent your assignment with Dalton, Cole, but our mutual friend has decided to take your advice and send a certain lady to a residence you recommended. I was asked to give this to you. It's from the landlord of the residence." Cole nodded and Atkins continued, "Now be a good man, Cole, and go flirt with the wench at the bar. Ask for a different drink or something."

Cole stood up and placed the two envelopes in his pocket and walked over to the bar. "I've a taste for a brandy if you have a good brand."

"Aye, we do, sir, be there anything else you'd like?"

"Yes, more than one thing, but I only see you here, so that limits my choices."

The girl smiled. "What would you be wanting, kind sir?"

"You, of course," Cole replied.

"Why, governor, if you really mean that I get off at six."

"Alas, I will be long gone. Would you have a good cigar?"

"Right down here, sir."

As Cole looked over the bar, the girl's hands slid down her top, exposing a breast. "Is this your kind?"

"Do you have others?" Cole asked.

The girl pulled her blouse down and wiggled, causing both exposed breasts to swing. "Is this more to your liking?"

"Aye, all the more so than my first choice, but still time is a problem." He took out several coins and laid them on the bar.

Dalton was now standing, so Cole downed the brandy and felt the fiery liquid burn its way down his throat.

The girl fixed her blouse and stood up. Seeing the coins, she placed them in a pocket that was inside her skirt.

"Don't forget to take out for the brandy," Cole said.

She smiled, "It's on the house, sweetie."

Atkins was grinning from ear to ear as Cole walked past him. Was this something that he'd setup? Cole suddenly felt like he was not the first who'd been given a private viewing.

***

THE NOTE FROM THE LANDLORD was from Lord Bickford, as Cole had expected. He said that he was happy to take on a new tenant and enjoyed renewing an old friendship.

Cole opened the other envelope. There was a brief note and another envelope inside. The note said 'to a fair lady's hand before the midnight hour'. The fair lady obviously meant Linda. It was now near seven p.m. Was it too early? The note hadn't specified anything but 'before the midnight hour'.

Cole was sitting in a corner of the Cock and Bull. Joe walked in but didn't see Cole in the corner. When Joe sat down at a table by himself, Cole stood and walked over. Chloe was on the way but returned to the bar and filled another tankard. Other than a pleasant greeting, neither man talked.

"Lawd, the two best looking men in Deal, and both of you are taken," Chloe quipped.

"If only you'd showed up before me darling had me in her clutches," Joe whined. "Fate, Cole, that's what it is." Joe acted like he was going to swat Chloe's bottom, but she swooshed her little butt enough for it to be beyond Joe's hand. Looking back, she gave a big smile.

"I see that she has gotten some practice dodging swats," Cole observed. With Chloe gone, Cole looked at his friend. "I've a need to know something. Between friends, is there a landing tonight?"

Joe picked up his tankard and brought it up to his mouth. Before taking a drink, he nodded his head. Cole finished his ale, asking if being married had made any big changes.

"Aye, Mary is used to being up at dawn, and in the past I've not headed to bed before dawn," Joe replied.

Cole laughed, "That's what you get from marrying a farmer's daughter."

"Is that so?" Joe said. "It beats cold sheets, though."

Cole laughed again, that was a true statement. A thought came to him then. *I never knew a woman could have such a hot little rear and still have cold feet.* He finished his tankard and rode out to Linda's house.

Saul must have heard him coming as he stood at the corner of the stable with a gun in his hand. He raised the gun in a salute when he recognized Cole. Linda had heard the horse as well, so she opened the door before Cole could knock. She was fully dressed, which surprised Cole, but he was glad of it. Linda was a lot of woman in the best kind of way.

"I have some coffee, or a brandy if you prefer," Linda said.

"You better make it coffee," he responded. He'd drunk enough alcohol for the day.

Linda took the note and while Cole sat in the kitchen drinking coffee, she read the note. In a few minutes, she came back and said, "I'm expecting a visitor later tonight. There is a question as to this visitor's loyalty. I need you to stay here until he's gone."

"If there's a question, why bring him here at all?" Cole asked. "This may be nothing more than a scouting trip, and I don't like it."

Linda didn't speak for a moment, and that encouraged Cole to continue. "Let's meet him near the landing. He can pass on his information and never know where you live."

"I think not, Cole. They have set this up, like they have, for a reason. Let's play it out."

Cole was fuming. "Stubborn! That's what you are," he shouted.

Linda smiled at Cole. She's never seen Cole angry with her. "Yes, I am, but you love me and are here to protect me."

Cole hushed then.

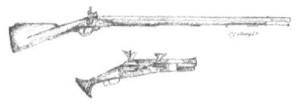

CHAPTER THIRTEEN

OLE MADE LINDA PROMISE WHEN the agent arrived, that she would stay either in the kitchen or the sitting room. Cole could always have her in his sight, that way, via the hall or her bedroom. He had time, so he went out and talked to Saul.

Saul, even from the outside, had a good view of the kitchen. Nearly the entire room since it was lined with windows on two sides. Double windows were in the sitting room. Though they were not as open as the kitchen windows, depending on where a person was positioned, Saul would have a fair shot if it came to it.

"Fear not, Saul," Cole told the old black man. "We'll get rid of the body, but if the shooting ever comes to light I will say I'm the one who shot the rogue."

Marge, Linda's servant girl, had left soon after Cole arrived. She would not be back that night. Cole couldn't help but wonder if she were warming Doctor Garrett's sheets. Well, it was none of his business, if she was. Cole thought of how many suitors the girl would have if she worked as a barmaid at the Cock and Bull or one of the other taverns. She definitely had the right 'wares.' He'd seen the girl flirt when she didn't think Linda was watching.

***

THE WALL CLOCK STRUCK MIDNIGHT. It wouldn't be long now. Cole finished off the coffee that he'd been drinking and went to the hall-way. Linda saw his worried look and smiled, her hand brushing his arm as he went by. At the table, over coffee, he'd checked the loads in her small pistol and his two pistols. He didn't want a misfire, should it come to it. Cole had put a chair in the hall so he wouldn't have to stand. It was situated so that even if you stood at the hall entrance it would be hard to spot him. If they were in the kitchen, he'd have to stand by the door and listen. In going over his plan, he found a board that squeaked entering the doorway into the kitchen from Linda's bedroom. He dropped a doily on the floor right where the squeak was. If anyone saw it, they would think that Linda had dropped it when putting up her crochet. Another thought came to Cole. *If I have to make a fast entry, it wouldn't make a damn if the floor squeaked or not.*

Cole looked at the clock to see that it had only been fifteen minutes since he'd looked the last time. He thought about having a quick brandy to steady his nerves. Damnation, a brandy would do away with the reason why he'd drunk two mugs of coffee. He wanted to be alert. He sat in a chair and found himself looking at Linda. She was a beautiful woman, one with class and bearing. Why hadn't she found another man? Did she want one? She had to get lonely; Cole knew that from the times he'd held her. *Major Letchworth*, now why did that name come to mind? He was a good man, a fine officer. But it had been his men who had killed her husband. Cole shook his head as he felt a chill. *Here I am trying to play Cupid or a matchmaker*, he thought to himself. Could he stand the thought of another man sharing Linda's bed? She dealt with the fact that Anne shared his bed. His thoughts suddenly cleared.

There was a noise outside. It sounded like the noise a horse's hoof makes when striking a rock. Did Linda hear it? He looked at her. She was leaning back in her chair with her eyes closed.

"Psst…" Cole whispered.

Linda raised her head and looked at Cole. He made a walking motion with his fingers and pointed outside. She stood up and went over to the windows, where she stood behind a curtain, looking out.

There were two horses out there. She recognized Joe on one of them. The other man was a stranger. Joe dismounted and held the other horse's bridle. The man who dismounted the horse was small in stature.

He walked to the door, gave two knocks, paused and then gave two more. Linda opened the door, a password was passed, and then Linda stood aside as the agent came in. Joe remained outside holding the horses' reins. Linda led the person into the kitchen.

The two talked in hushed voices. Linda listened and then clarified a few things. The agent was then up and gone. When the door closed, Cole walked out.

"Did you recognize the agent?" Linda asked.

"No, other than he was smallish for a man," Cole replied.

Linda laughed. "It wasn't a man at all."

Cole looked puzzled. "Lois, was it Lois Breeding?"

"Yes, and she's adopted her disguise so that even you didn't recognize her."

"I didn't get a good look," Cole countered.

Linda kissed him on the cheek. "I did and it was not until she took her hat off that I recognized her. She had dyed her hair and that really made a difference."

***

COLE WAS LATE WAKING UP the next morning. When he had gotten home, he had put his horse up, rubbing the animal down good and then giving Apollo a few rubs between the ears. Anne had woken up when he crawled in bed.

After a loving kiss, she said, "You smell like a horse."

"Do you want me to go back to the stable?" Cole asked.

"Only if we are going to play in the hay," she responded.

They snuggled close, horse smell and all. "I'll get us some bath water tomorrow when you get up," Anne whispered.

The next morning, Anne asked one of the maids to get some bath water and a clean set of sheets for them. The maid raised her eyebrows and smiled.

Anne laughed and said, "Not that. Cole came home smelling like a horse."

Mary, Anne's mother, said, "That's better than him reeking of cigars and spirits."

"Or worse," the maid said. When Anne and Mary looked at the maid, she added, "He could have smelled like another woman."

"I guess there's that," Anne said. "I trust Cole." She grew very serious and continued, "I don't think that Cole would ever hurt me that way."

Before the maid or Mary could speak, a voice said, "I would die before I hurt you or allowed anyone else to." Anne ran to her husband and, ignoring the horse smell, they embraced.

***

A CORPORAL, ONE OF ROD Letchworth's men, delivered the letter. Anne's mother gave it to Cole, who took it to the bedroom to read. After reading it, Cole sat for a moment and then he read it again.

The letter was from Lord Skalla. Cole would be needed in London for a few days but would also have a lot of time to do as he pleased.

Therefore, he was welcome to bring his wife and perhaps another couple.

Cole folded the letter and went looking for Anne. She was working with some roses, peeling back the loose petals of the bud. "Would you like to go to London for a few days?"

"Sure," was Anne's reply.

"There will be some work involved for me, but I will also have a lot of time when I'm not working that we can do a few things," Cole said.

"I'll go pack," Anne said.

"Wait! We can take another couple. What do you think about asking Joe and Mary to come with us?"

"I think it's a great idea. That way while you are working we can do things together," Anne replied.

"I'll saddle our horses. You can pack after we return."

***

The road to London was no better or worse than the usual trip, only less muddy. Joe, having no landings planned, had been willing to make the trip, stating he had a few errands to run for Sir George. Joe kept up a lively tale of some of the mishaps of the tubsmen climbing the cliffs during a landing. One, in particular, of a big woman tripping over her dress bottom and tumbling arse over tea kettle with her dress over her head and her drawers shining, kept Mary and Anne laughing.

Cole noticed how freely Joe talked in front of Anne. Did he have that much confidence that she'd never betray her husband's best friend? He didn't think Joe had become loose mouthed. The coach that they rode in was one of Sir George's. When the driver pulled up to Anne's parents, Cole had not missed the look on Sir William's face. He might have said something had Mary not squeezed his arm.

This prompted Cole to think, in the future, they might want to be picked up at the Cock and Bull. A few times of late, he'd considered moving from Anne's parents but decided not to, thinking that staying there would be better for Anne, and safer.

The coach slowed and, looking out the window, Cole said, "We're here."

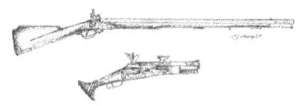

CHAPTER FOURTEEN

ORD SKALLA HAD BEEN PUNCTUAL, with a clerk showing Cole into his office a good five minutes before his nine a.m. appointment. Hot cocoa was served and since it was still early in the morning, a tray of pastries was also placed on the side of Lord Skalla's desk.

"I have invited you to bring your wife and another couple, as it will help with your assignment," Skalla said. "You need a cover, a front, as it were," the senior agent said. "As much as I wish it had been out of the goodness of my heart, it's not. We have a Frenchman here. He is an older man, who has provided us with good information. He is also of the social class that the new French government all but eradicated. For reasons I can't tell you, we've been led to believe that he may have been compromised. Over the next week, you will attend several functions. You will go to a play at the theatre; I did get you balcony seats. There will be a show of this new thing called a hot air balloon. He will be there, as well as thousands of others, I'm sure. While I can't do better, stands have been put up and you will be seated near him. Once you are in the crowd, I have other men to help watch. But I question their ability to watch and assess what they see. I've been assured that you have an eye to see what others do not, and that's what I need. A pair of eyes that see beyond the obvious."

"What is the name of this Frenchman, if I'm allowed to know?" Cole asked.

"Certainly, he is Monsieur Lee Bergevin. His hair is starting to gray, and he is taller than either of us, I'd say over six feet tall. He is a very distinguished looking man, very smart and very aware of his surroundings. In spite of his age, he is a very physically fit man. Before the revolution, he was part of a group that liked to climb the mountains of France."

"He should be easy to pick out," Cole said.

"Yes, he will be armed with a pistol and a sword cane," Skalla said.

This did not surprise Cole, as it was a popular gentleman's accessory. His father and Lord Bickford both carried one. Lord Bickford was rarely without his but Cole's father only carried his on occasions when he was dressed for some event.

Lord Skalla came around the desk to shake Cole's hand, ending the meeting. "My clerk will have your tickets." They had said their goodbyes when Skalla called Cole's name. "I believe if you go by White Hall, you may stumble into your brother. He is on an errand for Captain Atwater. He has been promoted over some and is Atwater's most trusted lieutenant, though not the first lieutenant."

The possibility of seeing Phillip excited Cole, so he had the coachman rush over to the Admiralty.

***

PHILLIP WAS MET BY COLE as he was leaving the Admiralty. Seeing Cole, Phillip rushed over and gave him a big hug. The first thing Cole noticed was that his brother was lean and hard. His handshake was strong, and his once smooth hands were now calloused. He was also much tanned. His hair was much lighter from being on a ship's deck and under a blazing sun for many hours a day in the Caribbean.

"How long will you be in London?" Cole asked.

"I'd say tonight and tomorrow, at least," Phillip said. "But in truth, until the Admiralty makes a decision as what to do with our ship." Cole had been aware that the ship had seen much action in the last eighteen months. Phillip continued, "Captain Best will probably retire an invalid. Atwater is acting captain and he should be given a command, as he deserves it. The Port Admiral thinks the ship is in need of an extensive overhaul. This will take a year or more. As bad as we need men, the navy is not going to let our crew sit on the beach until *Diamond* is seaworthy. Admiral Howe has recommended Atwater for command and included favorable comments about your brother. If Atwater is given anything less than a frigate, he wants me to be his first lieutenant."

Seeing Cole's questioning look, Phillip said, "I'm not senior enough to be first lieutenant on a frigate."

Phillip took hold of Cole's arm, as talk about the ship had died, "Where is your uniform, brother? Surely they haven't gotten rid of you so soon."

"No," Cole replied. "My deepest secrets have yet to be discovered." Both Phillip and Cole laughed. "No, we returned from the Caribbean and have been on training since. In truth, our lack of leadership in our army and with our allies has made our getting orders very unlikely. No one wants to see the Prince's own regiment captured or worse. So until such a time as a leader may be found, I'm on loan to the Foreign Office as a courier."

Phillip was about to step into the coach but stopped and stared at his brother. "You're a spy."

"No," Cole said. "Just a courier…"

"For spies," Phillip said, finishing the sentence. "Does anyone know?"

Cole shook his head, "Not unless they are on the need-to-know list."

Phillip put his hand on Cole's shoulder, "Dangerous work, brother, and little recognition for it. We landed and picked up one a few times. His name was Leo Gallagher. He is a man that I'd hate to anger. If you, by chance, run across him, you can mention my name but don't say that I mentioned his."

Cole nodded and told the driver to take them home. "You were going to our home, were you not?"

Phillip smiled, "Dear brother, you are looking at a man with months of pent up humors. Had I not run into you, I'd have found some willing maid worthy of my blade and vanquished her thoroughly. With my brother and his beautiful wife here I'll deal with my humors a bit longer. Who knows, I may even steal the beautiful Anne away from you."

"No chance," Cole shot back. "Why would she go from a thoroughbred to a plow horse?" A thought came to Cole: *I do know of two women who would love to bed you, I'm sure.* Phillip gave Cole a quizzical look. "Chloe for one, she is certainly in love with you. She realizes that she is beneath your station, but that has only made her sad. Anne told me that Chloe was about you as Anne was about me."

Phillip grew silent for a moment. "She is a lovely creature. I could never find a more beautiful wife."

Cole added, "Or one who loves you as much."

"Father would disown me," Phillip said, hanging his head.

Cole could see that he'd touched his brother. It dawned on him then. Phillip's feelings for Chloe were more…much more than lust.

He actually loved the girl. Cole wondered again, how the Earl would take that. Cole made up his mind. He'd speak to his father about the situation. Nobody was closer to the Earl than Peter Buckley.

Once they pulled up to the Earl's London house, the air immediately grew festive again. Anne rushed to Phillip and gave him a warm greeting.

"Is my brother still treating you like a lady should be?" Phillip asked Anne. "If not, I'm available. The most beautiful woman should have the best man, and not second best."

Mary, smiling, took all this in, "Is this the man that Belinda is so hopelessly in love with?"

"That's him," Anne replied. "Phillip, you remember Joe and Mary don't you?"

"Of course, they were at the wedding and how could I forget Joe after all we have been through." The two men shook hands, and Phillip said, "It's good to see you. Now, who is this woman that desires me?"

Anne explained who Belinda was, and Phillip said, "Of course, she is a lively and fun lass, as I recall."

Cole made a mental note to talk to his wife about Phillip and Chloe. Phillip's comment about Belinda satisfied the women but it let Cole know that she, Belinda, had done nothing to impress his brother. Had she bedded him, she still would be little more than a passing ship in the night.

Cole suddenly felt sick at Phillip's predicament. *Damn all the rules for society*, he thought. He was suddenly glad that he had the Earl's backing. *Had I not, would I be married to Anne? The simple answer was no.* There was no way in hell that he would have gained permission from her father.

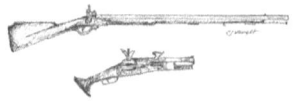

CHAPTER FIFTEEN

HE THEATER WAS CROWDED. COLE was not sure how much good he'd be, trying to keep an eye out for danger. He had taken Joe into his confidence. What Skalla didn't realize was that if he thought Cole was good, Joe was better. Years of being a smuggler had taught Joe to take nothing at face value.

Lee Bergevin had entered the theater. He was as Skalla described, a most distinguished man. On his arm was a beautiful lady. She was too refined to have been from Covent Gardens. A courtesan perhaps, but her demeanor didn't fit that mold either. The lady was twenty or more years younger than Bergevin.

Joe was watching as well and said, "Too young to be a daughter."

Cole and Joe took in the crowd, not just the immediate crowd, but throughout the theater. One individual got Cole's attention. "Joe, do you know our handler's name?"

"Atkins," Joe replied.

"Look at the man two rows behind Bergevin, he's wearing a brown coat."

Joe looked at the man, looked at Cole, and then back at the man again. It was Atkins. Joe was sure, but his reddish brown hair was now gray and he sported a goatee, whereas before he'd been clean shaven. "You are right, Cole. The gray hair does make him look much older."

The play was the first for Mary, and both she and Anne laughed at the antics and thought the comedy was perfect. After the play, a reception was given, being that it was the grand opening night. The girls were pleased their tickets included the reception.

Anne saw an old friend and both she and Mary went over to talk. Seeing Bergevin close to Anne's friend, Joe and Cole hurried over. As they neared the group, they heard Bergevin introducing the girl. She was his granddaughter, Phoebe. That answered that question, Cole thought. As Joe and Cole walked to their wives, Atkins passed them. Cole and Atkins' eyes met but they didn't speak.

When the reception was over, Cole watched Bergevin and Phoebe get into a carriage. The top was up, but for a trained assassin, the agent would have been an easy target.

When they got home a note was waiting, directing Cole to be at the office at noon. Anne had undressed and spoke to Cole, "Is that more interesting than me?"

He smiled, "Never!"

She walked over and helped Cole out of his shirt. As she did so, her breasts swept across Cole's face, lighting a fire of desire. He sat back down on the bed and gently caressed Anne's breasts. She moaned slightly as she pushed Cole down and lay beside him on the bed.

"Don't stop," she whispered.

Cole continued to kiss and gently nibble at her neck and breasts, and his hands began to move. He caressed Anne's stomach and as his hands drifted down to her thighs, he kissed his way down to her belly button.

Anne's breath was quickening. "God, Cole, take me now," she hissed. "I'm on fire, take me."

A partially opened window allowed a small breeze to enter the room. The lace curtain rose and fell with the breeze. The candle flickered creating shadows on the wall. The slight smell of rain drifted on the breeze as a slight sprinkle came down. This was not noticed by Cole or Anne as they cuddled so tightly, exhausted after quenching their burning fires of young love.

•••

COLE DIDN'T AWAKEN UNTIL NINE a.m. the next morning. He was entangled with Anne, with their legs together, her arm above his head, and her breasts in his face. *What a pleasant way to wake up*, he thought.

Anne stirred and then sat up. She looked down at her husband's smiling face and asked, "What are you smiling at?"

"Those beautiful catheads dangling so near my face. They are most inviting," he replied.

"I'm sorry, dear husband, but nature is urgently calling," Anne said.

Isn't that just like a woman, Cole thought. A man would have said, 'I gotta go piss.' It was more crude but very definitive.

Cole and Anne went downstairs for breakfast while their bath water was being heated. Mary was already drinking a cup of hot tea.

Cole asked, "Joe still in bed?"

Mary replied, "Yes, he said that while I was a farmer's daughter and was used to getting up early, his work was just ending at that time. So we've reached an agreement. He will get up by ten and I'll keep the house quiet until he's up."

Anne and Cole had their coffee and pastries and then they went back upstairs for their baths. This was one aspect of Cole's assignment that he liked. Being home more and having moments like this.

***

A FAINT COOLNESS GREETED COLE outside. He walked out from under the roof of the porch to get a better look at the sky. There was a bank of clouds moving in from the north. Thunderheads, his Uncle Angus would call them. The coolness touched his face, a breeze with the smell of rain in it.

The hot air balloon exhibition may have to be postponed, Cole thought. *Damn, I'm actually looking forward to seeing the show.* As he stood there a few drops of rain started to fall. Had he ever been to London that it didn't rain, at least a drizzle? Cole stepped back up under the porch. Anne walked out and saw that the rain was coming down hard, like a solid wall with the wind bending the trees and pounding the side of the house.

"We better go back in or we'll have had a second bath," Cole said.

The thunder came with the darkened sky, the far off beginnings of it until it reached an earth shaking boom. The boom thoroughly frightened Anne, who threw herself in Cole's arms. He kissed her and, as they turned to go in, a jagged flash of lightning struck something close by. The sound of it breaking something made Cole glad that they didn't have any trees so close to the house that one would fall on it.

"Damnation," Joe said as they entered in the room. "It sounds like the Frogs are attacking London."

Cole laughed, and looking at the wall clock, he quipped, "They waited until after ten o' clock, at least." Joe's response was a most obscene gesture, but with a smile.

The rain lasted an hour or so, and then moved on south. Venturing back outside, a tree was down in the street. It would take a while to clear the tree, and until then nothing could pass except a horse. A carriage couldn't get around it without detouring. The detour would mean going north a half mile, taking a left turn, and then coming back a mile to turn left to get back on the main road.

These directions were confirmed when Skalla sent a message saying that the hot air show had been rescheduled for the next day. He also had news about Phillip. When Phillip had left, he'd told them that he might have to report directly back to the ship. When he didn't return, Cole assumed that he'd done just that. He, in fact, did have to return but to a different ship, the *Dido*, a small twenty-eight gun frigate. He would be the second lieutenant. This was a big jump for Phillip, even if it was a small ship.

The ship was part of a group escorting a convoy to the Mediterranean. Cole had heard convoy duty was a thankless job but, to win the war, supplies had to be taken where they were needed.

***

THE NEXT DAY PROVED TO be a beautiful one. There was no hint, other than a few mud puddles, that yesterday's thunderstorm had even rained on London. Hyde Park was filled with people. Some of them with a genuine interest in the hot air balloons while others were more interested in whose purse they could steal.

People from the colleges with a background in science were all gathered over by the roped off area around the balloons. There were three of them looking at the balloons.

Cole thought to himself, *I wonder how in the devil I'm supposed to watch out for somebody when I can't even find him.*

After half an hour of being jostled and shoved around, and Anne having someone falling into her, they decided to go to the stands. It was a good decision, as they'd just gotten settled in when the agent sat down.

"Isn't that the same man that we saw at the theater?" Anne asked indicating Bergevin.

"Yes, it is," Cole said.

Anne looked at her husband for a moment. It wasn't unusual to see a person at different London functions. For them to out of the blue make a trip to London, though, and encounter the same man at both functions made Anne very suspicious.

The hot air balloon exhibition was interesting, but not the affair that Cole had hoped it would be. The balloons went up, came down, went up part way and then moved side to side before coming down again. At one point, Cole realized a rope was attached to the basket of the balloons. Tethered as they were, they'd only go up so far. He was pointing this out to Anne and Mary when a shot rang out. Cole and Joe each pushed their wives down. Cole looked to where Bergevin had been seated. He was down and didn't appear to be moving. Cole stood up and saw a man running between the stands and toward the rear.

"Joe," he shouted. "I'll be back." He took the three steps up to the top of the stands, then and jumped down. He saw Atkins and pointed in the direction that the man was running. Cole, hitting the ground hard, was still able to take off running. He saw Atkins weaving up ahead in the crowd.

BANG!! Another shot rang out. Cole burst between two carriages in time to see Atkins down in the street wounded. A man was coming towards Atkins with his pistol aimed at him.

Cole pulled his own pistol out and yelled. The man took another step towards Atkins, with murder on his mind. He'd not even looked at Cole, even when Cole shouted. Cole would never make it in time to tackle the man, so he stopped. He was breathing hard, so he took a deep breath to try and steady his hand holding the pistol. The man stuck his pistol to Atkins' head, so Cole fired. The ball hit the man, who still pulled the trigger on his own pistol. Cole's ball had hit the man under his arm and knocked him sideways, which threw his aim off, sending the ball into the street. The powder flash, however, singed the side of Atkins' head and ear.

Cole checked to see if the man was dead...he was. Cole looked at Atkins, fearing the worst.

"It's just a powder burn," Cole told the agent.

Two more of Atkins' men had shown up by then. One of them said, "Get him out of the street and to the office before the constables get here. Cole, you go on back to your wife."

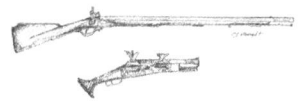

CHAPTER SIXTEEN

THE DAWN SPRANG UP WITH a gentle breeze coming off the sea. It was just enough to push small rollers up on the beach. Cole walked along the sand, dodging the water that crept up with the incoming tide. The smell of the salt and seaweed pressed against his face. The sound of a larger wave, up ahead, breaking on the beach came to him. A few birds were out scurrying around, picking out some morsel brought in by the tide.

He'd woken up an hour ago, leaving Anne in slumber. For a while, he had looked down on his wife as the moon shown through the window. They'd gotten back to Deal late, so they had stayed at the Cock and Bull, in Cole's old room. Anne had been frightened by the attempted assassination of Bergevin at the hot air balloon show.

Joe had said that when he had jumped off the stands in pursuit of the assassin, Anne had screamed, "No, Cole!"

Cole, in his determination to catch the shooter, never heard her. When he got back to the stands, she was still pale with fear and concern for her husband's life. He had taken Anne back to the house, with Mary and Joe returning as well.

Anne asked him that night if he loved her, truly loved her. Cole swore with all his heart that he did. She spit back, "Why did you leave me like that then? You could have been killed and I'd be alone. Cole, what's worse is, what if I was pregnant and you ran off and got killed. Your child would not have a father."

Cole couldn't find words to comfort her as guilt rushed over him. He had tried to come up with something to make her understand that England was at war. Soldiers were dying every day on the battlefield and he was safer here than he would be on the front lines. He did tell her that he'd saved a man's life.

"I'm glad," was her only response.

Near where they'd been sitting, the pistol ball had plowed a furrow on the plank between two women's legs. They were sitting directly behind her, so Anne had taken it all in...the bang from the pistol, the smoke from the barrel, the hat flying off Bergevin's head, and the thud as the pistol ball scarred the wood plank. She suddenly came to understand that but for a sudden movement, a man would have been killed. Her safe world was suddenly not so safe anymore. An innocent person could just as easily been killed.

Anne had come to bed wearing something like a winter gown, which was unlike most nights, when she was either nude or wearing a really revealing short gown. Where she had gotten it, Cole didn't know. While in the Caribbean, he'd heard men from the southern Colonies use the term 'granny gown.' While he'd never actually seen one, he felt that Anne's nightgown fit the description he'd pictured in his head.

Mary had squeezed his arm and whispered, "She'll be all right, just give her some time."

Cole was now up to some of the fishing boats that had been pulled up on the sand out of the tide's reach. The pungent smell of dead fish was strong, so Cole turned to retrace his steps back to the Cock and Bull and his wife.

✳✳✳

THE MORNING AFTER THE SHOOTING Cole had reported to Lord Skalla. Joe had gone on some errands for Sir George, leaving Anne and Mary to do as they pleased. They had planned to do some shopping, but while Anne went through the motions, Mary could tell that her mind was still on the shooting.

Lord Skalla shook Cole's hand immediately after he was ushered in the office. "It seems that I owe you for my agent's life. By stepping out as you did, though, you've compromised your cover. I've put a spin on it for the paper, saying that an officer in the Prince's Own Regiment was at the exhibition and, seeing firsthand the shooting, he lent a hand pursuing and apprehending the would-be assassin." Cole thought, *that was a good idea.*

Atkins came in, wearing a large bandage on his head and part of his face. He thanked Cole again and then left after a few private and hushed words with Skalla.

When Skalla returned his attention back to Cole, he surprised him, saying, "Take your wife to a nice dinner tonight and then return to Deal. You might even want to go to Canterbury for a few days."

Cole looked at Lord Skalla and said, "Thank you, sir. If Anne's up to it, we will."

✳✳✳

THE HORIZON WAS GETTING LIGHTER and a few lights appeared in some of the fishermen's houses. When Cole made it back to the low breakers wall, Anne was there in her granny gown and barefoot like Cole.

"Are you all right?" she asked.

"I am now," Cole said. "I was so worried about you that I couldn't sleep and I didn't want to wake you."

"I'm sorry that I got so frightened, Cole. I suddenly realized how fragile life is and how quickly you could be gone. I think I've suddenly awakened to the fact that my perfect little world is not so perfect. Cole, do you know you've killed another man? Yes, it was your duty, I know that. But, did this one have a family? Is there a relative who may search for you to get revenge?" Cole went to speak but Anne held up her hand to hush him. "How many, Cole? How many have you killed now? Three, four... How many and when will it stop? I don't blame you, but my world has just been shattered with the ugly truth that my husband is a killer."

Cole went to pull Anne to him but she pushed back. "I saw it, Cole. We were standing on top of the viewing stands and I saw you aim and fire your pistol at the man. I know that it was your duty, but I've got to think."

"It's war, Anne."

"Damn, Cole, don't you think that I know it's war," Anne replied.

Cole was suddenly glad that he'd not told Anne about those he'd killed to protect Josephine.

"I'm going back to our room," Anne said. As she spun around, the granny gown molded against her rear, with the breeze helping to push the material against her. *The granny gowns were not all bad*, Cole thought, admiring the view as he walked behind his wife.

When they got to the back door of the tavern, Cole spoke to Anne as she made the first step. "You sure have a pretty butt, Anne."

Anne spun around and being a step higher, she was face to face with her husband. "Damn you, Cole Buckley! You scare me to death and all you can think about is my arse."

"It's pretty," Cole said. "You should be glad that I'm looking at it."

They stood there for a long moment, eye to eye. Their noses were almost touching.

"God, you create a fire in me, you rogue." Anne started crying then. "I do love you so much. In truth, I don't care who you've had to kill doing your duty, I just don't want to lose you. I could see you lying there in the street, dead. I couldn't live without you, Cole." They kissed then, and it was a wet kiss with Anne's tears flowing down on his face. "Take me in and love me, Cole."

***

JOE SAT ACROSS THE TABLE from Mary. "Thank you for being a friend to Anne. Seeing the shooting unsettled her."

"It wasn't just her, Joe. It upset me also, only I'm older and a bit more mature. I knew exactly how she felt, though. I can still see you lying in the road, nearly dead. And if that's not bad enough, to have you shot at on our own porch. In my heart I've always known you could be killed. It's a dangerous game, this smuggling. I knew, however, who and what you were from the beginning. It doesn't make it any less frightening. I've come to just thank God for our time together. Anne will realize the same thing if she hasn't already. Seeing a man killed brings home the truth of just how fragile life is. I think that it affects women more than men."

Joe sat there. Hearing his wife made him think. It also made him realize the strain that he'd put on her. She didn't deserve it, nor did Anne. *After this war*, he promised himself. *I'll put this smuggling behind me, for her sake*, he vowed.

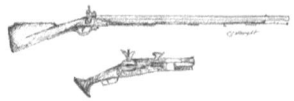

CHAPTER SEVENTEEN

FOUR WEEKS HAD PASSED SINCE the shooting. During that time, Cole and Anne spent most of the first two weeks at Belcastle. Cole talked with his father about the shooting. Peter Buckley listened, nodded and gripped his son on the shoulders. He also talked to his father about Phillip and Chloe. Cole thought his father understood the situation, but didn't make any comments or promises in regards to talking to the Earl.

Cole caught his mother looking at him a couple of times that night at dinner. Had his father already confided in her? If so, what caused the look? Was it the shooting or Phillip's loving Chloe?

Anne and Cole rode to Canterbury later in the week. Anne had gone into a dress shop and Cole went to get pipe tobacco for both his father and the earl. After purchasing the tobacco, he went to meet Anne. Entering the shop, he came face to face with Josephine. At first, Josephine was shocked and actually became flushed. Cole took her hand and greeted her.

She smiled and said, "I wasn't expecting to see you again, Cole."

He smiled back and replied, "This is where I'm from."

Josephine looked at him for a moment and said, "Belcastle's cottage was your idea, wasn't it?" Cole nodded his head. She continued, "I didn't put the two together."

"How are your wounds?" Cole asked.

Josephine's hands automatically went to her chest. However, before she could answer him, Anne walked up. Cole, still holding Josephine's one hand, took Anne's hand with his other one.

"This is my wife, Anne," Cole said. "Anne, this is Josephine."

Both women smiled with Josephine saying, "Call me Josie."

Cole asked her again, "Your wounds, how are they doing?"

"They are healed, but still sore. The surgeon says that it will be sometime before the soreness goes away."

"Have you met my father?"

"I'm not sure," Josephine replied.

"His name is Peter Buckley and my mother is Margaret. Should you need anything, call on them. I'm sure that father knows you are there. I will tell him that we are friends. If you get lonesome, my mother would enjoy a visit."

"Thank you, I shall keep that in mind."

Anne, not knowing the relationship, but sensing it was more than the usual spoke, "You'll love Mother Buckley and if you'd like...if you are able, we could go riding one day while I'm here."

Thank you, I shall be in touch."

On the way back home, Anne said, "She's French."

"She is," Cole answered, "although I noticed that she didn't use madame, mademoiselle, bonjour, or aurevoir."

"Who is she?" Anne asked.

Cole looked at his wife, thinking how much do I dare tell her.? "I met her through work," he replied, thinking the truth was in order. "She is a French spy. She was wounded trying to escape from

French agents. When the French found her in London, I recommended that she be taken to a cottage at Belcastle.

"She looked pale," Anne said.

Cole took his wife's hand, "You would be too, had you been shot in the chest. Anne!"

His wife looked over at him, "Yes?"

"You can't breathe a word of what I told you.. Not to anyone… understand?"

Anne nodded, "Oh Cole, I feel so sorry for her. She's alone in another country, knowing that she could be found and killed at any moment. She has to be lonely."

"Aye, lonely and living in fear of her life," Cole replied.

"Would you mind if I visited her, Cole, maybe your mother and I together? I will not mention a word of what you told me."

"I think that would be wonderful, Anne. I will tell mother that her presence here must be kept a secret."

Anne nodded and then added, "She loves you, Cole."

He smiled, "Don't be silly."

Anne responded, "A woman can tell. It's just like I know that Chloe loves Phillip."

"I helped save her life, Anne. She's just grateful," he replied.

"She's gratefully in love. I don't think that you did anything, Cole. I know you wouldn't betray me. I recognize the look, though." Anne laughed and continued, "Don't be shocked, husband. If you were not a man, you'd recognize it as well."

***

COLE DOWNED THE LAST OF his ale. "I think that's enough for me."

Joe belched and said, "Aye, that's enough for me, I'm thinking."

Dalton looked at the two men. "If you don't have one more round, how will I get Chloe to come over here again?"

"Call the lass and tell her you are in love," Joe commented, a bit too loud, thanks to three tankards of ale. He belched again and said, "Point me in the direction of the pisser."

Seeing Saul walk up, Cole stood, "That's two of us, Joe." He patted Dalton on the shoulder. "It's my time to buy next time."

Cole didn't hear if Dalton replied. He stopped at the front of the tavern and picked up two cigars and laid down a shilling. It was more than enough for two cigars, but it helped towards those that he'd taken without paying for. He handed one of them to Saul and said, "Evening, Saul."

"Thank you," Saul said, taking the cigar. He passed Cole a note as he took the cigar.

Cole didn't acknowledge the note; he took a lantern, raised the glass shade and lit his cigar. "Damme, but that's warm," he said, letting the shade down. He handed the lit cigar to Saul, who used it to light his cigar.

Cole asked, "Is all well with you?"

Saul replied, "Yes sir, doing well."

The entire town knew of Cole's past relationship with the widow, so anyone seeing him talking to Saul would think nothing of it. After lighting Saul's cigar, Cole walked around back to empty his bladder. Joe was coming back and he gave Cole a mock salute and then went on his way. When his screaming bladder was satisfied, Cole mounted his horse, Apollo, and rode home to Anne's parents.

Anne saw him ride up and waved, and then she walked down toward the stable. Her father had a groomsman but Cole always liked to take care of Apollo himself, unless he was in a big hurry.

Cole had just finished reading the note when Anne walked up. She saw the note and asked, "Work?"

Cole looked around the stable. When he was sure that no one was within hearing, he answered, "Yes. He then added, "For a few days."

Anne nodded and, determined not to let him see her worry, picked up a brush and started brushing the opposite side of Apollo.

Looking across the horse's back, Cole said, "You're going to smell like a horse, so we'll both need a bath."

Anne replied, "Won't that be fun?"

Cole, feeling wariness, walked around Apollo and took his wife in his arms. "I'll be back," he said, surprising himself, and not even sure why he said it.

Anne wiped a tear away, and noticed the smell of horse on her hand. "I believe this damn horse needs a bath as well."

Cole pulled her tighter in his arms. She never cursed unless she was very angry or worried. He didn't think that she was angry now. "We've had a long time together."

Anne replied, "I know, I was just dreading this day, knowing that it was coming. You know, I really understand how Josie feels. When you are gone, I can be in a room full of people and I feel alone."

Anne and Cole's mother had visited the French lady. "It was a good visit," Cole's mother said, promising Josie that she'd come back.

***

COLE WAS APPROACHING LINDA'S HOUSE and, just as he was turning on her lane, a riding officer came out of the woods. Cole threw up his hand and the riding officer waved back. A coach was there in the yard as Cole arrived at the house. Joe was talking to a man who Cole thought was the driver. As Cole got down, the man, who was obviously the coach driver, stepped up into the driver's box. Cole greeted Joe and the two of them walked into Linda's house. Lee Bergevin, the Frenchman, was there.

"How long has he been here?" Cole asked.

"I'd say half an hour," Linda replied. "Why?"

"When I turned on the lane, a riding officer was coming out of the woods. I surprised him, I think."

"Do you think that he was watching the house?"

"Why else would he be in the woods," Cole replied.

Joe thought for a minute. "He suspects a landing."

"My thoughts as well," Cole said. He knew that there had to be a landing, by Joe's actions and the presence of Bergevin. He had to get word to Letchworth before it was too late.

"Linda," Cole called, "get me a quill and paper." He then stepped out the door and called to Saul. "Come in," he said to Saul. He wrote the note which consisted of one word...'Withdraw.' "Take Apollo and go find Major Letchworth. He may be on the road or he still may be at the castle. Give this note to the major, and no one else. Take Apollo and ride. Ride like the wind, Saul."

Cole had not signed the note but with Saul riding Apollo, Letchworth would know who it was from and the importance of it.

Joe looked at the wall clock. It was nearly nine p.m. "I better go as well, Cole, and scout out where the duty men usually hide." This caused a chuckle. "I may not be back in time to escort you the entire way. Do you remember the first time you drove?"

Cole and Linda both smiled. "I'm sure that he does," Linda said. The two had spent most of the night together after Cole had driven a wagon full of smuggled goods for Joe.

Joe continued, "That's where you'll go. I'll be at the cliff if I'm not back here." He slapped Cole on the back as he rushed out.

CHAPTER EIGHTEEN

L EE BERGEVIN SAT ACROSS THE table from Linda and Cole. Tea had been poured and, while Cole would have wished for coffee, especially on a night like tonight, the tea was good.

"I understand that you are the one who dispatched my would-be assassin," Bergevin said.

Linda had not been told about this and, without thinking, she gripped Cole's arm. Bergevin, being a man who had spent most of his life reading people's faces and actions, immediately sensed that there was much more to this relationship than appeared on the surface.

The Frenchman, without waiting for Cole to reply, said, "I'm in debt to you, young sir," he said.

Cole didn't say anything for a moment. The feel of Linda's hand on his arm was bringing back memories that were best forgotten. "It was nothing," he finally said.

Linda, unconsciously, let her hand drop from Cole's arm to his leg. Linda, realizing what she'd done, moved it quickly away.

"What I don't understand," Cole said, "is you come to England where you are followed by assassins, one who come close to ending your life, and here you are going back to France. My uncle would say that you are daff."

Lee shrugged and gave a sigh. "I'm an old man, Cole. What have I to lose? Besides, the information that I stand to gain is worth it. My contact, also, trusts no one but me."

Cole had not missed how well Bergevin spoke English. You had to listen well to catch any French accent. His English was much better than Josephine's, or Josie's, as she liked to be called now.

Outside, the distant rumble of thunder was heard. Cole had his ears open, hoping to hear the sound of horse's hooves that would represent Saul returning. The chimes from the hall clock filled the room. The chimes were echoed by more thunder, only it was closer. *This could turn out to be a shitten mess,* Cole thought. It was eleven p.m., and Cole thought, *we can't wait much longer.*

"I saw one horse in a stall when I rode up," Cole said to Linda. "Do you have two?"

"Yes," Linda replied.

"I'll go saddle them. You two stay here. Don't open the door for anyone but me," Cole said. Linda nodded and Cole continued, "You have weapons?"

Linda and Bergevin replied, "Yes."

"Have them handy then," Cole said. "I don't like this feeling I have." He slipped out the door and stood in the shadows of the house. He had a feeling that he was being watched but didn't see anyone.

He saddled the horses and brought them up to the hitching post near the house. He knocked and was let back inside. He collected his bag of clothes and took his second pistol out of the bag and tucked it in his waistband.

As Cole went back out the door behind Bergevin, Linda laid her hand on his arm again. They didn't speak, but Cole smiled and

Linda returned the smile. When he was out the door, she grabbed her handkerchief as the tears started flowing. She had all but soaked the hankie by the time she was able to control her crying.

***

JOE AND SAUL WERE STANDING just off the road when Cole and Bergevin rode up. "Saul just got here," Joe said. Saul was nodding his agreement.

"Thank God," Cole said.

"Aye, I agree," Joe replied. "I'm thinking, though, that we've got someone with a loose tongue. Had it not been for him," Joe indicated Bergevin with a nod of his head, "this may well have turned out bad...real bad."

Cole told Joe about the feeling that he had at Linda's, like he was being watched.

"I'll stop by on the way home," Joe promised.

Saul took the horses' reins as Joe, Cole, and Bergevin started down the path. "Apollo can sure run, Mr. Cole," he called out. Cole smiled and waved, thinking that compared to what Saul usually rode, he probably thought that he'd straddled a lightning bolt.

Joe asked, hearing Cole chuckle, "What's so funny?"

"I was thinking that Saul was surely holding on for dear life if he gave Apollo his head," Cole replied. Joe chuckled then.

Bergevin had looked at the stallion earlier. He'd not want to ride the beast. No...he was too old.

When the three men were making their way down the path, several men spoke to Joe and a couple spoke to Cole.

Paddy O'Hare was down at the landing. "Two more are coming in," he said to Joe.

Joe nodded but didn't speak, though he fully intended to speak to him and Sir George about word getting out. With the Navy patrolling the Channel, they had been much more careful.

Joe walked over to where Cole stood out of the way. "You'll be with Captain Lunn on the *Blue Pearl*," he said.

Cole looked at Joe, "Stephenson's ship?" Joe gave a nod. Cole continued, "So Dalton is working with Sir George." There was no response but Cole hadn't expected one. Since Dalton and Sir George were working together, the risks were cut in half.

As the boat on the shore was unloaded by the tubmen, Cole touched Bergevin. "Ready?"

Bergevin replied, "As ever."

Two men helped Bergevin into the boat and, as Cole jumped in, the men shoved it off the beach and into the surf, where the oarsmen put their backs into it. They were soon alongside the *Blue Pearl*. Once on board, they quickly went into the small cabin.

The last time that Cole had made the trip, it had been with the woman, Lois Breeding. If all went well, he'd be talking to her soon. Cole decided that with Bergevin there, he would let him give the password. Cole had practiced it from Anne's to Linda's house and admitted to himself that he should have been practicing more. He was terrible at French.

When they neared the rendezvous area, Captain Lunn walked up to Cole and gave him a note. "Open it later," he said.

When Lunn walked away, Cole put the note in his breast pocket. He would have liked to have read it now, but knew the light from a lantern or candle could be seen miles away.

The same men were in the fishing boat that had picked Cole up the last time. Bergevin spoke to one of the men. The foul smelling fishing net was held up. Bergevin bent until he could touch the deck planks with his hand and then lay down. Cole heard the man's bones crack and saw him smiling at the sound. Cole got down after Bergevin, realizing that the man knew he couldn't move fast, so he took the spot closest to the hull. This would allow Cole not to be hampered if he had to get up and move suddenly. The agent definitely knew his job.

As the boat made its way to shore, neither man on the boat talked. At one point, Cole heard voices coming from another boat and the familiar reply from the men in his boat.

"Fishermen," Bergevin whispered.

The crunch was heard beneath the boat as it touched the shore, and one man jumped out and began tugging on the bow. Someone else spoke and the bow was pulled up much faster. The net was thrown back and Cole got up. He then took Lee Bergevin's hand and pulled him up.

Once they were ashore, the boat was quickly pushed off and a Frenchman spoke to Bergevin. Bergevin then turned to Cole. "There is much activity going on. One of our men has been captured. He was shot before he was captured and is not expected to live. I'm assured that the doctor caring for him will make sure he doesn't give anything away."

Cole raised his eyebrow but didn't say anything. He thought to himself, *That sounded ominous.*

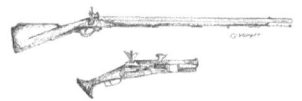

CHAPTER NINETEEN

HE TRIP TO HENRI'S HOUSE took a while. Two patrols seemed to be watching the coast road. Their guide spoke to Bergevin, who turned to Cole.

"They have more patrols now from Calais to Dunkerque, and Calais to Boulogne-sur-Mer. The patrols always return to Calais. They do this nightly. There's nothing north of Dunkirk now...but Oslend, Belgium," Bergevin said, and added after a pause, "but it is little more than a village."

Cole did a quick calculation. The patrols seemed to be moving along at a slow trot. It was about twenty-two miles to Boulogne, so at their pace it would take two hours and a few minutes. To Dunkirk, it was nearly thirty miles, so three hours. They should have more than enough time to get to Henri's and then to the next destination. Hopefully, as at this point, Cole was unsure as to where Bergevin would meet his contact.

Once they arrived at the house, Bergevin went up to the house while Cole waited in the shadows of an old tree. The knock was answered quickly.

"Bonsoir, Madame. Avez-vous un bateau à vendre?"–*Evening, Madame, do you have a boat for sale?*

"Oui, un skiff."—*Yes, a skiff.*

Hearing and remembering the password, Cole stepped out of the shadows and made his way to the door where Bergevin had already stepped in. Lois stood back and when Cole came in, she shut the door. Cole noticed that there was only a candle for a light... good.

Lois gave his hand a squeeze. "It's good to see you again, Cole."

"You as well, Lois," Cole replied, and leaned down and gave her a kiss on the cheek.

In the next room, Cole could hear Henri. "Lee, it's been a while, Monsieur."

The two switched to French, and for a few minutes Cole could not follow it. When they were finished, Bergevin looked at Cole and said, "We leave tomorrow for Gravelines. It's about fifteen miles."

Lois spoke then, "You can hear the patrols coming by. They have stopped here on occasion so we cannot break our normal routine. They go so far as to check bedrooms, looking for unmade beds, and they've checked at mealtime, looking for evidence that more than the two of us were eating."

"Jésus, si mauvais," –*Jesus, so bad*," Bergevin hissed.

"I speak better English than Henri, Cole will sleep in my room, and Lee in Henri's," Lois said. Cole thought, *That's nice.*

As they went into the separate rooms, Lois spoke again. "I see that Lee was able to avoid the assassins."

Cole nodded and said, "Why he came back is unthinkable, if you ask me."

Lois smiled, "He has lost a lot of money and property due to the Revolution. He wants to see a change for France...for the French people."

The bed was not a large one and the tête à tête, or *sofa*, was shorter still.

Lois said, seeing Cole looking around, "We can share the bed."

"Thank you," Cole responded. "I will be a gentleman."

"I would not have offered had I not thought so," she said.

Cole smiled, "Damned the luck."

Lois smiled and continued, "I've had reassurances from a mutual friend as to your gallantry toward women, damn the luck," Lois mimicked Cole.

She went around to the other side of the bed and got beneath the covers. Cole took off his boots and lay down on top of the covers.

"Comfortable," Lois asked.

"It beats the hell out of the boat's deck." Cole chuckled after saying that. "It smells better also." Lois chuckled at that. He asked, "Do you know this place we are going?"

"Not well, I traveled there with Henri once to visit a relative," Lois replied.

"A real relative?" Cole inquired.

"Yes," Lois responded. "His aunt and her elderly sister."

Cole rose up and took the pistols from his waistband. He lay back down and then rose again and removed his dagger.

"Comfortable now?" Lois asked.

"A massage along the small of my back would be appreciated," he replied.

"Humph, I bet it would," she responded.

***

THE SMELL OF HOT BREAD filled Cole's nostrils, waking him from a deep sleep. He was putting on his boots when Lois came in. She showed him where to wash up and get ready for breakfast. Cole was a bit surprised when he saw how late it was in the morning.

"I didn't mean to sleep so long," he said, when he'd finished his morning ritual.

"You had a long night," Henri reminded him.

The breakfast was little more than cheese, honey, and hot bread that was starting to get stale.

Henri apologized, "There's little to eat, I'm afraid. The soldiers take what they want." Bergevin waved it away.

Cole made up his mind to make sure London sent food the next time a crossing was planned. After the meal was finished, Cole wanted another tour of the property. He'd been there before, but that was a couple of years ago. He wanted to see it now in case he had to maneuver around after dark. He scouted out the property, moving things here and there that could make him stumble, or perhaps knock something off a shelf and give away his position.

A large tree was nearly centered in the backyard. Low limbs hung from it. He could reach the limbs, but climbing it with pistols in his belt could prove awkward. Cole saw a bench on its side across the way. He picked it up, and after wiping away the debris it had collected, he sat it where a quick step on the seat and he'd be in the tree in no time at all, and without one bit of strain.

Taking a small stick, he leaned it against the side door of the shop and another against the door to the boathouse. He warned Henri and Lois not to enter either door. Hopefully, if the wind didn't knock the twigs down, they would serve as a small warning that someone had entered and still might be there.

The sky had been overcast most of the day. When the sun went down, it grew dark quickly. Cole and Bergevin made ready to depart when it turned fully dark. Cole had just finished checking his pistols when Henri came in the room.

"It's time," he said.

Lois gave Lee Bergevin a hug and then gave Cole a hug and a quick kiss on the cheek. "Be alert at all times," she said. "Don't trust anyone," she paused and gave Cole a quick smile and then added, "but me."

They went out the door, with Cole following Bergevin. For someone his age, Bergevin walked at a good pace. They crossed the coast road and heard a whistle. Bergevin replied with two short whistles. A man walked out and motioned for them. Another man waited on a path and they set out at a brisk pace. They had walked a good hour when the guide ducked into what looked like a thicket of brush. Cole had to bend down and follow a short tunnel made in the brush and weeds. The center was a clear space of about ten to twelve square feet. A small fire was going, with the smoke being spread and dissipated as it went up among the brush. Cole was sure the fire could not be seen but what about the wood smoke. He then noticed the wind was blowing towards the sea, and that was good. But if the wind changed!!

Black, scalding hot coffee was given to him and Bergevin in old battered cups. They had barely had time to drink the coffee when a whistle was heard again. Their guide tossed the remaining contents on the ground. Cole took a big swallow, and then another one, almost scalding his mouth, and followed suit. He looked at Bergevin. The man's breathing seemed normal enough. Bergevin, unlike Cole who had stood the entire time, had stretched out. He held out his hand and Cole gave a tug, pulling the older man to his feet. They headed back down the tunnel of weeds and their guides bid them goodbye. Two new guides replaced them and they started out again.

It was almost dawn when they reached the outskirts of Gravelines. It was a sleepy little town, or so it appeared from where Cole now stood. They took a path that led them down near a farmhouse. A dog barked but the guide paid little attention to it. Some lights were starting to show in some of the houses. A few cows could be heard lowing, as they were ready to be milked.

The front guide suddenly turned down a path and walked about a hundred yards to another path that was beside a river. After eight to ten minutes they turned onto a path that was little more than a trail. A dog barked once or twice, and Cole could hear a voice trying to quiet it. The place was a shack, one that looked like it would fall down with any kind of wind. The man that stepped out was grey and old with sparse, stringy hair and a scraggly beard. However, behind him was a young boy, or so Cole thought...until she turned sideways.

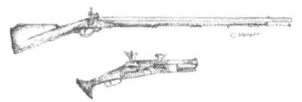

CHAPTER TWENTY

OLE SAT OUTSIDE ON A three legged stool with one leg short-er than the other two. A dog walked up and Cole rubbed his head and ears, causing the dog to wag its tail. When Cole stopped the dog nudged Cole's hand with his nose, wanting more rubbing. As Cole started again, the dog sat down with his butt on Cole's boot.

"You've a friend for life," Lee Bergevin said, as he stepped down from the shack. He nodded his head over his shoulder, indicating inside the shack. "She is Theresa Bodine. Her family is gone, like seventeen thousand others who were beheaded during the Reign of Terror. Robespierre's guillotine took her entire family...mother, father, brother, and older sister. Had it not been for her nounou... your nanny, she would have been killed, as well. She was in her play clothes when the mob came and the dear lady swore Theresa was hers. She now fights Robespierre's Committee of Public Safety with her wiles and quick mind. Napoleon has made vast changes in artillery."

Cole blinked and said, "I'm sorry." Bergevin had changed sub-jects too fast for him to comprehend.

Bergevin gave a sigh. It was clear the rapid pace from the last two nights was having its affect on the man. "Theresa has learned that Napoleon has been given charge of the committee's artillery. He has made changes so that the artillery can move at the same pace as the infantry. The carriages are lighter, as are the cannons. They have been standardized and are now all twelve pounders. These new field guns will pulverize any opposing forces that have nothing but small arms and bayonets. Napoleon, wanting to try out his new idea, massed his mobile artillery forward of his infantry lines. When the battle opened up, the Austrians were defeated before Napoleon's infantry ever joined in. The Foreign Office needs to make field commanders aware of this. If they see infantry, they will undoubtedly feel the metal of Napoleon's cannons as well."

Bergevin laid his hand on Cole's shoulder. "I tell you this, in case I don't make it back."

Cole felt that this admission meant the old man knew he might not make the return trip.

"Field work, I fear, is no longer for me," Bergevin said, echoing Cole's thoughts. "I will introduce you to Theresa at dinner tonight. You must never, even unto death, ever mention her name. After this trip, she will deal only with you." He paused and then continued, "Maintaining only one contact is how she has lived so long."

***

THE MOON WAS NEARLY FULL and the sky was clear. Cole wished it wasn't so. They had left an hour earlier than they normally would have, yet within a few miles it became clear that Bergevin could not keep up. The old gentleman had used his reserve getting to the rendezvous.

"Leave me," Bergevin said. He took Cole's arm in his hand. "My faith will not allow me to take my own life, Cole, so I ask you to do me the honor if it becomes necessary."

One of the guides spoke some English, so Cole said to him, "We need a horse for him," indicating Bergevin.

"Non, Monsieur, non," the guide responded.

Cole understood that there were none to be had. They cut two poles, and using two coats they rigged a stretcher of sorts and for the next half hour they made better time. They rounded a bend and the lead guide, who was scouting ahead, rushed up to them.

"A small patrol is just ahead," the guide said.

"How many are there?" Cole asked.

"Six," he said.

Cole nodded and thought, *That is double our number*.

Bergevin reading Cole's thoughts said, "I am able to take one of them."

Cole made up his mind and said to Bergevin, "Tell them to use their knives first."

"Couteaux d'abord," the old man hissed.

They obviously understood as they took out their daggers. They eased up to the small camp, thankful that it was just off the road on their side. Cole helped Bergevin into place, and then moved a pace or two to the left. A horse, hearing or smelling Cole's group, whinnied.

Damnation, Cole thought at first, but the French looked towards the horses instead of the bushes. This gave Cole's group the perfect opportunity. Cole's silent curse at the horses was replaced with, *thank you Jesus*, as he threw his knife.

All three knives hit their men. Cole quickly drew his pistols and fired but Bergevin was a second before him. Unfortunately, they had both aimed at the same target. The man went down with one ball in his chest and the other ball in his head. Two other shots rang out and two more men fell down. Cole aimed his second pistol at the last soldier and fired, killing the man instantly.

Cole quickly jumped into the camp. He pulled a dead soldier to the opposite side of the road. "Lee," he called, "check the saddle bags for any papers." Another thought came to him and he added, "And food."

The man, understanding what Cole said, went through the bags. He found food in each of the bags, rations for each of the men. One of the soldiers had a dispatch pouch around his chest. Cole tossed it to Lee. When the dead soldiers were all dragged out of sight, Cole took a piece of brush and swept out all the tracks and then sifted dirt over the brush marks.

One of the guides spoke to Lee, who turned to Cole. "He only wants to take one horse, as more would be so loud that he couldn't hear anyone approaching."

Cole nodded, although he would have rather ridden the horses, but agreed with the guide. A single horse turning up near where Henri lived might be overlooked. But four horses wouldn't be overlooked. However, the horse meant a big difference in Bergevin making it back to Henri's or not. Once they were at the path up to Henri's house, Cole divided the food up, giving each man a day's ration.

Once the guides were gone, Cole and Bergevin ran across the street and down the lane to Henri's house. A man, not in uniform, stood outside the front of the house. There were three horses, so that meant two men were inside.

It was early...way too early for a social call. The horse holder apparently had a striker, as Cole saw a flash. His back was to them but the flash reflected off the glass panes in the windows at the front of the house. A flame was visible for a few seconds and then it went out. It wasn't long before the odor of tobacco drifted their way.

"He has lit his pipe," Bergevin whispered.

"I'm worried about Lois and Henri," Cole spoke quietly. "I'm going for a closer look. If you hear shooting, don't let that man get away." Bergevin nodded his response.

It took Cole several minutes to get to the back of the house. A window in the kitchen gave a view of the table in the next room. Only a portion of it could be seen. Cole wanted to see it all, the table and the room. He checked and the twigs were still in place at both the boathouse and the workshop. Satisfied that he was safe, he worked his way to the window. A big man sat in the chair at this end of the table. Lois walked by then, carrying a pot of either tea or coffee.

When she came into the kitchen, Cole took a step so that she would see him. It startled her causing a small shriek. The Frenchman was up and coming toward the window so Cole ducked out of sight.

Lois turned to the man and was in his arms. "Un putain de rat," she said, meaning a damn rat.

The Frenchman gave her a hug, letting one hand drift over her breasts, while the other one slid down her waist and over her rear. He took the pot from Lois and sat it on the countertop. Still chuckling, he went back to the dining room and called to the other man. The other Frenchman came to the kitchen and sat down a cup. The two men then walked out of sight and Cole slid around the house.

It was now dawn and the sun was starting to rise over the horizon. A slight breeze picked up as the sun rose. It was nearing the fall season, and the mornings were cooler than they had been.

Lois spoke as the men walked out. "Au revoir, Victor."

After mounting his horse, Victor replied, "Au revoir, Madame, je reviendrai" (goodbye, Madam, I will be back). Lois smiled and waved, but they didn't look back.

Cole made his way to the end of the path and watched the men head toward Boulogne-sur-Mer. They could, of course, turn off and head toward Calais. Cole waited a good half hour before returning to the house. Bergevin was already inside.

"They got here late last night," Lois was saying when Cole walked in the back door. "Their story was that they had a ways to travel and needed a rest before they started the next leg of their journey. They requested some coffee so I made it. When none was taken to the man outside, I took him a cup. I lit a candle as I took the coffee to the man. However, Victor blew out the candle, saying the man didn't need it."

"Did you say Victor?" Cole asked.

"Yes, Victor DuFort, I believe."

"This is not good," Cole said and told them about Josephine. "He is not trying to catch an agent, with a man and horses outside. He either has a notion as to who you are, or is maybe thinking that you might even become an informant for him."

"There's another possibility," Lee Bergevin said. "He may have his mind set upon making you his mistress."

"His mistress," Lois repeated.

Cole swallowed hard, and he took Lois's hand. "Do not overly reject his...his advances. He is a cruel and brutal man. To reject him means death or worse. Remember they have several ways to demean you. The things that they do are worse than death."

"Like shoving a hot fireplace poker inside of me," Lois replied.

Cole swallowed hard, thinking that was one he hadn't heard yet. He made up his mind if Lois was abused, Victor DuFort was a dead man. His death would be slow and painful.

CHAPTER TWENTY ONE

THE GUIDE WHO MET COLE and Bergevin was worried. The bodies of the patrol they had attacked had been found. Several people had been taken in for questioning. There were reports that a few had died under DuFort's hand. It had been decided that it must have been a roving band of thieves, as all the food had been taken. Cole, hearing this, wished that they had taken the soldiers' weapons also.

The guides, who came for the trip back to the boat, had also brought a horse with them. It was an old horse, not near in the shape as that one taken from the French patrol. They made it to the rendezvous site but there was no boat there. The guides gave them a partial loaf of bread and some cheese. A wine skin was given to them as well. Cole eyed it all. The wine skin was the most suspect. However, an hour later he took a timid swallow. It was better than he expected, so he took another swallow and handed the bag to Bergevin.

They had been in place for an hour when the boat appeared out of the night. "Quickly," the man called. "The guard boats are out tonight as if they expect something."

The crew, using poles to push the boat away from the shore, was turning before Cole was fully on board. When they went to get under the net, the man shook his head, "Non."

A rope was slipped out of a scupper on each side of the small poop so a person could slide over the side and hold onto the rope without being visible to the bateau de garde, or guard boat. Cole was not worried about himself being in the water, but for Bergevin there was a bit of concern. His concern was put to the test not fifteen minutes later.

A man that Cole had seen but wasn't paying attention to jumped down from the poop deck. "In the water, in the water," he hissed.

Cole went over quickly and Bergevin followed. The boat crew had put a net over not more than fifteen minutes ago, and when the guard boat came alongside they were busy pulling the net up and dumping what few fish they had on deck. Words were exchanged that sounded pleasant to Cole.

Cole, looking through the scupper, saw a fisherman take a swig from the wine skin and then offer it to a man on the guard boat. The man looked aft towards the officer and then declined the offer of the wine. The guard boat pushed off after wishing the fishermen well. The men continued with the net for a while and then pulled Cole and Bergevin back on board.

The sails were up and they sailed towards their rendezvous with the *Brazen*. It was a cutter, but not one that Cole was familiar with. He was surprised further when it turned out to be a Royal Navy armed cutter. By the time they were on board, Cole found out that they were headed to London and not back to Deal.

Bergevin went below as soon as they were on board. Cole helped him out of his wet clothes and into some dry ones. A blanket was wrapped around him. A crew member identified himself as a surgeon's mate and brought each of them a glass full of brandy. While it wasn't the quality served at Belcastle, it was the best thing Cole had tasted since leaving Deal. As he sat in the little cabin, Cole felt himself dozing. He looked over at Bergevin, who was fast asleep. Remembering the note that he'd been given before they left, he took it out of his pocket. He had to handle it carefully, as it was soggy and the ink had run. Cole swallowed hard after reading the note. It read that under no circumstances must the Frenchman be left or captured. Take action to prevent it. *Damn*, Cole thought. He'd been ordered to murder Bergevin, if necessary. He was glad that he'd forgotten about the note. He was not sure he could kill the man.

After reading the note, Cole nestled himself in the corner of the small stern cushions. He dozed, dreamed of Anne, and then dozed again. When he woke up it was daylight and they were in the Thames River near London.

A coach was soon at the dock and Cole and Bergevin were whisked away to the Foreign Office. There, they met with James Atkins and Lord Skalla. Atkins' bandage was gone and his face looked like it had healed. Skalla had a smile on his face but it quickly changed when he saw the shape that Bergevin was in.

"Lee, it appears that you are a bit under the weather," Skalla said.

"I'd likely be under the dirt were it not for Cole. But everything went satisfactorily and a connection has been made. We are also bringing news of a change in the French's warfare tactics." When Bergevin finished with his narrative of the new artillery pieces, Skalla gave a sigh.

"This Napoleon is making a name for himself," Skalla said.

When Bergevin made his departure, Cole advised Skalla of DuFort's appearance at Henri's and his apparent interest in Lois.

"It might prove beneficial," Skalla said.

"It also might get her raped or killed," Cole retorted.

"True, but she was well aware of the possibilities and dangers before she volunteered," Skalla returned.

Cole was fuming but held his anger in check. *At what point was information worth a person's life? How far must Lois or anyone degrade themselves to get this information?* Skalla would say one person's life was a small price to pay to save many lives. It was the logic that most superiors would have. *Had they laid so close to a person as to feel their heartbeat, to smell the soap in their hair, or to lie under a stinking fish net wet together? No, they were never that close to the actual person...or had they, at one time, been so?* Cole dropped the subject, knowing that it was a point they'd never agree on.

He then remembered the raid on the smugglers that he'd called off. "It would be good if you sent word to Major Letchworth prior to an assignment, Lord Skalla." He then related what had almost transpired.

"A good point, Cole. I shall draft a message for you to deliver to the good major. I expect that you're ready to get back to Deal now."

"It would be nice, sir."

✦✦✦

COLE HAD TIME TO BATHE and change clothes before a coach took him and James Atkins to Deal Castle. Since Cole hadn't been given any correspondence to give to Letchworth, he assumed that Atkins would deliver it or speak to the major personally. Letchworth's job was not one Cole relished. Raid this landing but ignore the next one. *What would his men think? What would Sir William think?*

At the castle, Letchworth greeted Cole as he got out of the coach. Seeing Atkins, he merely said, "Come this way."

Since Cole's job was finished for the time being, Sergeant Duncannon rode to Linda's house with Cole so that Cole could get his horse, and then the good sergeant would go back to the castle. Linda, hearing the horses, looked out the window. Seeing Cole, she came outside.

Cole had been speaking with Saul, who went to saddle Apollo. Linda gave Cole a welcome-back hug and a quick kiss on the cheek.

"You look tired," she said.

"I am," Cole admitted. "I believe that I could sleep for a week." He said a quick goodbye and let Apollo have his head, only slowing as he rode through Deal.

When he got home, he let the stable boy take Apollo, hoping the horse would forgive him. He didn't see Anne as he entered, but he did see Sir William.

"Cole, could I speak with you a minute?" Sir William asked.

"Yes, sir," Cole replied. He followed his father-in-law into his office, letting his bag drop on the floor.

If Sir William took note of Cole's disheveled appearance, he gave no sign of it. Cole could tell that Sir William was upset.

Sir William started, "Cole, I never faulted you for your dalliance with that widow woman before you married Anne. I, in fact, encouraged it, if I'm truthful. But son, you are married to Anne now. It angers me to no end when I have reports coming in telling me that you are spending time with ..."

"That nice lady." Sir William looked up and Cole turned around. Anne was standing in the door.

"Anne," Sir William said. "I..." He was not able to finish.

"There are things that you don't know, Father. You mustn't know. I know and that's all that you need to know. I'm aware that my husband, as part of his new duties, goes there. I'm comfortable

with it, so you should be too. Come on, Cole, you need a bath."
When Anne closed the door to their room, they embraced.

"I thought that I was about to be shot," Cole said. "Thanks for the rescue."

"I saw you ride up, so I was ordering hot water for you for a bath."

"I could use one," Cole said.

"Yes, and you also look like you could use some rest," Anne replied.

"I'm good for a while," he said.

A knock at the door let them know the water was ready. As the tub was being filled, Cole sat down and took his boots off. They were tight, very tight, after being immersed in salt water. It was a good thing that he hadn't taken them off. If he had, he probably wouldn't have gotten them back on.

Anne came over and helped undress him. He eased his tired body into the almost too hot water. He closed his eyes as the heat eased his aching body. He felt two arms wrapped around him from behind. Anne had stepped out of her clothes.

"Mummm..." Cole groaned.

"Does the water feel good?" Anne asked.

"Uh huh, but not near as much as what's lying on my shoulders," he replied.

"You mean me catheads," Anne said, mimicking the tavern wenches.

"Yes," Cole said.

She moved from the side of the tub and asked, "Would a view be better?"

"Aye, but this would even more so." Reaching around Anne, he pulled her so that he was able to bring her lips to his.

Anne's hand went down in the tub to balance herself. "I believe the bath has rejuvenated you, husband."

Cole still tasting Anne's sweet lips replied, "It was not the water, dear wife."

It was some time later, as they lay in each other's arms, that Cole said, "That's twice you've come to my aid this morning."

"And you mine," Anne said. She'd never admit the fear she had been living with these past few days. Her man was home now, though, and while he was home, all was well in her world.

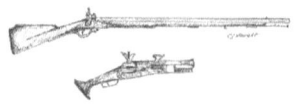

CHAPTER TWENTY TWO

IM JORDAN SET A FINE table at the Blue Post Inn. Joe and Mary sat with Mary's father, John Stuart. Cole and Anne were there as well. John had lost a few pounds since Joe and Mary had got married. While he had lost a few, it was easy to see Joe had found a few extra pounds. John was saying it was all Mary's fault. If she were not such a good cook, Joe wouldn't be putting on the added weight.

Several people were eating dinner when the front door opened and a hush fell over the crowd. A Navy midshipman walked in. Outside there was a shout followed by a curse. It was the press gang.

The midshipman walked through the crowd and stopped at Cole's table. "You three get up and move over by the door. Nobody spoke or moved. The boy made the mistake then of laying his hand on Cole's shoulder and giving it a squeeze. Cole quickly grabbed the boy's hand, swung him around and flipped him onto the floor of the inn.

"Bosun," the boy yelled. A burley man rushed up, a belaying pin in his hand and tapping the side of his leg.

"Before you find yourself in the same amount of trouble as this snotty," Cole said, using a term that Phillip had told him. "I'd suggest you stop and reconsider your actions. I'm Lieutenant Cole Buckley of the Prince's own regiment." The midshipman started to rise but Cole put a boot on his chest, pushing him back down. "If you have an officer about, go get him." The bosun stood there a moment, not sure what to do. "I gave you an order," Cole snapped. "Move!"

The bosun rushed out the door. The people in the inn clapped as he ran out.

"Stay there," Cole said to the midshipman. Several minutes later, after Cole had started eating his dinner, a Navy lieutenant walked in, with the bosun pointing out Cole.

The lieutenant walked over to the table and said, "I'm Lieutenant Cory of *HMS Dido*."

Cole looked at the lieutenant and spoke, "Did you say *HMS Dido*, Captain Atwater's ship?"

"I did."

"Is your second lieutenant Phillip Bickford?" Cole asked.

"He is," the lieutenant replied.

"Well, son," Cole said, looking down at the bewildered midshipman. "You have just been given a reprieve."

Cole turned to Cory, "I'm Lieutenant Cole Buckley. Your second lieutenant and I are brothers." The Navy lieutenant took on a look of surprise. Cole continued, "In light of this snotty being from my brother's ship, I shall not press charges. He needs to learn, though, that he doesn't lay a hand on a person or attempt to intimidate them with pain. I assure you, had he gripped my sergeant there, he not only would be on the floor, but he'd be missing a few teeth. You may get up now, son."

The lieutenant helped his midshipman up, as Cole said, "Another thing, Lieutenant. This is not the type of establishment you enter to find able seamen. With the exception of the sergeant and me, there's not a man here under the age of fifty. There's another place in town where you could get your quota."

"I'm sorry, sir. We were told the only place to stay away from is the Cock and Bull."

"I'm sure that whoever gave you those orders probably thought the young sir had enough common sense to know a gentlemen's inn when he saw it," Cole responded.

"Yes sir," the lieutenant said. "If that's all, we'll be on our way."

"Ah,..just a minute, Lieutenant, I'll walk you out," Cole replied.

Outside the door, Cole asked, "Is my brother ashore?"

"No sir, but I believe that he plans to come on shore later."

"Good, I'd like to talk to him," Cole replied.

"I will send word immediately," the lieutenant said.

"Thank you. One more thing, I know that your young gentleman feels he is doing an important job. Take it from me, though, this is a town of hard men. Most of them would have slipped a dagger between his ribs for what he did to me."

"I understand, sir, it will not happen again." They said their goodbyes and Cole went back inside the inn.

"There will be some unhappy people tomorrow, I'm thinking," John Stuart said.

"Aye, and not only from Deal," Cole responded.

Just as they were about to leave, Major Letchworth came in with Sergeant Duncannon. "I'm here to hopefully save a few," Letchworth said.

"I wondered if you had a hand in the press gang coming," Joe said accusingly.

"No, not me, but I'd think higher up the local ladder," Letchworth replied.

Anne turned pale as her hand went to her mouth, "Not father," she said, but knowing the answer even as she spoke.

Letchworth asked, "Would you come with me, Cole, since it's your brother's ship?"

"Aye, I will. Joe, would you escort Anne to our room at the Cock and Bull?" Cole asked.

Joe nodded, but Mary spoke, "We'll stay with her until you return, Cole."

"I'll head home, then," John said. "Thanks for dinner, Joe."

Joe threw up his hand in goodbye and they left. They passed a group of men being herded down toward the beach.

"I wonder if they have taken any men out to the ship yet," Anne said.

"Let's hope not," Joe replied.

Cole saw Lieutenant Cory and introduced him to Major Letchworth.

Letchworth said, "It's my understanding, Lieutenant, that Sir William pointed out that Deal was prime for hands. That's true on the surface. However, our magistrate is not always privy to everything. There are several men who are under government contract to carry out certain tasks that can't be done by those in uniform."

"Humm...I see, sir," the lieutenant replied. A boat came ashore and Phillip was in it. "There's our second lieutenant, sir. I'm sure that he can work it out."

Cole walked up to Phillip and the two men embraced each other. "I understand that you showed one of our midshipmen the error of his ways," Phillip said.

Cole smiled and said, "It was better me than someone with a dagger."

"Aye," Phillip responded.

"We have a problem on our hands, Phillip."

"Oh," Phillip said.

"Yes, there are certain men here who have...who are under contract to the government to carry out certain activities that cannot be done by others."

"It's just you and me, Cole, speak plain," Phillip said.

"The Foreign Office has employed certain smugglers to perform various operations that the Navy can't do," Cole replied.

Phillip looked at Cole, "Spy work."

"I didn't say that."

"You didn't need to, Cole. We've been told to ignore certain craft unless they appear to be in distress, and then lend a hand."

Cole nodded, and Phillip asked, "Do you have a list?"

"No, but Major Letchworth has already spotted one captain and I see another one," Cole replied.

"Cole!"

"Yes!"

"Father is concerned about your being involved with the damn spies."

"No..." Cole said softly. He'd not wanted the family to worry.

Phillip said, hushing Cole, "You know too much not to be involved to some degree at least. There are not too many people who belong to the Regiment that you do, who are away as you are. Have a care, Cole. I wouldn't know what to do if something happened to my big brother." It was a very emotional moment. "Is Chloe working?" Phillip said finally.

"Yes, she is."

Phillip called Lieutenant Cory over. "You've met my brother."

"Aye."

"Good, but don't believe a word that he tells you. He wasn't tough enough to be in the Navy so they put him in the Army." Cory smiled, and Phillip continued, "Get with Major Letchworth. He will point out certain men who are captains. They in turn will call out their crew. I imagine that there would not be more than ten per ship."

Looking at Cole, Phillip said, "Make that twelve each, and not another one. You can then take the other men to the ship."

When Cory left to do as he was told, Phillip looked at Cole, "You know damn well there's not a lugger, ketch, or yawl that has a crew of more than six."

Cole laughed, "I'll buy."

"Damned right you will, and even if you have to serve, you'll get Chloe off for the rest of the night," Phillip responded.

"Consider it done, brother."

"I already have, Cole, I already have. One last thing, Cole, somebody needs to talk with Sir William. He wrote Captain Atwater encouraging him to come." Phillip looked at Cole when he didn't speak. "I don't mean you, Cole. Maybe the good major or whoever you report to. Captain Atwater was told to bring one hundred men back to Portsmouth."

"Phillip, you can't mean that."

"I do, I read the letter."

"Damn," Cole muttered.

"It's war, Cole. I know that the Army is not doing much, but the Navy is taking the fight to the damn Frogs and we need men...lots of men that know the sea."

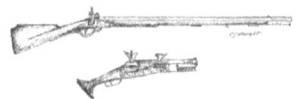

CHAPTER TWENTY THREE

T HE WEEK WENT BY FAST. Word must have gotten out that Cole had tried to come to the aid of the local people when the Press Gang made its raid. His dropping the midshipman at the Blue Post Inn had certainly been the talk of the town.

While Dalton Stephenson and Sir George Aylward sent notes of appreciation, Cole's father-in-law was very distant. Things got worse when Anne asked her father if he had ever once thought about the women and children who would have no man to look out for them.

Anne said to Cole at one point, in front of her mother and father, "Perhaps we need to move into your room at the tavern...or better still, Linda has a big house. She would love our company."

Sir William had responded, "We are at war and the Navy needs men."

Anne shouted, as he rushed off, "Then you feed those women and children."

Mary tried to ease the moment but it did little good. To top it off, Saul had showed up with a note to report to Linda's house.

Anne said, "I'm going with you. I'll wait at the tavern."

They talked of Phillip and Chloe being together, as they rode. They were both so obviously happy.

"They are hopelessly in love," Anne said. "I know that you spoke to your father, but I'm going to speak to your mother. Margaret will make both of them listen to reason."

"Mother!?" Cole asked incredibly.

"Cole Buckley, if you don't think your mother rules Belcastle, then you haven't paid attention. Mother said that Charles may be the earl, but Margaret ruled the manor."

"You know, Anne, the earl has had lady friends, but in all my years he's never brought a woman to Belcastle. I've wondered at times. Phillip and Catherine have both called her mother...all their lives. Well, Catherine knew her mother, I guess."

"She doesn't remember her," Anne broke in. "She told me that. I'm sure the earl has a mistress. Most men in his position do. I'd bet that she's younger and he's probably given her a house. I'm sure that she knows a house and money is all there'll be." Anne looked at Cole, who had a blank look on his face. "What, Cole, what is it?"

"What if he fathered a child?" Cole replied.

Anne said, "I'm sure that he'd use a sheepskin."

Cole looked at Anne, "How do you know about sheepskins?"

"Belinda took one of her father's and we put it on a cucumber to see what it looked like."

Cole was astonished, "A cucumber!"

"Yes," Anne responded.

"Anne!"

"Well, it seemed to be about the right size."

"Damn," Cole swore. "You never cease to amaze me! Penny novels from Covent Garden, and now sheepskins and cucumbers!"

"Mr. Stephenson shouldn't have left so much around for us to look at. Don't look at me like that, Cole Buckley, the man...or boy looking through cracks at girls bathing."

Cole held up his hand. He knew better than to get into it with Anne. She would bring up things that he'd forgotten about. Things before he'd even met her. Catherine...blast her big mouth. She didn't know when to hush.

As they rode along, Cole realized that they'd been in such a heated conversation; they had already passed the turn-off to Deal. He said, "Just come on. If somebody is there we'll just go to the stable." He looked at his wife as he said that and saw that she was smiling.

"You saw the turn-off and didn't say anything," he accused.

"One must never correct her husband," Anne said.

Cole just looked at her and then leaned over and gave her a kiss.

"That's the way, Govenor," a man said, clearing weeds from a fence. "Give the lady a good one."

Cole kissed Anne again and looked back after he'd finished. The man gave a toothless smile and waved his hat.

"It will be all over Kent before you know it," Anne said.

Cole smiled, "Who cares."

"Not I," Anne said. "Not I."

They rode up into Linda's yard. Saul waved and walked over to them. Linda came out and said, "Go on in, Cole. Anne and I will walk a bit."

"I'm sorry," Anne said to Linda. "I shouldn't have intruded."

Linda took her hand and replied, "You are never an intrusion. I was worried about what you'd think, with Cole coming out here as he does."

Anne smiled, "I trust you both." She gave a chuckle then. "Father was ready to shoot Cole, however." Linda looked dismayed. "A riding officer spotted Cole coming here. Of course, he had to go straight to Father."

"I never thought of that," Linda said. "He didn't tell Sir William what he was doing?"

"No, I told father that I knew he came here and if I was not worried, he shouldn't be either." Linda now looked concerned. "Linda," Anne said, "Cole never mentioned what it was that you or he does. He just said work made it necessary for him to come here. If I couldn't accept that, then he wouldn't take the job."

"And you accepted it?" Linda said.

Anne stopped and looked at the older woman. "Whatever Cole is doing means that he's able to spend more time with me. After he was gone for a year, you could dance naked in front of him if it meant that I got him at home every night."

Linda reached out and embraced Anne, "I promise you I shan't do anything of the sort. You have shown more maturity than most, Anne. I am proud of you. If I'd had a daughter, I could only hope that she'd be like you." She gave Anne a motherly kiss on the cheek.

Hearing a noise, they turned to see Cole coming down the steps. A man was with him that Anne had seen in London. Apparently their meeting was over.

Lord Skalla introduced himself to Anne, describing himself as head of the Foreign Affairs. "I wanted to meet you," Lord Skalla said. "You letting us borrow your husband from time to time has been most beneficial. He has saved two of my people's lives."

Two, Anne thought, *I only know about one*. She smiled and said, "He saved my father's life as well."

"I will be meeting your father tomorrow," Skalla said. "We have a bit of business to discuss."

Anne looked at Lord Skalla a moment and then said something that shocked them all. "I take it your office is higher up than father's. So you could do me a favor and tell him not to send for the Press Gang anymore. I know he thinks that he did right, and was trying to get rid of smugglers, but he never thought of the women and children who no longer have their men to care for them."

Skalla looked at Cole, who shook his head, denying he'd mentioned anything.

Anne continued, "I've said something to him but I'm just his daughter. Mother and I are the ones who see the accusing faces when we go to town."

"I see," Lord Skalla said. "Well, I shall certainly bring it up when I see him. It's unusual, someone your age caring so much for people."

"Anyone who sees how hard the people here in Deal have it, and doesn't say something ought to be..." Anne looked at Cole. "What did Phillip say the Navy did to bad characters?"

"Flog them," Cole replied.

"Yes, that's it. They ought to be flogged."

"Would you do the flogging?" Skalla asked.

"Damn right, without hesitation," Anne replied. Everyone laughed at Anne.

Linda wrapped her arms around Anne and said, "That's my girl. We women could show these men a thing or two, I'm thinking."

Lord Skalla took Anne's hand and kissed the back of it. "You are a woman I could get along with, Anne Buckley. I wish there were more as passionate as you. I shall take my leave now."

Linda took Anne's hand, "Let's go in, dear. I believe that we might find something pleasant to drink."

Once they were gone, Lord Skalla looked at Cole. "You have a very passionate wife, Cole. I wish some of our generals had her passion."

"You should have seen her talking to her father," Cole said.

"Yes, I can imagine. Your report was well written, Cole. I'm glad that the situation turned out as well as it did. Thankfully, it was your brother's ship. They still took a large number of men, didn't they?"

"Yes sir, but not the one hundred that they hoped for. I will say they cleared out a few hard bargains."

"Well, there's that. I have passed on the information you brought back, Cole. It will take time for us to be able to counter Napoleon. But we will…in time."

"How is Lee Bergevin?" Cole asked.

"He's coming along well. He told me that you refused to end his life."

"It was not necessary, Lord Skalla."

"Could you have done it, were it necessary?" Skalla inquired. Cole looked at Skalla, but didn't speak. Skalla continied, "Of course you could have. Atkins just got back. They've lost another guide. I may send you to bring out Bodine soon. Reports are that the guide we lost basically stayed back to give her time to escape."

"Did they find the shack?" Cole asked.

"No, they were nowhere near it."

"What about Lois?"

"Lois is doing her job." Skalla was abrupt with his answer which didn't appease Cole.

Cole thought, *if I go get Theresa, I may damn well bring Lois back as well. What can he do? Send me back to my regiment.*

The trip back home was quiet.

"Did I make a fool out of myself, Cole?" Anne asked.

He leaned over and took her hand. "No, you let it be known in no uncertain terms that you didn't like to see people treated unfairly. Lord Skalla said he wished that we had just one general with your spirit." Cole then added, "No, Anne, you didn't make a fool of yourself. You showed that you care. I was proud of you, so proud I wanted to cheer."

Anne smiled, "I think I get some of it from you."

"Me?"

"Yes, a lot of men would have let Linda go to jail. A lot of men would have ducked down when the killer was shooting at us. But you cared enough to go after him. And you saved two of Lord Skalla's people," Anne said. "Was the other one Josephine?"

"Yes!"

"I knew it. The woman loves you. I know it was not an affair. But to love someone like she does you, usually means you have done something exceptional for them."

"What did I do for you?" Cole asked.

"It's not what you did; it's what I did when you came to my party. I gave you most of my dances and I kissed you."

"A little peck," Cole replied.

Before Cole knew it, Anne was leaving her horse and seated in front of him on Apollo. "I'll show you a peck, Cole Buckley."

When they broke apart, Anne said, "Do you think we can make it home or do you want to stop in the woods?"

Cole turned off the trail with Anne's horse, Pandora, following them. Cole sat on a boulder and Anne straddled him.

"Damn you are excited, Cole."

"Look who got me that way!"

"Do you remember when we were in the stable and Sidney walked in?"

Cole managed an "Um huh."

"Well, right now I wouldn't give a damn. Take me, Cole, take me now."

"I'm trying," he hissed, and then he did.

When they were spent from their frenzied lovemaking, Anne said, "Will you still want to do this when I'm old and fat?"

"If I'm able to."

Anne looked at Cole. "I hope I'll always be able to please you, one way or another."

Cole looked at his wife as the stars started to twinkle in the sky. "I have no doubt of that, Anne."

"Cole."

"Yes."

"Is sex different when you love somebody?" Anne asked.

Cole thought for a minute. "Phillip and I bedded a couple of trollops. There was nothing there but satisfying our lust. With Linda, at first it was just sex. But then I started to like her and felt that life had been cruel to her, so I developed a relationship with her. It was then two people caring for each other's needs. But you, my darling, I've never felt the way I do with you, with anyone else. It's like you have my very all. Every feeling, every sensation, it's you."

Anne kissed Cole, "There's never been another nor will there ever be another, Cole."

Cole kissed Anne then, feeling the closeness...her breath on his face, her heart beating against his chest.

"Do you still care for Linda?" Anne asked.

"Yes, I'd be a liar if I said no. Mind you, it's not as a lover, but as a loyal friend."

"I'm glad you said that because she cares about you. She cares enough about me that she'd want a daughter to be like me if she had one."

Cole smiled. "I'm sure that she would."

"You have a way of drawing people, Cole. Joe, Linda, and others that I'm sure I don't know."

"Well, you are the one that I feel drawn to," Cole said.

Anne wiggled a bit. "I can see that, you naughty man."

"You started it," Cole said.

"I'm going to finish it too," Anne said, French kissing her man.

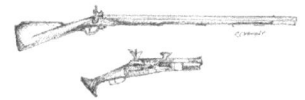

CHAPTER TWENTY FOUR

L ord Skalla's visit with Anne's father did little to improve his disposition. He grew morose and snapped at Anne and her mother. Mary asked him at dinner a few nights later what had gotten him so upset. He then said that he didn't take it kindly when people in his own house went behind his back.

Cole stood up, having taken about all he could tolerate. "Sir William, if that comment was directed towards me, sir, it was misplaced and you have been misinformed."

"Father," Anne started, but Cole, on a rare occasion, put his hand on his wife's shoulder and told her to be quiet. Since Cole had never spoken so forcibly to her, she grew flushed but held her words. Cole knew that no good would come of it if Anne admitted that it was she who addressed Lord Skalla. The truth was, it wasn't Anne who instigated it, it had been Major Letchworth. However, Cole didn't want Sir William to know of his relationship to Lord Skalla and the Foreign Office. Sir William had pushed back from the table but did not stand.

Cole addressed Mary then, "It appears that this situation has reached a point where I'm no longer comfortable being here, nor do I wish to see my wife subjected to this behavior. So while I've consented to live here so that Anne could be close to you when duty calls me away, I feel these arrangements have reached a point where we cannot continue. I will have no man treat my wife so rudely... not even her father. Were it someone else, I can assure you that I'd already have sought satisfaction."

Cole knew that he'd laid it on a bit thick, but it got results. Anne squeezed his hand, and Mary's hand went to her mouth as she gasped, and Sir William turned pale but did not speak for a long moment.

"Anne, gather your things. At least, what you will need for the next few days."

Sir William now stood and said, "My apologies to everyone."

Cole nudged his wife. "Thank you, sir. However, we've made a decision to leave, for the time being."

Anne and Cole left the table and went to Anne's room. She packed enough in a bag to last a week.

Cole said, "If we decide to stay longer, I will send a wagon for your things."

"Where shall we go?" Anne asked.

"Tonight we will go to my room at the tavern, but ultimately to Belcastle. I think that your father is not at ease with what he thinks I'm doing."

Anne looked at Cole and asked, "What's that?"

"Since I'm not with my regiment, rumor has it that I'm in bed with the smugglers," Cole replied.

"Oh Cole, can't you tell my father that is not true."

"I can't tell him anything, Anne, as much as I'd like to."

Anne had been holding Cole's arm and pulled it to her body, holding it tightly.

"Anne, another thing, you must not tell anyone of my relationship to Lord Skalla. When I told you to be quiet, I was afraid that you'd admit talking to him," Cole said.

Anne looked up and nodded but didn't speak as tears flowed down her face. The door was slightly ajar. Sit William had come to apologize and overheard most of the conversation.

So that's it, he thought, *the damn Foreign Office of secrets is using Cole as a spy*. He undoubtedly was taken back and forth to France by the smugglers. That's why Skalla didn't want their operation to be disturbed. He walked back to his office. Anne had no idea the danger her husband faced. He'd wondered how Cole was able to be away from his regiment. He knew that answer, as well, now. He also knew his son-in-law was an honorable man. He'd known that if something happened to Cole, Anne would need her parents' support. For his wife's sake, Cole had consented to live here instead of at Belcastle.

Damme, Sir William thought. *I'm an old fool and I may have driven a wedge too deep between my daughter and myself, to see it changed. I will try*, he thought.

Mary was waiting when Cole and Anne came out. "I've sent for the carriage," she said. "You can tie your horses to the back." She then embraced Cole. "I love you, Cole."

"I love you, Mary," Cole returned.

Anne hugged her mother then and they both started crying. When they got in the carriage, Henry, the driver, held Anne's hand as she climbed in. Before he let go of her hand, he kissed it and smiled. Anne laid her hand over Henry's.

"You've always been so sweet to me," Anne said.

Henry smiled and then got in the driver's box. As they rode down the road, Cole touched Anne's arm and pointed into the woods. It was where passion overtook them and they'd recently made love in the woods. Anne laughed and hugged Cole closer.

Henry heard the laugh and while not sure of the cause, he was glad to hear it. Anne had always been a girl with deep thoughts. She was far more mature than most girls her age. She was like a shining star, Henry decided. He'd heard her give Sir William hell for leaving so many without their men. *It's what the man deserved*, he thought and Anne was the one who could do it.

***

THE NEXT TEN DAYS WERE idle. There was more war news coming in. The armies of England and her allies were taking a thrashing. Many felt that it was only a matter of time before France would invade England. Only the Navy prevented that.

Every time a Gazette made its way to Deal, it was filled with naval victory after victory. One report told of the *Dido* taking on a French thirty-two gun frigate that was defeated after a four hour battle. The ship's first lieutenant had been struck down and Captain Atwater had mentioned his Second Lieutenant Phillip Bickford's actions and bravery that had help win the day.

Cole was certainly proud of Phillip, but it worried him that he'd been in the heat of so many battles in this war. "I wonder if he'll continue as first lieutenant," Cole said, speaking to his Uncle Angus.

Cole called Chloe over and started to read the paper to her. However, surprising Cole, she took the paper and read it herself. Cole mentioned it to Anne later.

"She's a smart girl, Cole. We've become good friends," Anne said.

Cole had noticed the two of them together when Chloe wasn't working. Last Saturday evening, Anne surprised Cole even more.

When the crowd got really big, Anne went behind the bar and filled pitchers and tankards with beer and ale, and even helped in carrying a tray to a large table. *If Sir William hears of this, we're doomed,* he thought, *making his daughter a tavern wench.* Cole smiled at his uncle.

"I'd not tell her to stop, mind you," Angus said.

"Nor would I," Cole admitted.

He'd mentioned it to Anne who snarled, "Men. Chloe was having her monthly curse so I helped her."

"You like Chloe, don't you?" Cole asked.

"Yes, and I wish there was a way to make her aunt and uncle give her the money back."

A bit surprised, Cole looked at his wife, "Tell me about this," Cole said.

Anne's anger when speaking had made him curious. "Chloe's father was a silversmith in London. He had a very good business. Chloe said that he'd made custom silver pieces for a lot of wealthy people, including the Earl of Belcastle. She said that her father made the earl a set of goblets with the family crest on them."

"What was her father's name?" Cole asked.

"Alfred Hester."

"I know the name," Cole admitted.

Anne continued, "They lived above his shop. A fire broke out one night. Her mother and father were both killed. A good sum of money had been put up and it was given to her mother's sister and husband. She was to be educated and cared for. She was for a year. She was then required to work at home while her cousin went to school. She was starting to mature and was often touched by her uncle, accidentally of course. One day when the aunt was gone, her uncle tried to bed her. He had her dress over her head when her aunt walked in. The husband said she was forever tempting him and leading him on until she succeeded in seducing him. Her aunt took his word for it and ran her off with only a few of her clothes and none of her belongings."

"I will have Lord Skalla check into this, if not him, then the Earl," Cole swore. He paused and then said, "You're sure she is telling the truth, Anne."

"Yes," Anne spat. "Why would she lie to me?"

Cole smiled, Anne was so naïve...very loyal, but naïve. He'd still have it checked into, though.

"Anne."

"Yes."

"The good thing about Chloe having her curse," Cole said.

"Yes."

"She's not pregnant."

Cole got a slap on the arm for his remark.

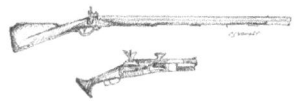

CHAPTER TWENTY FIVE

HE BOAT GROUND INTO THE sand as James Atkins and Cole Buckley jumped out and ran up the rocky beach to where their guide was waiting. Lois Breeding had been able to get word to Lord Skalla that things were deteriorating fast for Theresa Bodine. A reward had been posted for information on Theresa. On top of that, there had been beatings, and at least one death had been attributed to people thought to be hiding her or passing information to her. That didn't include the man who was killed holding off the French soldier, thereby giving Theresa time to escape.

The rendezvous, this time, was near Boulogne-sur-Mer. It was in a different direction than Cole had traveled on previous trips. Atkins, however, seemed to know his way around. At the top of the hill from the beach, the guide was waiting. His name was René LeFébure. He and Atkins had a brief conversation and then they started out.

Atkins spoke over his shoulder to Cole, "We'll have horses waiting up the road but we need to set a brisk pace until we get there."

Cole threw up his hand in acknowledgment but didn't speak, saving his breath for the walk. He had not gotten much exercise in the last week beyond strolls with Anne. One night after the tavern closed, Chloe walked down to the beach with him and Anne. Anne coaxed Chloe into repeating her story about her aunt and uncle to Cole.

Cole sent a letter to Lord Skalla, afterwards, asking if he could have someone find out about Chloe's inheritance. He'd not heard back from Lord Skalla, but there'd not been enough time for a reply. Finding out that Chloe's father was a noted silversmith was better in regards to her being a tavern wench when it came to the Earl, but Cole didn't think it would help with his approval of a marriage. Cole's mind was on Phillip and the Earl when he stumbled into Atkins. The man had raised his hand to stop, but Cole ran right into the man's back. Thankfully, Cole was able to reach out and catch Atkins to keep him from falling. Voices could be heard ahead, loud boisterous voices…a patrol. It was obvious, hearing them talk, that they'd been drinking.

The sound of somebody being slapped rang out. The cries came from a girl or a woman and were followed by the angry voice of a husband or father. Cole's group inched forward. A man was tied with his hands behind him and close to him a girl or young woman had her hands tied together. They were held over her head by a sergeant who was holding onto a rope. The woman's top was torn into shreds and most of her upper body was exposed. A man was squeezing a breast so hard that the woman was grimacing in pain.

The man was unfastening his britches and saying, "Putain, ouvre ta bouche"—meaning *Whore, open your mouth.*

Cole pulled a pistol out. Atkins wore a belt with a place for two pistols plus a harness of sorts that fitted over his shoulders and held two more pistols. As the Frenchman stepped near, the woman spit at him. **Slap!!!** Blood gushed from the woman's mouth.

The sergeant holding the woman's rope dropped it and then leaned close and whispered. It was then that Cole could see the man's epaulettes. The rogue was an officer. Cole could not hear what the sergeant said to the man, but the officer laughed and said, "Oui."

The woman's husband was dragged across the little clearing to the fire. His arms were pinned down over his head and someone lay across his legs. The sergeant put the tip of a bayonet into the fire. The end was soon glowing hot. The sergeant pulled the bayonet from the fire, showing the woman the glowing red tip. He held it close to her breasts, letting her feel the heat. She tried to pull back but couldn't. The sergeant smiled and stuck the end back into the fire. When the tip was a bright red he took it from the fire. He straddled the man on the ground.

The officer now had his manhood exposed. Pointing at it, he said, "Ceci ou cela"—meaning *this or that*.

The woman was crying but shook her head *yes*. As the fat French officer took a step to her, all eyes were glued on the woman as she gave a sigh. It was then that Cole stepped out and shot the sergeant in the back of the head with his left pistol and then shot the officer in the back with his right pistol. Cole dropped his pistols and pulled out his sword. He lunged, and the man holding the male prisoner gagged as the blade ran out the front of his throat. He heard two quick shots, and then a third. Atkins had killed three more of the French soldiers.

Their guide was screaming, "Non, non," when Cole shot the first man. He now stood with his head hanging, obviously mad. They cut the ropes that held the man and woman, and helped them to their feet.

"Gather the weapons," Cole said.

The woman obviously understood English, as she started picking up the weapons. Their guide did nothing but watch with hands crossed and looking angry. The girl was suddenly aware of her exposed breasts and pulled a jacket off of a soldier that was near her size. She then removed his shirt and put it on.

Cole spoke to the woman once the weapons were all gathered, "Take the horses and go far away from here and turn them loose."

The woman walked over to Cole and placed her rough hand on his face. "Merci, brave monsieur." Seeing that Cole didn't understand her words, she repeated them in English, "Thank you, good sir." Looking at Atkins, she repeated, "Merci."

She gave Cole a kiss on the lips, letting the kiss linger a moment, and then she got on the horse. She and the man set out, leading the extra horses. The dead soldiers were dragged over and pushed over the bank. The guide had not helped like the previous guide, which caused Cole to be somewhat suspicious.

Atkins and the guide had words. Atkins spoke to Cole to have him move up alongside. "He thinks that we wasted too much time helping the peasants. We could be risking Theresa's life by doing so."

They got to the horses, and the two guides exchanged hot tempered words. Finally, they got on the horses and started off at a trot. Something kept eating at Cole as they rode. Atkins seemed to not be upset or acting strangely. They finally drew up and the guide spoke to Atkins and rode off.

"He's going to scout up ahead," Atkins said.

"I don't like it, James. I don't trust that man." Cole dismounted and continued, "The previous guide had no qualms shooting the French soldiers. This one didn't fire a shot. He also called the man and woman peasants. I've never heard that remark from anyone who was supposedly one himself. Also, the other guides were worried about horse travel. Why is this man not worried? Lastly, he took off at a gallop, and that's not what I'd call trying to remain silent."

"You're right," James said. "What shall we do?"

"Let's get rid of these horses first and then we'll go forward on foot," Cole replied.

Cole's boots stepped on something sharp. It was a small rock and an idea came to him. He ran his hands over the ground until he found another rock. He raised his saddle up and placed the rock beneath it, with Atkins following suit. Tightening the cinch down tight, Cole slapped his horse on the rump. James did likewise and the horses took off back the way they had just come.

Cole dusted their boot tracks as best as he could and the two set out, following the road but just off of it. They had walked about twelve to fifteen minutes when they picked up the sound of horses coming. They ducked down as the horses went by. It was their guide with three French soldiers. The horseman stopped as they passed where Cole and James now hid.

Cole whispered as he watched, "He's setting up an ambush. Were we to have waited and ridden back with the blackheart, they'd have had us."

"Aye, let's move out and see if we can find Theresa. She may have been captured," Atkins said.

"My thoughts exactly," Cole replied.

They set out at a brisk pace, with Cole trying to keep his ears open for the sound of horse's hooves, both in front of them and coming up from behind. When they spied a glow up ahead, they slowed to a careful walk. Their guide and his men, so far, had not returned. Hopefully, he was still chasing their horses. A glow such as was ahead usually meant a campfire.

Cole was sure that, as big as it was, the people were not concerned about being spotted. Why would they be? Cole decided. The ambush was to have been set up several miles back down the road. A quick survey showed at least sixteen men were present, plus those that followed the guide. An officer was probably in the large tent. A wagon was parked away from the fire. Theresa sat, with one shoulder bloodstained, and tied to a wagon wheel.

"We have to move quickly," Cole whispered.

Little embers from the fire drifted skyward as someone tossed a piece of firewood into the fire.

"Look," Cole said, "they are lucky that they haven't set the countryside ablaze."

James said, "Maybe we can help."

"I don't see why not," Cole replied. "Give me eight to ten minutes to get behind the wagon. The wind is blowing toward the camp."

Atkins pulled a huge watch from his pocket. "Get moving."

Cole faded into the night as Atkins pulled up several tufts of dead grass. He could only use the striker once; otherwise the men in the camp might hear it. When he pulled several more tufts, he looked at the watch. *It was past time*, he thought. He lit the first tuft just below the crest of the hill. Once the brush caught, he ran stooped over, letting burning tufts fall into the dry brush. It was catching up fast. Now if Cole could do his part, they'd have part of their mission done.

Cole had made his way behind the wagon and was about to crawl under when he saw a pair of boots. The soldier was about to relieve himself. Cole didn't want to be urinated on, but if he couldn't move fast enough he'd be wet. He stood up, pulling his dagger. The man's eyes opened wide when Cole stood up. The dagger went up from under the man's chin and into his brain. Cole eased him down and then crawled under the wagon. He looked out to see the orange blaze coming up the hill towards the camp.

Theresa's head was hanging down. *Damn, was she unconscious?* Cole touched her and then pushed her hard. She stirred as he did so.

"Can you hear me?" he whispered. She nodded her head. "I'm going to cut the ropes on your hands but don't drop them." There was another nod of her head.

Suddenly he heard a shout, and then several excited voices rang out. Men ran towards the fire and as they did so, Cole hissed, "Roll over. I'm going to pull you."

Theresa rolled over and Cole grabbed her coat along the shoulders and pulled her to the other side of the wagon.

"My feet, my feet," Theresa hissed. "They are tied."

Cole handed her the dagger. It was sharp and she quickly cut through the ropes. As she stood, she could feel the pin pricks as circulation went back to her feet. Cole, sensing the problem, threw the woman over his shoulder and took off.

"Over here," Atkins called once they'd crossed the road. "Which way do we go?"

"Into the dark," Cole advised.

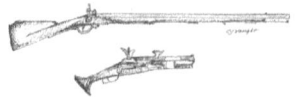

CHAPTER TWENTY SIX

THE SKY WAS GETTING LIGHTER. The sun would soon be up. The wind was slight but cool. For the first time, when Cole inhaled, he didn't smell the ashes from the fire they had set last night. Theresa was beat. Cole had carried her at times. She now felt feverish. When it was light enough, Cole would look at her wound. It had not started to bleed, but Cole wasn't sure if that was good or not. He'd heard Doctor Garrett say 'it's sometimes good to bleed out the morbid humors that build up in a wound.'

Atkins had gone up to the top of the hill to see what was on the other side. Cole knew that they needed to head back towards the road and the sea. They'd not return to where they'd met the guide. That spot was now compromised.

Theresa turned and moaned. She had been dozing. Cole was concerned about her. The woman needed medical help but he had no way to get it for her. He didn't even have water for her. He was looking at her when it dawned on him that he could hear footsteps. They were not from the direction that James had taken. Where they were hid, for the most part, was out of sight, but not completely.

He put his hand over Theresa's mouth and shook her gently. Her eyes were immediately open. She nodded her understanding to be quiet.

It was a boy who appeared to be driving a milk cow somewhere. It meant that a house or village was close by. Behind the boy a dog barked. *Damn*, Cole thought. The dog walked straight towards the brush. The boy called the dog back. Walking towards the thick brush, he called the dog again.

He put a rope around the dog's neck and then he spoke. Theresa softly replied, "Oui, merci." She then whispered to Cole, "Soldiers are near. They are looking for two men and a wounded woman. A reward is offered if she is found but death will be long in coming to anyone who aids them."

Cole stayed down but drew his pistols. He had charged them last night but now he rechecked each pistol.

The dog started barking again and the boy shouted at it. Voices were then audible. Now, Cole knew the boy was saying no to something.

"He's telling them he had come to find a cow that had gotten out," Theresa whispered. "He'd found her and was headed home. He told them that he hadn't seen anything but the damn cow. That must have been when a soldier had laughed."

Cole tried to peek through the brush, but the cow stood between him and those speaking. The boy had deliberately turned the cow to block the view. The soldiers walked off and the boy whispered, "It's clear. I will come back tonight."

Theresa thanked him again. As he left, he dropped a wine skin that he'd been toting. *Hopefully it's water*, thought Cole. It was, and not too warm. Cole gave the skin to Theresa. She took a timid sip and then passed it to Cole. Taking a sip, he handed it back to her.

"Non," she said.

"You must," Cole said, so she took two more swallows. He then pointed to her shirt. "I need to examine your wound."

"Oui," Theresa replied.

Cole found the dried blood had stuck the shirt to the wound. "Lay back," he said and unbuttoned the shirt. He then dripped some water onto the shirt and let it soak before peeling it back. Opening the shirt, Cole was quick to see that she had on nothing beneath it. Cole was not sure how old Theresa was, but she was not as old as he thought.

"You have seen women before?" Theresa asked.

"Yes, I'm married."

"It's all the same then…Non!"

"Oui, it's all the same," Cole said, while doing his best to expose the wound without exposing the young lady. Finally, he took his knife and cut a slit in the shirt so that it wouldn't have to be opened up.

"You have gentle hands," she said.

"Thank you, I'm trying not to hurt you," he replied.

"You're not," she said, but her grimace told the real story.

Once the shirt was open around the wound, Cole was surprised. "You were not shot."

"Non, baïonnette," Theresa said.

Cole was not sure if that was good or bad. It was bad if the blade was dirty. The skin appeared to be closing over. He remembered stepping on a screw and puncturing his foot as a young teen. The doctor had pulled on the wound opening it so that it could drain. Puncture wounds need to drain, he remembered. The skin around the wound was red, hot to the touch, and very tender. It seemed to be pushing out like a boil.

He rolled up the tail of her shirt, which appeared to be a man's shirt, as it was so large on her. "Bite on this. I need to open the wound."

Theresa took a drink of water and then bit down on the cloth. Cole put a finger on each side of the wound and stretched the skin.

"Ummph!" Theresa gasped in pain.

He stopped and Theresa looked up at him and nodded, with her eyes wide. *At least she's brave*, Cole thought. On the second attempt, Cole used his thumb and index finger on each side of the wound, and pulled at each edge. Pus shot out, nearly hitting him in the face.

Theresa cried out, sat halfway up, and then lay back down. The pus drained from the wound and continued to do so. Cole took out a handkerchief and wiped the pus away, using more water to clean it. He took off his jacket, his top shirt and then his bottom shirt. It was the cleanest thing he had, so he tore it to make a dressing. He tore a narrow long strip to fasten the dressing about Theresa. Once he was finished, he looked into her face and saw that Theresa was watching him.

"It feels better already," she said. "It doesn't feel so tight."

"I'm glad. Let's get you fastened back up and ready to go before James comes back," Cole said.

Theresa touched his hands, "I think you are in the wrong profession. You should be a doctor."

"What makes you think that I'm not?" he asked.

"You are too gentle," she replied. "The doctors just do it."

Cole smiled, "Rest now."

James still had not returned by dusk. Cole was worried, but emphasis had been made that Theresa's rescue was above all else. A rendezvous had been set up for two different places, if they were to get separated. It was just dark when Cole could hear someone walking. He thought, at first, that it was James; but again the direction was wrong.

"Mademoiselle, Mademoiselle."

"Oui."

The boy was without his dog. "I think it is safe now to come to the barn. The soldiers found a man, and killed him. They have now moved on out of the area."

Cole felt his heart skip a beat when Theresa repeated what the boy had said. "Can he described the man that they killed?" Cole asked.

Theresa asked the boy and then looked at Cole, "Non! The boy didn't see the man, he was just told about him."

Cole took his dagger and scratched "1/2" on the tree. If James was not dead and returned to the spot, he would see the numbers and know that Cole was going to the first and then the second rendezvous areas.

✶✶✶

IT WAS COLD NOW THAT the sun had gone down. Cole looked at the barn door as it creaked with the wind. The farm boy, Jules, Theresa said, had led them down to his family's farm. The barn, which was not much larger that a shed, at least kept the wind off.

Jules had brought some bread, cheese, and another wine skin, only this time it contained wine. The wine was surprisingly good, although a bit sweet.

Jules spoke to Theresa again and when he left, she explained, "There is no blanket that he could get but there was a saddle blanket if it got too cold. He cautioned against lighting a candle as the light would shine through the cracks in the boards. Lastly, he said, the soldiers were coming back and checking for two escaped prisoners. Therefore, we must be gone by dawn and leave no trace of having been here. He said that his father was afraid of the soldiers and the secret police, so he had not mentioned us to him."

Jules' last comment Cole had understood, even in the boy's French. "Va avec dieu," which meant *go with God.*

Cole opened his eyes. He had not really slept but had dozed just for a minute. Something had alerted his senses. He listened but heard nothing, yet he was uneasy. A feeling that he'd learned to trust. In the past, it had often stemmed from some subconscious awareness. It was not unlike the guide's use of the word 'peasants.' The man DuFort was a brutal, cruel man, but very clever. It would not surprise Cole if he withdrew his men only to return after everyone was asleep.

Cole could not see the face of his watch, but his mind told him it was about 2:00 a.m. Careful to make no sound, Cole gently shook Theresa. Her eyes opened immediately and she could see him put his finger to his lips for silence. Cole stood up and went to peek out between the boards at the door. The air was chilly standing near the door, in fact, it was very chilly.

One of the two horses in the small paddock blew, not loud, but a soft blowing sound. Cole thought, *the horse felt it as well.* He pulled one of his pistols and gave it to Theresa. He didn't need to tell her not to shoot unless it was necessary. It was silent still; and nothing seemed to be moving...*nothing*! When he started to think that it was just his imagination, he heard it, just the whisper of a sound. Someone was moving in the brush to the left side of the barn towards the rear. *They were not in a good position, being in the barn*, Cole thought.

He walked carefully back to the rear of the barn. A board had been propped against a piece of loose siding. *Could he move it quietly*? Theresa followed Cole so that she could help him. He lifted the post that was wedged in the ground with only the slightest sound. Theresa had her back against the piece so that it would not fall. Cole put his hands against the siding. It didn't offer to fall. He grasped the twelve inch wide board that had to be ten feet tall and lifted. The board came up and he slid it sideways and looked out. It was clear.

Cole then picked up the board, which was at least two inches thick, very heavy and took a full step. He, ever so gently, sat the board down and leaned it against the back wall. He thought that the board didn't have enough of an angle, as it wanted to tip back.

He whispered to Theresa, "Get that post." He pulled the bottom of the board back six inches, and then let it go and it didn't tip backwards. He still leaned the post against it, wedging it as best as he could.

A man walked by the side of the barn. His movement was visible through the cracks. The dog growled and then growled again. The man spoke to the dog, but the dog continued growling, and it got louder each time.

Someone spoke and another man answered. They heard a third voice speaking out. All the voices were to the front of the barn, between the barn and the house.

"Let's go," Cole said.

They crouched down and crept slowly away from the barn. Cole looked back and saw a light on in the house. A soldier, probably an officer, called out and a brief conversation transpired. Two men finally went in as Jules walked out rubbing the sleep from his eyes. A few more words were passed and then the soldier left.

The officer asked the farmer if he'd seen anyone and was told no. The officer then asked again, was he sure nobody passed.

"The dog hasn't growled until you walked up," the farmer said. "If anyone had passed, the dog would have growled and barked as he did with you."

The men in the house returned, saying no one else was in there. They didn't even look in the barn. Cole thought, *That was close, but it could have been worse.*

"How do you feel?" Cole asked. "Are you ready to continue?"

"Oui, I could not go back to sleep," Theresa said.

When they started off, they skirted the farmhouse and Cole headed back towards the coast, he hoped. They made it to the coast road an hour later. Patrols were coming and going.

"They must be hunting for us," Theresa said.

"Aye, I think you are right," Cole replied.

When the road was clear, they crossed over and Cole said, "Look there, Theresa."

Men were carrying torches and walking down near the beach.

"They know that for us to escape, we have to reach the sea," Cole said. "They are trying to cutoff that means of escape."

"Oui," Theresa answered and slumped to the ground.

She's very weak and exhausted, Cole thought while admiring her bravery.

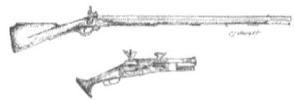

CHAPTER TWENTY SEVEN

OLE LET HER REST FOR a while as he watched the cliff and the beach, where there was one. He finally got up after he'd let Theresa rest as long as he dared, since a patrol had just gone by. However, huddled together in the brush behind a tree limb hanging from a dead tree, they would have been nearly impossible to see from a group of men rapidly riding by on horseback. Though it had not been planned that way, their clothes blended well with the dead brush.

Cole didn't ask Theresa how she felt. It was obvious, from her pallor and beads of sweat on her forehead when she moved. He hefted the wine skin and saw that there was not much left. He gave it to Theresa to drink, and then after she had drunk, he took a mouthful. He swished it around his dry mouth and then swallowed. All that mattered, at this point, was that it was wet.

Cole's thoughts returned to James Atkins. Was he a prisoner, was he dead, or hiding some place? His biggest concern was if he had been captured, he might give up information about Lois Breeding.

How far were they from Henri's now? he wondered. Theresa was up and they made it back across the road. Staying out of sight of the road, but following its route to the best of Cole's ability, they came upon a fast-running stream. Cole took the wine skin and, emptying the last little bit, he rinsed it out using the stream's clear water. Once the skin was full he gave Theresa a drink. He then soaked the dressing that was stuck again to the wound. Removing the dressing he sniffed it, and found that it didn't smell. "Thank you, Lord," he said to himself.

Theresa jumped when the cold water touched her skin. Cole said, "I'm sorry, I don't have anything to heat the water in."

He gave the woman the last of the bread and crumbles of cheese. There was little to be shared, so he gave it all to Theresa. They started out again and walked for an hour. Cole knew that they had to stop, Theresa was exhausted. They stopped just below the crest of a hill. Cole sat her beneath a tree and then pulled a small deadfall around her to give some cover.

"I'm going to scout around," he said. He gave her the water and placed a pistol in her hand. "Don't go anywhere. I'll be back."

Cole crested the hill, crawling on all fours. There was another farmhouse below. A man was in the field plowing and a woman walked out the back door and went to the barn. Cole, keeping to what cover was available, made his way down to the house. The woman that he'd seen was walking toward the field with a bucket in hand.

Cole, seeing this and hearing no sound, rushed around the side of the barn and into the house. A new loaf of bread was in a bread pan in the window. He looked about quickly and saw some ham. He put it on the table with a kitchen knife. He looked out the window. The woman was still walking toward the man.

He spied a clothes basket and took out a freshly washed shirt and a pair of under drawers. The under drawers would serve as a clean dressing. There was also a sack lying across a chair back. He grabbed it and put in the ham, knife, and the bread pan. He saw a jug and smelled it...brandy. He put it in the bag also. The under drawers he stuffed inside his shirt. He was about to leave when he saw the cheese. He put it in the bag with the other food.

He looked out and the woman was almost on him. How did she get back so fast? He ran through the house looking for another door. He saw an open window in a room. He ducked into the room and as he went out the window he saw a child looking at him, a little girl about three years old at the most. She sat up in the bed and rubbed her eyes. Cole smiled and then went through the window, a notion hitting him as he did so. He took out several gold coins the Foreign Office had given him and sat them on the windowsill. They'd be found soon enough.

He noticed an old crumbling fence as he made his way back up the hill. A tree was there, as were several downed limbs, one of them very large. He decided to move Theresa there. By the time that he got back to the agent and got her moved, it was growing dark. The sky was turning dark quickly and felt like it would rain. Using some downed tree limbs and stones, Cole soon had a snug little corner. He made a lean-to using dead tree limbs, as best as he could for the roof, not unlike what he and Phillip used to do building forts. By the time he finished, he had a fairly tight little hiding spot. It would not be completely waterproof, but close to it. If it got too bad, he could slip his tarpaulin jacket over them. He crawled inside their little hideout and, using the sticks and broken off branches he'd collected, made a fire using dead grass to start it. He didn't build a big fire and as the smoke drifted up through the limbs and branches, it would dissipate. Since he'd used only dried wood, it wouldn't smoke or smell that much anyway.

He cleaned the bark off a small stick and, cutting a piece of ham, he heated it up. Outside the wind was picking up and in the far off distance thunder could be heard. When the ham was dripping, Cole cut two slices of bread and then cut the ham in two pieces. Putting a slice of ham between the bread he handed it to Theresa.

"We call that a sandwich," Cole said smiling, "named after Lord Sandwich."

Theresa took a timid bite, chewed it up and then a bigger bite. "It's good," she said. "I didn't know that I was so hungry."

Cole cut a piece of cheese, and seeing crumbles fall he gathered them up. After eating, Cole opened her shirt where the wound was.

She eyed him but said nothing, appreciating his gentleness.

Cole was perplexed as he looked at Theresa a moment and then he smiled.

In the firelight, Cole could see the wound was closing over again. He cleaned out the bread pan and put water in it and then put it over the fire to heat. He let the water come to a boil and then pulled the pan off the fire. When it was cool enough, Cole tore strips from the under drawers and used them to bathe the wound. He pulled the wound open but only got a little pus from it.

"The warm water feels better," Theresa said.

Once he cleaned the wound, he took the crumbled cheese and put it on the wound, and then applied the dressing.

"A ship's surgeon told me that, for whatever reason, moldy cheese makes some wounds better."

"It feels better," she said. He thought, *It's probably the hot food and brandy*.

"I've a clean shirt for you," he said. "I'll turn so that you can put it on." When this was accomplished, Cole took the old shirt Theresa had been wearing and burned it.

The rain came about midnight. Cole was quickly awakened. Water dripped through his makeshift roof. They had slept four hours.

"Do you feel like traveling?" Cole asked.

"Now?" Theresa asked.

"Yes, we have to find a way to get to the sea. This rain will keep most of the patrols in, so we can travel with less possibility of getting caught."

Theresa made to get up and Cole said, "Wait." He put everything together and took off his tarpaulin and put it on Theresa. Almost immediately, cold drops of rain dripped down on his neck and back. He took the sack of food and other things that he'd stolen and put it all in the bag.

He said to Theresa, "See if you can keep this under that jacket." She nodded her reply.

Cole crawled out first, feeling his clothes get immediately soaked. He then helped Theresa out. The tarpaulin was so large on her that she could wear it like a hood over her head. Cole checked their little hideout once more, making sure that he'd left nothing. When he was sure of it, he used his foot to kick the little hideout down. It had served its purpose.

***

AT THE LITTLE FARMHOUSE THAT Cole had raided, the farmer and his wife sat wondering what had happened. Their food had just disappeared. They'd yet to discover the other things that Cole had taken. The father was playing with the little girl when the wind got up. The mother, remembering that she'd left the window open in the little girl's room, went to close it. As she did so, she saw the gold coins.

"Louis," she yelled. "Louis, it's a miracle."

She showed the coins to him. The coins were more than they made in a year. As happy as they were, they had to be careful spending them. It would not pay for news to get out that they had gold.

***

COLE HAD BEEN RIGHT. THE road was deserted. Theresa felt much better with the warm food, clean shirt and freshly dressed wound, not to mention the brandy. It was bad that the other agent had disappeared, but Cole had done a wonderful job. She followed his lead without question, and this was something she'd never felt comfortable doing before. She was a bit torn. She was used to men wanting her for sex. She'd even let a few have their way with her to get the information she needed. Those who had their way often regretted it. Some of them died in their sleep with a dagger plunged into their heart. But Cole had not acted the least bit interested in her sexually, even when her chest was bare on one side, when he initially examined her. Her thoughts were conflicted. *Was she no longer desirable*? Most men she had known would have been trying to seduce her, especially back at that little hideout. She finally admitted to herself that she would have allowed his advances, as tomorrow they could be in DuFort's hands or worse, Joseph Fouche. A thought came to her. *Did he like boys?* Several French men she knew did. Some even liked both. No, that was not it, she told herself. Her thoughts were suddenly interrupted.

Cole was speaking to her. "There's a path going down to the sea. We'll try it. Maybe we can even find a means to escape."

Theresa squinted, trying to see through the rain. She couldn't see anything; still she took the hand that he offered and headed down to the sea. His hand, she noted, felt cold. It dawned on her that she had his coat.

Tugging Cole to a stop, Theresa spoke, "You are cold. Take the jacket for a while."

Cole replied, "Not yet. I'm looking for either a boat or a shelter. We should be close to where our boat landed." Theresa nodded, and then followed as Cole continued walking.

They had walked another mile when Cole abruptly stopped again. A glow from a fire was up ahead. Who was it? Cole and Theresa walked cautiously down the narrow strip of beach. As they neared the fire, a boat that had been dragged up on the beach came into view. Higher up the hill towards the road, a group of men sat under a cave of sorts. It was not deep, no more than six or eight feet back in the hill, with the front open. There were four men there; actually three men and a boy, maybe a teen at most. Two of the men were in uniform.

Cole walked back a few steps and talked to Theresa. They had kept their pistols out of the wet as much as possible. There could still be a misfire, and that would not be good at a time like this. He had always been told that action was better than nothing. So with Theresa voicing her understanding of what he wanted her to do, he walked up to the fire.

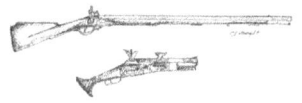

CHAPTER TWENTY EIGHT

T HE MEN AT THE FIRE were laughing and passing a wine bottle. They were busy telling each other stories of their exploits with the local mademoiselles. One of the men shouted, "Mademoiselle, c'est une pute." Cole knew enough to know that the one man had called the other man's girl a whore. It seemed like a good opportunity to get their attention.

"Silence," Cole ordered.

The banter was immediately stopped. The men, who had been looking into the fire most of the evening, could barely make out Cole, who stood across the fire.

One of the men stood up and said, "Qui es-tu, Monsieur?"

Cole only understood one word but Theresa spoke, saying, "Laissez tomber vos armes," meaning *drop your weapons*.

The man who had stood up shouted, "C'est eux," meaning *it's them*.

Shouting as he did caused another man to jump to the side, grabbing his musket. Cole fired—a misfire. The damp powder hissed and smoke came from the barrel, but it didn't fire. The bigger of the two men jumped out, hitting Cole square in the chest and knocking him to the rocky dirt. Cole felt his breath leave his lungs as the big man landed on top of him.

Cole fired his second pistol, more from instinct than realizing what he was doing. It misfired as well, but the powder flash such as it was burned the bigger man's face causing him to roll over and cry out. Cole felt air rush back in his lungs, and then the smaller soldier dove into his legs. Cole, still on the wet ground, got his knees under him and kicked out, throwing the little man into the edge of the fire.

Cole felt a burning sensation as the big soldier slashed at him with a small sword. Cole had gotten his blade out now and made a cross-the-body slash, having the satisfaction of feeling the blade bite into flesh and bone. Cole rolled away from the big man, who was coming for him again. Instead of rolling further away, Cole jumped into him. Surprised, the big soldier raised his blade. Cole thrust up, catching the man in the throat under the chin. The blade came out the back of his neck. Cole jerked his blade free and hurled it at the charging little man. The blade went in his mouth and out the back of his skull. When the man hit the ground, Cole rolled him over and, placing his boot on the soldier's forehead, he pulled his blade free. He wiped the blood off on the dead man's shirt and walked under the overhang out of the rain.

The two remaining men who sat under the overhang looked like a father and son. They sat still, staring at the madman who had killed the two soldiers. They were obviously fishermen. Theresa stood there covering them with her pistol. Blood was flowing down the back of Cole's arm.

Theresa spoke to the father, "You check his arm." She emphasized her words with her pistol.

The father looked at her and replied, "Your powder is just as wet as his was."

Cole hadn't understood what was happening when Theresa stuck the barrel of her pistol in the boy's ear and pulled the hammer back. "Ton choix," Theresa said, meaning "your choice."

The man held out a hand, "Non, s'il te plaît," meaning "No, please," he said.

Cole had a nasty gash across the back of his arm. They emptied out the bags of the dead soldier and. finding a shirt, they bound up Cole's arm.

Cole said, "Tell him to get the dead soldiers on his boat. The rain will wash the blood away."

"The dead men?" Theresa asked.

"Yes, and their belongings. I want nothing left here but the fire," he replied.

When everything was loaded, Cole used one arm on a pole to help push the boat off the beach. "Tell him to head for the Channel," Cole said to Theresa, who passed along his orders.

Once they were out in the Channel, Cole helped the boy roll the soldiers' bodies overboard. They had put rocks in their bags and sunk them as well. They were nearing the Goodwin Sands when they sighted a ship. Cole didn't think that a French ship would be this close to England, so he had the father signal the other ship by lighting a lantern and dipping it up and down.

When the ship came close, a lieutenant hailed, and Cole called back, "I'm Lieutenant Cole Buckley of the Prince's Own. I require assistance."

The lieutenant was talking to somebody. Cole called again, "My brother is the first lieutenant on the *Dido*, Captain Atwater." When he said this to the lieutenant, it decided things.

A boat was put over and they picked up Cole and Theresa. Cole took out three more gold coins and gave them to the fisherman. "If you get caught, tell them that I killed the two soldiers and we held a gun to your son's head. However, if you are not asked, I wouldn't tell." Theresa recited Cole's words to them.

When they were on board the ship, Cole spoke to the captain, only telling him enough to get him to do as he wished. The surgeon then looked at Theresa. He cleaned the wound and properly bandaged it. He said nothing about the crumbled cheese.

The surgeon then looked at Cole's wound. He cleaned it and spent thirty minutes suturing it up. Cole and Theresa were then given cots in the sick bay to rest until they made port.

Theresa looked at Cole, "I feel that my life is your life."

Cole smiled and said, "I'm glad we made it."

She came to him then and said, "Why is it you were not attracted to me?"

Cole took her hand. She was close to Anne's age but had been through hell for years now. "I am very much attracted to you," he said. "More than you know, but you are so much like my wife. I would have felt guilty had I touched you."

Theresa leaned over and kissed him. "I am lucky. They sent a good man for me." As she turned and got into her cot, she said, "Dors bien, mon amour," meaning "sleep well, my love".

Cole knew the 'mon amour' meant my love, but he didn't get the rest of it. He went to sleep thanking God that he was headed back to Anne. He'd had enough of the Foreign Office and sneaking around a countryside where he couldn't understand a damn thing the people were saying.

***

THE FRIGATE, ACTIVE, PULLED INTO Portsmouth where the port admiral approved a coach to London for Cole and Theresa. During the trip, Cole thought about Anne. He had not given her a time when he was to return but he knew that he had been gone long enough for her to start worrying. What was to have been a two day trip, three at the most, had turned into five and he was not home yet. Having been constantly in the company of Theresa hadn't helped either. She'd exuded a certain sex appeal, without even trying. *Damnation*, he thought, must he always be teamed up with beautiful spies.

There was one difference in the three women. While all of them were beautiful, each in their own way, Theresa and Josephine would kill a man at the blink of an eye, but would Lois? She had lived enjoying the finer aspects of life. She was a refined lady. Neither Josephine nor Theresa could say that. But with all of Lois's ladylike behavior, could she pull the trigger? Cole hoped she wouldn't have too, but Victor DuFort's continued interest in her made that outcome a high probability.

Cole's mind turned to James Atkins. What had happened to the man? Cole looked at Theresa, "Have you had previous contact with Atkins?"

Theresa had been reclining in the rear seat. She sat up, hearing the question. "No, I'm not sure after just the one meeting that I would recognize him. Why do you ask?"

"It almost feels like he abandoned us," Cole said. "Jules, the farm boy, said that a man was shot and they were still looking for two others. How did they know that it was only two others?" Cole asked.

During the time they were trying to escape, something had been in the back of Cole's mind. Atkins hadn't picked up on the use of peasants by their supposed guide, nor did he think it odd that the guide hadn't shot at the French soldiers, who were forcing themselves on the man's wife. Then there was Atkins's sudden disappearance. Maybe he was putting too much into it, but again, maybe not. There was something else bothering Cole. How did the assassins know which coach to follow in their attempt to kill Josephine? It was something that he'd bring up in private with Lord Skalla.

Chloe came to Cole's mind then and with that, the lawyer Chantry. He'd been to Chantry's office with Joe. The most capable man in the profession, Joe had said. If Skalla found out Chloe was what and who she said she was, Chantry would be the man to go to.

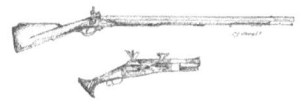

CHAPTER TWENTY NINE

HE COACH DROPPED COLE OFF at the Cock and Bull. Cole was surprised, but maybe Lord Skalla had taken pity on him, wounded as he was. There was a shriek as he walked in the door, and Anne rushed to him. She grabbed Cole's wounded arm, causing him to grimace.

"Your arm, you're hurt," Anne said.

"It's nothing major," Cole replied.

They walked into the tap room. Seating Cole, Anne went and got a brandy for him. *Damned if she's not turning into a regular tavern wench*, Cole thought, the way his wife went behind the bar and expertly poured him the drink.

Angus and Florence came out after hearing Cole's name. "It's glad we are to see ya, lad," Angus's voice boomed. As Angus went to slap his shoulder, Anne cried out, "No, Angus, he's been wounded."

After several minutes of well wishes and general talk, Cole stood up. "I'd love to talk longer, but I'm exhausted and would like to lie down for a while." *Especially to people whose language I can under-stand*, he thought.

Anne led Cole to their room and helped her man undress. Seeing his wound, her hand went to her mouth. The wound was at least eight inches long. What had Cole done to be wounded so? As she looked closer, she saw the bruises on his back and hips. He'd been in a big fight, she knew at once. He had obviously won, as he was home. She said nothing about the bruises. Instead, she continued to help him out of his clothes.

"I'll go get a pan of water and sponge you off," Anne volunteered.

"I had a bath this morning," he replied. "I just want you beside me now."

Anne removed everything but her chemise. If Cole wanted that off, he'd remove it or let her know to remove it. With just a sheet and thin blanket, she slid in next to her husband. Fighting back tears of worry, she snuggled close to her man. They would make love later, but for now they'd just hold each other. Soon after laying down, Cole was asleep. Anne went to slide over to give him more room but he pulled her closer and said, "No."

Anne thought that whatever Lord Skalla was having her husband do, it was having an effect on him. She had never seen Cole so drained of energy. It was near midnight when Cole woke up. Anne was next to him but facing the wall. Her hair was over her shoulder, revealing her neck.

Cole eased up on his elbow and began to kiss on Anne's neck. In less than a minute, she was moaning...Mumm. Had he seen her face, he would have seen her smile. His hand went across her chest and grasped a breast. He began playing with her nipple and it soon became hard and erect. He pulled her waist to him. He could feel himself getting excited. He pulled her chemise up over her buttocks and up to her shoulders. He kissed the lower part of her back moving up to her neck. He laid her on her back and she could feel him. She thought, *whatever he's been doing hasn't lessened his desire.* She rose up to meet him then, her passion matching his. *Damn,* she thought as her whole body quivered, *how could he continue to take her to such heights each time they made love*? He had never made love to her so passionately. She let out a sigh. She was the one who was totally exhausted now. He moved off her and rolled her on her back. He started kissing her face, eyes, lips and her throat. The chemise came off and he devoured her breasts with his hands stroking her thighs. The exhaustion gave way to a heightening passion, and they made love again.

"Where does your energy come from?" she asked.

"You," Cole said whispering in her ear. "I missed you."

"I can tell," she replied.

Their bodies were both clammy. He moved the sheet back, leaned down and then kissed her stomach. *She tastes salty*, he thought.

"Are you working up for another round?" she asked.

"I might be, if you think that you can revive me," he replied.

Anne rose up and swept her hair back from her face. "You think I can't?"

"You are not the question," Cole said. "A horse can only run so many races."

"Let's see," Anne said, as she started applying her womanly wiles.

Cole pulled his wife to him later, "You win."

Anne smiled, feeling a sense of satisfaction. She collapsed across Cole, her breasts plastered to his chest. When they woke up again, Sidney was singing to the milk cow.

***

KIN CHANTRY HAD A REPUTATION as the premier barrister in not just London but all of England. He employed twenty lawyers and as many clerks. New lawyers were known to join his law office for no salary, just so they could say that they had been instructed by the best.

Chantry had one weakness: horses. His stable was a palace compared to many homes. When he sought advice in regards to a horse, he'd consult with Peter Buckley, Belcastle's stable master. Cole, having met the famous lawyer on several occasions, felt that he would be able to see Chantry.

Cole and Anne, along with Mary and Joe, made the trip to London, bringing a reluctant Chloe with them. Angus had agreed to give Chloe the time off, saying she'd rarely taken a day off since she'd been there. Once they were in London, they went to the Earl's house and put their things away. Joe and Mary had a few odds and ends that they wanted to take care of, so Cole, Anne, and Chloe went to Chantry's law office. Cole didn't expect to see the barrister that day, but rather get his name on the books for an appointment. Entering the office, the room was wall to wall with people. The chairs were all filled and people were standing.

Cole pushed his way to the clerk's desk. The man didn't even look up, but said, "Yes?"

"I'm Cole Buckley and I'd like to see Mr. Chantry."

"It appears so would half of London," the clerk said. "Maybe you should write a letter and then we could get back to you in a month or so."

Irritated by the clerk's lack of concern, Cole reached over and grabbed the clerk's chin so that the man was now looking direct-ly at Cole and wincing from the hold on his chin. Cole smiled but didn't let go of the chin. "I feel like I have your attention now...do I have your attention, sir?"

"Yes," the clerk replied.

Anne and Chloe looked on in awe. Anne was seeing a side of her husband that she'd never seen before.

Cole was staring hard at the man and said, "I have no tolerance for rudeness and less for fools."

"Yes, sir."

"Now, sir, I want you to get up from that chair and go see whoever makes the appointments and tell them that Cole Buckley from Belcastle stables would like to see Kin as soon as possible."

"Yes, sir."

Cole emphasized, "From Belcastle's stables."

"Yes, sir." The man stood and when Cole turned loose of his chin he almost ran to the back. He returned very quickly, with his chin still a bright red. "Please follow me, sir."

Cole, Anne, and Chloe followed the clerk. After going through a door and turning down a hall, Cole saw the barrister. He was talking to another gentleman, maybe a senior employee.

Kin Chantry was a man of medium height. His hair was snow white and he was developing a bit of a paunch to his stomach. At seventy-six years old, the man still had the look of a man you didn't take for granted.

Chantry looked up as the man walked away. "Young Buckley," Chantry said with a big grin on his face.

"Mr. Chantry," Cole returned.

"I understand that you are in the Prince's Own Regiment."

"Yes, sir."

"I know that you didn't stop by to talk about horses, although my mare *is* ready to breed," Chantry said.

Cole replied, "I'll be glad to take her back with me and have her bred with Apollo."

Chantry's face brightened, "Would you, Cole?"

"I'd be glad to."

Chantry thought a minute, "Are you free for dinner tonight?"

"Yes, sir," Cole said.

"Good, come to my house by eight o' clock. We'll talk business and horses."

"Thank you, sir." Cole had noticed Chantry looking over his shoulder. He stepped back and said, "Mr. Chantry, may I introduce my wife, Anne. She is the daughter of Sir William Brabham."

"Deal's magistrate," Chantry finished the sentence. "And who is this charming young lady?"

"This is Chloe Hester. She is the reason for our visit."

"Splendid, I will see you tonight," Chantry said.

Chantry touched Cole's shoulder as they were leaving. Cole turned and Chantry asked, "What made you assault my clerk?"

"I apologize, sir, but the man was very rude, treating me or us, I should say," with his hand pointing out Anne and Chloe, "as if we were just street urchins."

Chantry nodded, "I shall speak to him as to how to address my clients."

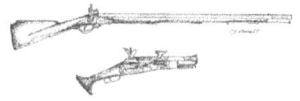

CHAPTER THIRTY

T HE MEETING WITH KIN CHANTRY had turned out well, over a tasty meal of pheasant with potatoes, carrots, and acorn squash diced and roasted in the pan with the pheasant. Apples had been sliced and were cooked around the margin of the cooking dish. A very tasty Riesling was served with the meal. After the pheasant was finished, a black cherry tart was served, with a sweet cream being available for the tart. Sherry was served for the ladies while Cole and Chantry enjoyed a brandy after the meal.

Once they got down to business, it came as no surprise to Cole that Chantry had known Chloe's parents. At one point, he showed some silver pieces to Chloe. She looked at a set of mugs and turned them over, looking at the Hallmark.

"Pitman made this. That piece over there is very old. It looks like a Paul de Lamerie," Chloe said. Above the fireplace was a beautiful picture frame. "My father made that," she said without even taking it down.

Cole thought he saw Chantry wipe a tear from his eye. "It was to frame a painting of my wife...of my wife and son. Sadly they were killed in a coach on an icy road," Chantry said.

"I'm so sorry," Chloe said, reaching out and touching his shoulder. Anne and Cole watched, both of them thinking it was a tender moment.

Chantry asked a few questions about who Chloe's father's lawyer might have been. He was old, Chloe remembered.

"He was a Mister Drummer, I believe."

"That makes sense," Chantry replied. "Jeremiah Drummer had an office not far from your father's shop."

When the ladies retired to freshen up, Cole took Chantry into his confidence. "My reason for being so interested in Chloe is selfish, although she and Anne have become good friends." Cole told Chantry that Chloe worked for his uncle's tavern, but was not the typical tavern wench. He told him how Phillip was madly in love with the girl but knew that Lord Bickford would never agree to the marriage.

"She is a charming girl," Chantry said. "It does not surprise me that she's not a regular wench. She has breeding. Her father was the illegitimate son of Lord Cambridge and his mistress. Cambridge loved the boy and set up a trust of one hundred guineas annually. I know because I set up the trust. That's something I need to look into. I will get back with you by Friday. Now, about that mare of mine and Apollo..."

***

THE NEXT THREE DAYS WENT by quickly. The women did some shopping, and Anne bought Chloe a dress to wear that night as they went to the theater. Cole and Joe sat behind Anne, Mary, and Chloe as he was able to get a box in the balcony. Cole and Joe had as much fun watching their wives and Chloe as they did watching the play.

The next evening they dined at Rules. The place was known for Dover sole, salmon, lobster and oysters. Several people known to Cole were there dining. A few of his fellow officers were there also, and none of them could take their eyes off of Chloe. The girl was embarrassed by the attention that she was getting. When they got home that night, there was a note from Chantry waiting on them. He had arranged an appointment to meet at ten o'clock the following morning. He had included some papers for Chloe to sign. One of them was a paper attesting to the fact that Chloe Elizabeth Hester gave Kin Chantry, Esquire her 'Letter of Attorney' so that he may conduct all legal business and proceedings for a period of up to her twenty-first birthday. Chloe signed the paper and Cole signed as a witness.

The day looked to be a chilly one, with the sky clear but a whipping wind from the south. After a breakfast of strong coffee for Joe and Cole, and hot cocoa for the ladies, the group ate lightly, having stuffed themselves the night before.

While Cole and Chloe called on Chantry, Joe, Mary, and Anne would run a few errands. Mary wanted a piano, and Monro & May, at 60 Skinner Street at Snow Hill, was the shop that was recommended by Dan Thompson in Deal.

Entering Chantry's office at a quarter to ten, the clerk looked up from his desk. Seeing Cole, he stood and asked Cole and Chloe to follow him. They were taken to another desk in the back where, surprisingly, a woman greeted them. She introduced herself as Miss Yates, Mr. Chantry's personal secretary. Cole had never seen a woman working in a law office. However, to be Chantry's personal secretary, she had to be excellent in her job. She appeared to be sixty with graying hair but she had a slim figure. The male in Cole also noticed the abundance of her breasts for a woman so slim. He also wondered if she might not offer old Kin Chantry more than secretarial services. He immediately felt guilty for thinking such thoughts.

Miss Yates introduced herself and collected the papers that Chloe had signed. She looked at a wall clock and asked Cole and Chloe to follow her. She took them to a small waiting area to wait until being called by Chantry. Another man sat in the waiting room.

When Chloe sat down, she got a better look at the man and then spoke, "Mr. Drummer, is that you?"

Jeremiah Drummer looked up and then smiled. "Chloe Hester, you've grown up."

"Thank you, sir."

Cole looked at the portly man. His eyes were bloodshot and the veins on his face spoke of his affection for either gin or rum. Knowing how many people in London had an unbelievable yet destructive love affair with gin, Cole guessed that was also Drummer's poison. It had not been very many years ago since gin was introduced. However, London now had seven thousand gin shops and dens. He'd heard his Uncle Angus discussing it with his mother and father. To the working class, gin had become more than a drink. It drove away desperate hunger pains, and it also drove away the cold and offered an escape from the brutal slum life. There was many a man that would let you sleep with his wife or daughter for a quart of the poison. 'It was a sad commentary,' Cole's mother had said.

When it was ten o'clock, Chloe, Cole, and Drummer were called to a room with a long table. Miss Yates sat to the right of Chantry. Chloe was seated next to Chantry on the left and Drummer was beside Miss Yates.

Chantry got right to business. "Chloe, your father was a wealthy man. Your aunt and uncle were given one hundred pounds initially to make whatever changes were needed to provide for you, and to provide you with an education. Apparently, none of that was accomplished. My investigator has found out that the money was spent buying farm land. Also, Mr. Drummer here has signed receipts for fifty pounds a year that was to be your allowance, but was given to your uncle. It has also been found that your uncle bragged to men at a local tavern how he was caught trying to molest you, but your aunt believed him and she set you out. However, they still collected your allowance. I propose to rectify that situation. Was there anything else, Miss Yates?"

"Yes, sir. It appears the aunt confided to the butcher's wife about having Chloe's allowance but that not having her around has made life easier for them."

Cole handed Chloe his handkerchief. Hearing the report had made Chloe heartbroken and teary eyed. Finding out that her aunt and uncle, whom she had loved, would treat her so unjustly was unthinkable. But it had happened.

"You will no longer have to work in a tavern, Chloe. Mr. Drummer here failed to fulfill his obligation to you and your trust by making visits and checking on you. He, therefore, has agreed to pay all legal fees associated with seeing you repaid for the illegally spent funds or make payment himself. Are we done, Miss Yates?"

Miss Yates replied, "All documents have been signed by both parties."

"Thank you," Chantry responded. "Now, Cole, if you and Chloe would stay a moment, the rest of you may leave." Drummer followed Miss Yates out of the room.

When the door closed, Chantry put his hand over Chloe's hand for a moment. "Young lady, you have been treated most unkindly. I know it hurts to hear how unkindly it has been, but that's about to change. I understand that you are in love with Phillip." He continued on without giving Chloe a chance to speak. "Cole assures me that Phillip feels the same about you. However, as a bar maid that love could never end in marriage." Chloe nodded her understanding, while wiping away tears. Chantry said, "What I propose is to make you my ward." Cole and Chloe were both speechless. "I thoroughly enjoyed you being over at the house the other night. I realized having someone in the house made me fill younger, more alive. Were you not a bar maid, but my ward, your chances of marriage to Phillip will be greatly enhanced. We may even take a weekend and go to Belcastle, so that the Earl will get a chance to meet you and see how charming you are. You don't have to decide today. Cole is going to take my mare to...to meet his Apollo. When he returns you can come back with him if you decide to take my offer."

"Why are you doing this?" Chloe asked.

"Your father was a friend. The picture frame he made was a gift. I should have been his lawyer but he knew that I wouldn't charge him so he used Drummer. In his day, Drummer had a bright mind, but drink has destroyed the man."

Chloe looked at Chantry. "I don't have to think about it, sir. I will accept your offer. I do have a few things to get in Deal, and a few goodbyes to make."

Chantry smiled, "Don't worry about a wardrobe. We shall take care of that when you return."

Chloe took Chantry's hand and squeezing it she leaned over and gave Chantry a kiss on the cheek. "What shall I call you?"

"Kin is fine. If the day comes and you feel comfortable doing so, you may call me grandfather."

Chloe kissed Chantry again. "Thank you, Grandfather."

Cole saw the old gentleman wiping away tears as they left.

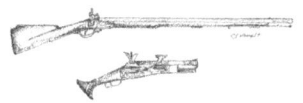

CHAPTER THIRTY ONE

A NNE AND COLE STOOD AT the paddock behind the Cock and Bull and watched Apollo act up around Chantry's mare. While Apollo was trying to impress the mare with his dominance, she basically ignored him. She was brought to the paddock in full heat and during that time she had allowed Apollo to be the stallion that he was. Now that the breeding cycle was over she showed not the slightest interest in the big boy.

They would return to London tomorrow taking the mare and Chloe. The tavern had given Chloe a farewell party the previous evening. Many a young man was saddened to see her go, not the least of whom was Dalton.

Lord Skalla had sent a message to Cole via Linda. James Atkins had been killed. While the news was very sad, Cole was glad the man had not turned out to be a turncoat. Linda had welcomed Cole and Anne over for tea. While they were there, she had related what the latest agent had said. The French Army showed no signs of slowing down or being defeated. Napoleon was gaining the reputation of being the best artillery commander the French had. This had been disheartening.

While they were at Linda's, Joe stopped by. He actually was headed to the smuggler's warehouse and saw Cole and Anne. Mary's new piano had arrived so the three of them, Linda, Anne, and Cole were asked to come to dinner the next night.

***

THE DINNER AT JOE AND Mary's house turned out well. The women squawked away, as Mary's father called it, while the men enjoyed a good cigar and then Mary played the piano. The woman sang several songs. It was an overall good evening.

On the way home, Anne related that she'd gotten a letter from her mother asking them to come visit. She had assured Anne that her father, Sir William, was most distraught over their not being around. It was decided that the next time Cole had to work; she'd go stay with her parents. Surprisingly a note came from Linda saying she needed to go meet Lord Skalla at the London office. Anne and Cole had mentioned taking Chloe back to London, so if Linda would like to travel with them, they would plan when to go.

"Apollo is not going to know how to act, losing his girlfriend," Anne said.

"He'll find another," Cole joked.

"You men," Anne hissed, but smiling.

Anne looked at Cole's wound later that night. It seemed to be getting better. Doctor Garrett had removed the sutures, and the wound had closed but the arm was still a bit sore. They woke up the next morning to find a coach sent by Major Letchworth waiting in front of the tavern. Cole invited the driver in for breakfast. The driver, who had made a few trips with Cole, gladly accepted breakfast.

"It has to be better than the swill at the barracks," he confided, causing Cole to smile.

The trip to London proved uneventful. They went to Chantry's house first. The old gentleman was glad to see his mare but seemed more excited to see Chloe. Her few belongings were taken to her rooms. She had a bedroom, sitting room, and one of the closets had been converted into a bathroom. Miss Yates was there to help Chloe. It was her job to see Chloe installed into her new quarters and then take her shopping. Once the women were out of the way, Chantry spoke to Cole."Chloe is now a landowner of two hundred acres with a house, barn and the extras."

Cole looked at Chantry and said, "That was fast."

"The facts were presented to the man in front of lawyer Drummer and the magistrate. He could turn over everything to the estate or go to Newgate."

"What happened to them?" Chloe asked.

"He is now a sharecropper and the aunt cleans and cooks at the local pub. The daughter is a bar maid at the pub as well," Chantry said.

"I'm glad that it turned out right. I was a bit concerned about reprisal," Cole said.

Chantry smiled at Cole. "That was addressed. Should anything happen to Chloe, the uncle knows that he's headed to Newgate."

When everyone had said their goodbyes, Anne was taken to the Earl's London house while Cole and Linda reported to Lord Skalla.

***

THE NEWS COULD NOT HAVE been more severe. In addition to the death of James Atkins, two other agents had been caught. Both of them had been tortured and executed. Had they talked under torture before they were put to death? The answer was not yet known. Neither of those caught knew about Henri or Lois. Lord Skalla was sending a man back that night to pick up the latest news. He was to make his way to France via a smuggler, but he was not to leave the city of Calais. Tomorrow was the day Lois would make her routine visit to the city. Hopefully Lois and the new agent would both return to Deal with the smuggler. If they made it back, they were to remain at Linda's house for three days.

Major Letchworth was to keep some of his men stationed about to see if any unknown visitors showed up. If so, they were to capture the spy and hold him until Skalla could get there with a team to interrogate him.

When Skalla had finished with Linda, he said, "A coach will return you and the agent back to Deal."

When Linda left, Skalla turned to Cole, "You, sir, are about to return to your regiment. Major Huntington will be promoted to light colonel. He is to take over the daily operation of the regiment. He has made it known that he would like for you to be promoted and placed on his staff. There is a captain who feels the distinct possibility of going to war is more than he had bargained for. I have arranged it for you to purchase his captaincy."

"I ...I don't know what to say," Cole began.

"Say nothing," Skalla said. "You far exceeded our expectations, so the purchase of the commission was a bargain. I brought you to London so that you may obtain the uniform for your new rank."

"I hope that I don't disappoint Sam," Cole said, a bit of doubt edging into his thoughts.

"Sam has no such doubts nor do I," Skalla replied. "I will do my best to drop by the Regiment soon. By the way, Catherine is in London at the Major...ere Colonel Huntington's townhouse."

"We will go see her," Cole said.

"Good," Skalla responded.

It was apparent that Cole's time with the spy master was about over so he asked, "One question, My Lord. How are Theresa and Josephine doing?"

Skalla smiled, "It's hard to be so closely entwined as you were with those ladies not to harbor some concern for their welfare. Josephine is doing well. We couldn't have chosen a better spot for her. Theresa should now be in Scotland."

"Why so far?" Cole asked.

"DuFort and Fouche have long tentacles," Skalla responded, and then opened the door for Cole.

Cole told the driver, "To Bickford house." He wondered as he got in how long he'd be able to keep the coach. He would surprise Anne with the news of his promotion. She could then accompany him to the tailor. Once they finished there, they could go to the Regiment. Hopefully, Cole's being dressed in civilian attire would cause no problems.

***

COLE SAW HIS OLD SERGEANT right off. The sergeant came to attention, saluted and said, "Good day to ye, Captain."

Cole returned the salute. "So it's common knowledge that I've been promoted?"

"Aye, it was within the hour of your promotion and Colonel Huntington's taking over of the regiment. Our good colonel let it be known the regiment would be whipped, and that be his very word, sir, whipped into combat readiness before the New Year. He said if any officer was in the regiment for any reason other than to fight the Frogs, he wanted to know before the end of the day."

"Any hint as to what my duties will be?" Cole asked. He'd already learned that if you wanted to know what was happening in a regiment, you asked the sergeant. "Is there any word as to what my new role is to be, Sergeant?"

"Aside from being in charge of a company, I think our new governor wants you to bring in some durable horses and not just a bunch of pretty high steppers," the sergeant replied. Cole laughed in spite of himself.

The sergeant kept Anne company while Cole reported to the headquarters building. Sam Huntington glanced up from his desk, and looked back at the papers on his desk, and then back up again. A smile creased his face.

He stood and shook Cole's hand and asked, "Have they turned you loose yet?"

"Not entirely, but I feel like it will be soon."

"It won't be soon enough for me," Cole's hrother-in-law said. "Someone fired a shot the other day when the horses were being exercised and half the lot went crazy. I remembered you saying how nervous some were around loud noises last year. We could never go into combat with the majority of these horses. I want you to see that we have decent horses beneath us when we are deployed."

"Any word on when that might be?" Cole asked.

Lieutenant Colonel Samuel Huntington stepped closer to his brother-in-law and whispered, "For some of us a lot sooner than for others. I will fill you in more when you get back. But Wellington would like to take a few companies of Dragoons with his infantry in March." Sam held up his hand to prevent any more questions. "Is Anne with you?"

"Yes, Sergeant Boone is watching over her," Cole said.

"I'll go out and speak to her. We'll have dinner tonight if you've no other plans."

"None, sir."

"Good, Catherine will be happy to see you both. I warn you, there'll be no talk of leaving. She can't understand the reasoning behind my trying to get the Tenth ready, only to leave her waiting."

Cole nodded. It was not an easy subject with most women.

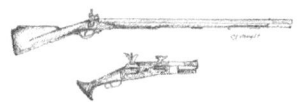

CHAPTER THIRTY TWO

HE SMUGGLER'S KETCH WAS NAMED the *Dorset*. The captain had made his landing just south of Deal, about halfway between Deal and Dover. It was not the first time that he had anchored in the area. Any further south and the going for the tub men would be too rough. He had taken on board mostly a cargo of spirits, which included some fine French wine and brandy. There was also some port that the ladies loved so much and a few hogsheads of tobacco. The *Dorset's* captain was smiling and thinking, old Angus at the Cock and Bull would be happy with this load. He wanted to light his pipe, but even with the promise that he'd not be harassed by the Customs boats, he didn't take anything for granted. He'd made a good bit of coin smuggling, but his purse had never been so fat as it had been since the war had started. He had taken word to a contact in France a few times and had even carried an agent across once. By doing so, he'd ensured that the *Dorset* would have a safe crossing.

He also knew that not every captain had been so fortunate. He'd done as he was told though, and had kept mum on this arrangement. He only hoped the war wouldn't end too soon. While his crew didn't know of his arrangement with the Foreign Office, they benefitted from it. He'd always shared the wealth with the crew, and there'd been more to share lately.

Tonight, after the landing was finished, they'd go back to France. When they got there they would tie up at the dock, get a good night's sleep and tomorrow night make the run back to Deal, and then go home for a few days. It would give the men some time with their families. One of his crewmen needed the extra money, as his wife was due to have a little one soon. Would he be worth keeping once a family had been started? With some, it made no difference, while many other men gave up the free trade.

A boat bumped alongside. A man he didn't recognize sat in the stern of the boat. No word passed as the man climbed on board the *Dorset*, and went aft to sit by the stern. Once the boat was brought back aboard the ship, they come about and set sail for Calais. Standing by the wheel, he caught the helmsman yawning.

"Keep a sharp eye," the captain growled.

They were close to port when a hand called out, "Ship to larboard, Captain."

A few lights were twinkling at Calais when the lookout got the captain's attention. The other ship was closing fast, much faster than what the captain was used to. It was a French gunboat. The agent who'd been sitting near the stern started to rise.

"Stay where you are," the captain advised. "If it looks like they are going to board, slip over the side."

The French gunboat was almost upon them when a voice called out in French, "What ship are you?"

"The *Dorset*, Captain Zackery Nunnelly."

The helmsman was striking the captain's shoulder and pointing aloft on the French ship. A man was hanging from the yardarm. It only took a moment for Nunnelly to recognize the man as the spy that he'd brought over last week. The man had been captured and must have talked. That was the last thought that the good captain would ever have. The guard boat had four guns per side. All four on this side fired at once. The captain saw the leaping orange flames belching from the guns but their thunder fell on deaf ears. The little ketch was no more...not a man survived. The explosion was heard in Calais. The usual corporal on duty at the harbor heard the explosion like everyone else on the waterfront.

The *Blue Pearl* had arrived only an hour earlier. The guard boat had stopped them as well but let them pass once Captain Lunn identified his ship and himself. He was sitting with the French captain drinking coffee laced with brandy when the explosion was heard.

The corporal stuck his head in the door and confirmed what they knew.

"Please Capitaine Lunn, do not let them talk you into bringing an unwanted guest to France," the French officer said.

Lunn replied, "Not me, my owner wouldn't risk the business association that we have."

"Monsieur Stephenson is a smart man. I think that he is smarter than his father," the French officer said.

"I agree," Lunn said, trying not to think of the times that he'd carried an agent in the *Blue Pearl*. In the future he'd do his best to get out of transporting spies. Hell, smuggling was risky enough.

The following evening when the *Blue Pearl* landed its cargo ashore, Lunn spoke to his mate. "Ask if Joe is working tonight. I must speak to him, if he is."

Lunn had to make a run north and it would be days before he could speak to Dalton in person. The guard boat had followed them out when they left port. They were, Lunn guessed, making sure he didn't rendezvous with anyone. When they were heading out to sea, they saw pieces of the *Dorset* floating. They saw a couple of bodies still floating along with the debris. The men grew very silent.

Lunn's senior mate sided up to him. "I don't want to end up like that lot, so I hope you don't intend to carry any more passengers, Captain."

"I hope not as well. But remember, Richard, we are at war," Lunn replied.

"If you do, you'll do it without me. Let the bloody Navy carry the spies," the mate responded. Lunn had to agree with him.

A boat returned to the ship an hour later and Joe was in it.

"Come with me," Lunn said. "Richard!" The mate turned to his captain and Lunn continued, "When the boat is loaded, let me know and Joe can return to shore in it."

"Aye, Captain."

Lunn took Joe to his cabin and poured the man a full glass of rum and had one for himself. Lunn quickly explained what had taken place. He then repeated the mate's recommendation. "Let the Navy take them close enough, they could get to shore on their own."

"Makes sense," Joe said, but he'd seen the government do very little that made sense.

The mate knocked and stuck his head in the small cabin. "The boat is ready, Captain."

Joe shook Lunn's hand and headed back to the boat. He'd have to tell Angus about the *Dorset*. Old Captain Nunnelly and Angus had been friends for a long time.

***

COLE HAD JUST LEFT THE tailor's shop when the messenger found him. "I'm glad that I found you, sir. Lord Skalla would like to see you immediately." He didn't say it but from his actions something most urgently had come up.

Anne's fingers gripped Cole's arm. She was already upset that her husband would be going to France and now this. She took a deep breath trying to control her emotions. *Damn, damn, damn,* she thought.

The messenger was on a horse, so Cole took the carriage from Bickford house. They'd been using the carriage the last few days.

"I'll wait in the carriage," Anne said once they arrived at the Foreign Office.

Cole replied, knowing that the place was likely under surveillance, "I think it would be better if you came in."

Seeing Anne, Lord Skalla ordered tea for her and told Cole to follow him. Once the door to his office closed, Skalla came right to the point. He told of the *Dorset's* sinking and the loss of the agent he'd sent to bring Henri and Lois Breeding home.

"We can only assume that the agent who went over on the *Dorset* talked under torture. He didn't know Henri or Lois's name but he did know who their contact was. You have to go bring her home."

Cole was stunned. He'd not envisioned another trip to France. "When do I go, sir?"

"Soon...as soon as possible," Skalla replied. "Take Anne home and I'll have you met at Deal with a ship to transport you." He looked at Cole and said, "Are you up to the trip, Cole?"

"Yes sir, I'm just a bit shocked. I wish James Atkins was going with me. He spoke French like a Frenchman."

Skalla smiled, "Take Anne home and I will send word to your regiment. I understand that you've been training horses not to be ...what's the word dammit."

"Gun shy," Cole said. "We are training those that we can and replacing those who have no promise."

Skalla nodded and said, "I will send word if something comes up."

"Thank you," Cole said, thinking Anne was not going to like this.

Cole looked over at his wife sitting in the waiting area. She hadn't touched her cookies, and the tea looked untouched as well.

She stood up and spoke one word. "Work?" Cole nodded his yes to her question.

They went back to Bickford house and packed everything up but his new uniforms. He'd not need them where he was going. Since the coach they'd arrived in had gone back, Cole realized that it hadn't come to mind for him to ask for transportation home. Skalla had already considered that though, and had a coach at the Bickford house by the time they were packed. In spite of, Skalla's promise to inform Lieutenant Colonel Samuel Huntington of Cole's orders, Cole wrote a short note to him. It was short and to the point:

Sam,

I find myself in the clutches of my other employer. He states that this is my final task. I shall return as soon as possible.

Cole

While Cole wrote a note to Sam, Anne wrote a quick note to Catherine. They were to have gone shopping that afternoon.

Catherine, dear sister,

Something has come up at Cole's other job. It must be urgent as we are leaving for Deal in a few moments. I'm sorry I can't make it as we planned. I hope to see you soon. Damn this war to hell.

Anne

The driver for the Bickford carriage was given the notes to hand deliver to Sam and Catherine. He'd only yesterday driven both Catherine and Sam to dinner with Cole and Anne. "I will make sure they are delivered, sir."

"I've no doubt," Cole responded.

***

COLE HELD ANNE CLOSE TO him much of the first leg of their journey. When they spent the night at a coaching inn, Cole saw Mercy. The girl remembered him well. She looked at Anne but didn't say anything about her not being Josephine. *Hell*, she thought, *he could be my husband for a few nights if he wanted. The man sure had a way with women.*

Cole was very polite to Mercy and told Anne that she had helped nurse Josephine.

"I believe that she wouldn't mind nursing you, dear husband," Anne said.

"Shall I ask her?" Cole responded.

Anne replied, "Not if you want to live."

They slept in each other's arms that night. They left at daybreak the next morning. The driver lit the coach's lanterns, as a heavy fog had set in.

"Hopefully it will clear soon," the driver said.

It didn't clear up so they stopped at the next coaching inn. They had breakfast and when they were finishing the driver asked, "Do we push on?"

"No," Cole said. 'I'll not risk the horses or an accident with a fog this thick."

"I could walk ahead with a lantern," the driver offered.

Cole thought, *that would offer little over all*. He knew it was the right decision to stop but Lois was on his mind. He was worried that he wouldn't make it in time. He thought of Josephine's friend and the cigar burns on her body and nipples. That had to be a very excruciating pain. Well, he'd already made up his mind: DuFort would die for what had been done to Josephine. If he harmed Lois, he'd still die, only more slowly...much more slowly.

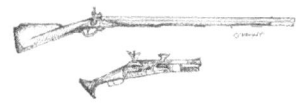

CHAPTER THIRTY THREE

As part of the Channel Fleet, it was time for HMS *Dido*, of twenty-eight guns, to return to Portsmouth to repair and replenish. The ship was in good shape, lacking only in water, fresh vegetables, and some fruit if any was to be had at Portsmouth.

Captain Atwater, however, dreaded returning to Portsmouth. By now a senior lieutenant would almost certainly have been assigned to the ship as first lieutenant. He didn't particularly want a new lieutenant. In fact, after facing a superior French fleet in the waters off the west coast of Brittany in June, the Channel fleet had suffered the loss of several officers.

When Atwater told Vice Admiral Cornwallis that he would promote from within the ship, the commander was more than happy to let Atwater man his ship as he saw fit.

The French had attacked the Channel fleet with twelve ships of the line and eleven frigates, while Cornwallis only had five ships of the line and two frigates. The British fleet had turned away the

French fleet, though they largely outnumbered the British, and it would not soon be forgotten.

When one of Cornwallis' captains showed no desire for new lieutenants, he was more than willing to grant the man his wish. He had enough calls from the other ships that had more need.

While the commander had listed those that had been killed in battle, the *Dido's* first lieutenant would not be long missed by the Admiralty. Someone would want to put a favorite son, nephew, or protégé in the billet.

Atwater dreaded this, he had trained Lieutenant Phillip Bickford since the first day he'd come aboard HMS *Diamond* as a mid. The boy turned into a capable midshipman very quickly. The boy had asked for no favors, even though his father was an earl. He'd shown a desire to learn and was willing to listen to anyone who could help him regardless of rank or station. The crew, especially the old salts, liked him. Because he showed them respect for their knowledge, they did all that they could to help him learn. Six months after coming on board *Diamond*, he had far excelled in his knowledge and abilities when compared to the other mids in the cockpit.

When Atwater had been given temporary command of the customs cutter, he was told that he could take a junior officer. He chose Bickford to accompany him. The young man, as first lieutenant of the *Dido*, had the ship and crew operating as a crack frigate. Atwater didn't want to see that changed.

When Dido dropped anchor in the harbor and a young lieutenant came on board with a message ordering him to report to the port admiral immediately, he was certain that he'd be bringing back a new lieutenant. *Damn the luck*, he thought as his gig tied up on shore.

The port admiral surprised Atwater. "Tell me, Captain, what do you need most so that you can return to sea?"

Atwater was caught off guard. "Ere...water, sir, that's our biggest need, beyond that, fruit and vegetables."

The admiral nodded, "What about man power? I read that you lost your first lieutenant."

Here it was, Atwater took a deep breath and spoke, "What I'd like, Admiral, is a junior lieutenant. My second officer has taken over as first lieutenant. Frankly, Admiral, he's done an outstanding job, so much so, that I don't want to lose him."

The admiral smiled, "Let's not upset your balance then, Captain. I have a number of young lieutenants I could send you. Tell me, Captain, would you mind a passed over master's mate?"

"Certainly not, sir, I welcome him," Atwater said.

Atwater knew that some captains didn't like having a man who'd once been 'before the mast.' But his first senior lieutenant, when he'd been a midshipman, had once been an ordinary seaman. The man had imparted a wealth of knowledge to him.

"I will always welcome an experienced man," Atwater told the admiral. "Is he someone's protégé?"

The admiral smiled. "Commodore Sir Gabe Anthony felt the man had what it takes to be a good officer."

Atwater smiled to himself. Gabe Anthony, the younger brother to Vice Admiral Lord Gilbert Anthony. Their father had been Admiral Lord James Anthony. A titled family but one whom had gained their reputation in battle. Sir Gabe was once called the bastard son. That was a long time ago, and those speaking the loudest then now wouldn't even be considered to clean his boots. While his father and brother had been flag officers of some repute, Gabe was the one who had won more victories and done more damage to England's enemies than any two of the better known commanders, including Nelson.

"Has Sir Gabe raised his flag yet?" Atwater asked.

"No, not officially, but soon I'm told. He is still in America or Antigua," the admiral replied.

"When he does I'd gladly serve under him," Atwater said without thinking.

"So would several others," the port admiral said. "Now, for your assignment, you will sail to Deal. There you will take aboard two of the Foreign Service's agents. You will take them to within rowing distance to Calais. They will leave the ship there. They may return the next night, or several nights later. You are to stay in the area until they are picked up but not longer than a week. If they have not returned to the ship within the week, we have to assume that they are lost." Atwater nodded his understanding.

The port admiral continued, "Very well, sir. Your orders will be waiting at my clerk's desk. Your new officer is probably lurking about the halls now."

"What's his name, sir?" Atwater asked.

"Levi LeDoux," the port admiral replied.

"Is he French?" Atwater inquired.

"He is an American. His grandfather was a French Canadian and his grandmother was an Indian. His father was Jacob LeDoux. He married an American girl. He was a farmer and fisherman. Levi appears to have liked the sea more than the farm. Anthony signed him on. Before long he was rated a master's mate with high recommendations to become an officer. One of the members of the lieutenant's board spoke to me and said that they asked the man a question and he didn't reply. They asked if he understood the question and he said yes, but they didn't tell him the prevailing wind or what type of coast he had. They made up something and when Levi had finished answering, they were all scratching they heads in amazement. He answered every question asked about seamanship. When asked a question about social standards, he admitted that he did not know the answer but said if he found himself in such a position he'd watch the senior officer and follow suit."

"He can think independently," Atwater said.

"Yes, it appears so," the admiral replied. "Now, make your needs known to my clerk. I will see that they are met."

"Thank you, sir," Atwater responded and picked up his hat and left feeling much better than he had that morning. Now he had to go tell Lieutenant Bickford that his job was secure.

***

ONCE COLE AND ANNE WERE back in Deal, they went to visit Anne's parents. They let them know that Cole had been promoted to Captain. Sometime later, when Cole and Sir William had gone outside to smoke a cigar, Mary sat her daughter down.

"Something is wrong, Anne, I can tell. Your mother knows you, so tell me."

Anne rushed to her mother and started crying. "Something bad has happened. I don't know what it is, but Cole is being sent to France to bring home an agent. Several agents have been killed and one is now in particular danger. Mother, I eavesdropped. I walked around pretending to eat a cookie and drink tea, but I had my ear against the wall at times and know they are depending on Cole to bring her back."

"Her?" her mother said.

Anne thought for a moment. "Yes, Lord Skalla said don't return unless you have her or she is dead."

Mary handed her hankerchief to her daughter. "Does Cole know that you know?" Anne shook her head, no. Her mother continued, "He must not know then. He can't leave here worried about you. There's nothing that can make a man make a mistake like worrying about his wife. You must make him a happy man."

Mary took her daughter's arms and held them in her hands. "You must make love to him like you've never done before."

Anne was shocked. Her mother was telling her to have sex. Well, why not, she was married.

Mary looked at Anne and said, "You have him leave so full of joy that he'll only think of coming home to his wonderful wife and not what was worrying his wife. If he's a happy man, he'll more-than-likely return a happy man. God forbid, if something did happen to him, you and he both will have the satisfaction of knowing how special those last few nights were together."

Anne smiled, "I love you, Mother. We have more privacy at the tavern, but when Cole leaves, I'll come back home."

Mary smiled, "I will look forward to it."

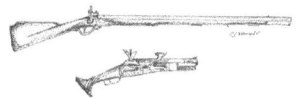

CHAPTER THIRTY FOUR

OLE SNAPPED AWAKE. HE LAY very still with his arm cramped by the woman who lay next to him. She lay on her side, but her still firm, young breasts jutted out. Would they be like that in a few years? He had heard women talk of the change in their breasts after having children. They no longer stood out ripe and proud, but tended to sag a bit. The more children, there was more wear on the breasts. Did he care if Anne's breasts lost their firmness? No, he decided, he'd love her regardless.

The sound came again. It was the sound that had awakened him. They had made love long into the night. Anne had been like a tigress. When he grew sated and was dozing, she'd awaken him with her hot breath on his neck, chest and going downward. Before long he'd be fully aroused again. When they'd finished he wondered if he'd have enough energy to even get up the next morning.

Cole eased his arm from beneath Anne's head. Looking out the window, it was still dark. He walked over to the window and heard men talking. He put on his britches, picked up his pistol and looked outside. There was nothing, so he eased out of the room and down the hall to the back door. He opened it and saw that there were two men unloading barrels. Cole smiled to himself. The smugglers had made a run tonight and Angus was having his supplies unloaded.

One of the men looked up, saw Cole, and froze. He whispered and the second man looked up. A third man that Cole didn't see stepped from the shadows with his pistol drawn. It was Paddy O'Hare.

"Sorry," Cole said. "I got to piss bad and could never get the hang of pissing in a pot."

Paddy smiled and tucked his pistol into his waistband. The other two men went back to work.

"I didn't know that you were out here," Cole lied.

"As loud as those two idiots have been, it's a wonder that Florence hasn't sent Angus out here," Paddy said.

Cole smiled; he was sure that Angus knew of the delivery and would have just turned back over and went to sleep.

"They wouldn't have woken me up," Cole said with a smile. "I had a work out last night."

Paddy smiled, "Aye, it's still a young blade, ye are, Cole. But with such a pretty young lass as you got, I envy you."

"Excuse me," Cole said, and took a few steps. His bladder was now truly in need of being relieved.

"Make sure that ye shake the dew off yer lily when ya finish," Paddy joked, and Cole laughed at him.

When Cole was finished and was heading back to the door, Paddy touched Cole's arm. "A frigate is offshore, Cole. It anchored not long after the lugger left."

Cole frowned, and his first thought was another press gang. He then thought, *the frigate was here to get him*. It was no secret to Paddy, who, like Joe, had been present on occasion when Cole had made some of his previous runs over to France. Cole knew that, like Joe, Paddy would not talk.

"It's better that ye go with a frigate," the Irishman said.

Cole nodded, "I'm truly sorry about the *Dorset,* Paddy."

"Aye, lad. We all are, but using the Navy may be best. At least, that way the Frogs will have to match a force that can give the same as what they receive."

One of the men unloading cleared his throat.

"We best be going," Paddy said. "We still have two more stops and these dullards are slow. Have a care, Cole. I want to see ye in your new captain's uniform." He gave Cole a slap on the back and walked off.

Two things came to Cole's mind. *So it's to be this morning that I leave,* he thought. The other was *how does Paddy know that I've been promoted to captain.* As he opened the door, Anne was standing there. She startled him, making him take a step back.

She smiled at Cole and said, "I woke up when you got out of bed."

"You shouldn't have come out," Cole said.

"I was checking to make sure that some wench wasn't trying to steal my man," Anne said, smiling.

"It was Paddy."

"I know, I recognized the voice," Anne replied.

Cole opened the door and the moon shone down so he could see that Anne only had on a sheer robe. "It's a good thing that you didn't come out," he said. "I'd have had to take on three men."

Anne smiled and playfully said, "Just so you know that I can be a wench me self."

Cole slapped her butt as she turned. "Oh, Governor, you like to play rough, do you," she said.

"Where did you hear that line?" he asked.

Before she could speak, Cole said, "Don't tell me. It was in a penny novel."

"Actually Belinda said one of Mr. Stephenson's trollops used to say things like that. She even liked to be tied and whipped with a strap."

"You need to stop talking to that girl," Cole said.

Anne turned, "I haven't much of late. I told her that I was sure Phillip was in love with someone. I didn't say who, though." Cole nodded his head. Anne turned to her husband and said, "I am worried about Belinda. I think that her father was a terrible influence on her. She never fails to say that she wonders what it'd be like to have a group of men ravage her body at once."

Cole was shocked and dismayed.

Anne looked at Cole and continued, "She could end up poxed and die a dreadful death."

"I know," Cole responded.

"I hope that she finds a good man soon," Anne replied.

I do too, Cole thought.

***

COLE HAD JUST FINISHED BREAKFAST when there was a knock at the tavern's door. Florence stood and said, "I'll get it." She was back a minute later, and Phillip was walking with her.

Cole broke out in a sigh. "As I live and breathe," he said, as the brothers embraced.

Anne was next to greet Phillip, and then Angus, as Florence poured Phillip a cup of coffee.

"I've come to get you, brother. We sail as soon as you can gather your stuff," Phillip said.

"I'll get it," Anne said and went towards their bedroom. She'd dreaded this moment and promised herself that she wouldn't cry but when the moment came she felt the tears start. She ran to their room and dried her eyes on the end of the sheet hanging from the bed. She smiled and thought, *if that bed could talk, it would put all the penny novels from Covent Garden to shame.* She picked up Cole's bundle. One thing was for certain, Cole would leave a thoroughly satisfied man. And truthfully, so was she. He'd given her as much in return as she'd given him.

She handed Cole his bundle when she was back in the kitchen. She then said, "Wait," and rushed out and returned with a letter. She handed it to Phillip with a smile and said, "To keep you warm."

Cole embraced his wife and said, "I shouldn't be gone long."

Trying to sound like Angus, she responded, "Then be off with ye, but be back before me bed grows too cold."

Phillip laughed, "If that don't hurry you back, I don't know what will."

Anne flushed, not believing what she'd said in front of everyone. Florence put her arm about Anne and said, "That's the way, girl."

Cole and Anne kissed once more and then the men left. Outside the tavern, Cole found himself surprised once more. Dalton stood there, dressed as a peasant.

Dalton smiled, "You didn't think that they'd let you go by yourself, did you, with your French being so terrible."

Cole smiled and put his arm over Dalton's shoulders.

***

ONCE ON BOARD THE SHIP, Cole and Dalton found a place so that they'd be out of the way. Captain Atwater had shaken their hands and briefly welcomed them aboard.

He then surprised Cole, "Get us underway, Mr. Bickford."

"Aye, Captain," was Phillip's reply.

Cole sat in awe as his brother barked out orders and the men in bare feet ran about obeying them. Some men went forward and started turning what he was later told was the capstan. He watched as a man yelled for the men to put their backs into it, and telling another man that he was a laggard. Other men went aloft while some others seemed to be pulling the yard arms around.

"Damme, Thacker, you move slower than an unpaid whore's drawers. Move it there. Watch were ye be steppin', Hardy, ye daff bugger, the cap'n's watching you."

Whack!! Whack!! A man was hitting the side of his leg with a rattan.

"Anchors aweigh," someone called from the bow.

"Make sail," Phillip called. "Let go, haul taut."

Chaos is what it looked like to Cole, but Phillip seemed perfectly in control, and before Cole knew it, the ship had turned, or come about as the sailors say, and was gliding across the water.

Cole knew the frigate was among the smaller of what he considered warships, but compared to the luggers and ketches that he'd crossed the Channel in previously, she was huge.

Captain Atwater called for Cole and Dalton, once the ship was underway, to report to his cabin. They were given a glass of sweetened lime juice once they were there. Cole had been expecting something a bit stronger but didn't complain.

A few minutes after being served, there was a knock and a marine sentry announced, "First lieutenant, sir."

"Enter," the captain responded.

Atwater got straight to the point, once Phillip was in the cabin. "My orders are to drop you off a mile offshore. My men will take you ashore in one of the ship's boats. We'll be back at the rendezvous area each night for a week. If you have not been picked up by then, we sail away and you are on your own."

Before a question could be asked, the captain continued, "Ships from our Channel Fleet are continuously peeping into ports along the coast, so seeing us shouldn't create much of a stir. We may even make a few runs closer inshore to drive the Frogs' attention away from where we'll actually rendezvous."

Captain Atwater pointed to a place on the map. "I'm told that this is the best place to put you ashore."

Cole looked at the spot where the captain was pointing and said, "I disagree."

Atwater and Phillip looked at Cole, as he continued, "That's the same location that I've always been put ashore. They were waiting on us the last time. My partner was killed and I nearly was." Cole heard Phillip take a deep breath. "Since then, we have lost three more agents and a ketch."

When no one spoke, Cole said, "It's also several miles from here to where I hope we will be met by agents."

Cole said pointing to the map, "Here is Calais. Between Calais and Dunkirk is a well-traveled path. About midway is a place where fishermen land. I'd prefer to be put ashore and picked up there. If necessary I could take one of their boats."

"I have no written orders that say I have to let you off at any particular spot, so I'll go along with your wishes," Atwater said.

"Thank you. I also have one more request. I don't trust our previous signals to still be a secret any longer. In the past we've used a lantern. I'd rather use a smuggler's system."

Atwater raised his eyebrows, "Oh!"

"I'd rather use a striker. Three strikes, say fifteen seconds apart. Your reply is only one strike. I shall be expecting it, so I'll not miss it. If I've taken a boat, it will be three quick strikes. If you see three long strikes followed by three short strikes, fire away as we are in danger," Cole said.

Atwater agreed and looking at Phillip, he said, "You have that, Lieutenant?"

"Aye, Captain, I have it," Phillip replied.

Once out of the captain's cabin, Phillip looked at Cole. "So it's not been all parade and claret."

"No, it hasn't," Cole admitted. To change the subject, Cole talked about Chloe.

After a while it came to him that even when Phillip was laughing and joking, his eyes and ears were on the ship. Cole also realized then how much had changed since the day they'd been caught watching the servant girls' shower at Belcastle. They had gone from frolicking teenage boys to men...hardened men. Damn it all.

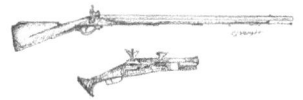

CHAPTER THIRTY FIVE

THE NIGHT WAS DARK AND the sky almost blue when the moon peeked its head around the clouds. A young lieutenant was in charge of the ship's boat that carried Cole and Dalton ashore.

"Levi Ledoux," the lieutenant said, introducing himself.

"It's nice to meet you," Cole replied with Dalton nodding his head.

Lieutenant Ledoux sat in the back of the boat next to a man, a seaman, holding the tiller. The seaman sitting next to Cole said, "First time the cap'n's cox'n ever took a boat 'thout the cap'n in it."

Cole wasn't sure of the significance of the remark but felt that it was a compliment. "Lieutenant Bickford is my brother," Cole said.

The man smiled, "'Ear that mates, we got the first lieutenant's brother with us'n's." All the men smiled but said nothing.

"Silence," the cox'n ordered, and it became very quiet.

The seaman leaned close to Cole and whispered, "Lieutenant Bickford is the best officer that the Navy's got. I'd sail with him anytime."

The conversation died then and, before he realized it, Cole saw the frigate had disappeared in the dark. Cole went to ask how they'd know how to get back when the seaman put his fingers to his lips. He leaned over so close to speak in a whisper, that Cole felt the man's hot breath on his ear.

"Voices travel a long way on the water."

The seaman looked back even as he pulled on his oar. "The lieutenant has a compass," he whispered again.

Cole nodded his understanding while thinking how stupid of me. The trip to shore didn't take as long as Cole anticipated. Of course, a boat load of seamen at the oars was far different than a fishing boat with patched sails and a crew of two to three men. As soon as Cole and Dalton were out of the boat, it shoved off again with hardly a sound.

"That was easy enough," Dalton whispered.

They could see a fire down the beach, beyond the big boulders, on the spit of sand where they had landed.

Cole said, "That's where the fishermen pull in at times."

"Think it could be soldiers?" Dalton asked.

"It could be, but it's probably only a few if they are," Cole responded. He recalled the soldiers that were with the fishermen when he escaped with Theresa.

The tide was coming in and the sound of the rollers breaking on the shore was a peaceful, lulling noise. Hopefully, if there were any soldiers about, it had lulled them to sleep. To go down the beach to the path up the cliff was impossible with the tide coming in. Therefore, climbing over the boulders, the two men headed up the beach towards the fire, hoping they wouldn't have to go that far.

It would be good to know when and what time the tide came in, Cole thought. *But the time changed with the tides.* They found a path by accident. They'd gone nearly one hundred yards when Cole stopped to speak to Dalton. As he looked back, he saw a path leading up the hill behind a boulder that they'd just come around. The path had a few switchbacks but came out close to the road. Cole and Dalton made their way along the road, and with a clear path and no obstructions, they made good time.

They halted in a half an hour, and Cole motioned to Dalton to follow him. They were at a place where he and Lee Bergevin had met their guide the first time that they'd had a rendezvous with Theresa. Following the trail between high brush and the path several yards, they made it to the drive at the front on Henri's house.

"Damnation," Cole hissed.

He knew that it had gone too smoothly to last. A candle was lit in the front of the house, and from that small amount of light, Cole picked out two sentries. The last time there had only been one. They walked down past the drive and crossed the road, and using the trees for cover, they made their way up close to the house. Pausing to catch their breath, the silence was shattered by a scream. The sound caused Cole's heart to jump. The one sentry spoke to the other one. He was shaken by the screams, it seemed.

Dalton touched Cole on the shoulder. When Cole turned, Dalton whispered, "He said that DuFort has just taken another fingernail."

Cole grabbed his hand reflexively. He took Dalton's arm and motioned for him to follow. They'd gone only a few yards when Cole stopped abruptly. A man was standing near the back door but was looking in the window. He had a rifle slung over his shoulder...another sentry. Were there more? With the man's attention on what was happening inside the house, Cole told Dalton to stay. He then darted across the open yard to the tree that he'd scouted out on the previous visit.

Cole felt a chill run through him as he looked from behind the tree. Lois had her hands tied and was hanging from the beams inside the house. Her back was striped and Cole could see dried blood across her naked back. He heard another scream and saw that DuFort was bending over and when he stood he had a bloody pair of pliers. He was thankful that it had not been Lois but felt pity for the man. Cole felt that they didn't have much time so with the sentry still looking in the window he darted back over to where Dalton waited.

"We have to do something quickly," Cole said and explained what he saw. "We need to get rid of the sentry and create a diversion."

A horse whinnied and Dalton said, "I've a thought."

"Let's get rid of the sentry first," Cole said.

Dalton watched Cole go back to the tree where he'd been. Once Cole was in place, Dalton got on the ground, making a slight noise as he did so. The sentry's head came around and he spoke. Dalton crawled a few feet and groaned. The sentry was looking at Dalton now.

Dalton, speaking in French, said, "Help me, I've been stabbed. Help me." He moaned, "Ahhh!"

The sentry, with his musket in hand but not aimed, took several cautious steps towards Dalton.

"Oh God, please help me," Dalton whined.

The sentry almost ran to Dalton then. He moved so fast that Cole had to dive to catch him. Cole clamped his hand over the sentry's mouth and plunged his dagger in his neck, hitting the jugular and watching blood spurt out of the wound. Dalton took the man's musket and laid it on the ground. He then took the man's feet and with Cole at his shoulders, they placed the man deep into the shadows.

"The ones in front?" Dalton asked.

Cole nodded and asked, "Can you throw your knife?"

"Fairly well," Dalton replied.

Joe had taught Cole how to throw a knife, and while he was in the Caribbean, he had practiced nearly daily. He had grown very good at it, but had not equaled Joe's ability. Joe could call his target and hit it while on a horse or riding in a wagon. Cole went to the corner and came up to the front on the house. The two sentries were between the front door and the window with the candle in it.

Cole didn't think that it was over twelve to fifteen feet to the sentry on his side. Dalton possibly had another five feet. With the sentry's back to him, Cole took his dagger in his hand and gave it a throw.

"Ahhh," the man moaned as he sank to his knees. Cole's knife was imbedded up to the hilt in his back.

The other sentry turned and Dalton let fly with his knife. The man either took a step or Dalton misjudged it. The handle of the knife hit the second sentry in the back of the head, knocking him down. As the sentry turned and stumbled to his feet, Cole ran up and clubbed him twice with the barrel of his pistol.

The first aspect of the plan was over, now for the second part. Dalton would wait a full minute, giving Cole time to get to the back of the house. After one minute, Dalton would enter the house from the front and Cole from the rear. They each picked up a pistol from the downed sentries. They also took the muskets and threw them behind the hedges. Cole took the opportunity to pull his dagger from the man's back. He wiped it clean on the man's coat.

Cole was soon in place and watched. Suddenly there was a crash of glass. Dalton had jumped through the window. The damnable door must have been bolted. When the French agent turned towards Dalton, Cole entered through the back door as silently as he could. One of the Frenchmen was standing slightly behind his fellow agent and had a pistol in his hand. He was about to fire when Cole pulled the trigger on his pistol, blowing off the side of the man's head. The agent in front tried to jump into the hallway, out of sight, but Dalton's ball caught him at the bottom of the throat. The man made a gurgling sound as he died choking on his own blood.

The last of the Frenchmen, the one closest to Cole turned quickly to face him. The man may have thought that he had a chance, since both men had fired their pistols. He was wrong, though. Cole had fired the sentry's pistol, but he also had four more charged and ready. However, a loaded pistol was not needed. Cole clubbed the man good with the barrel of the spent pistol. The French agent dropped.

"Lois...Lois...can you hear me?"

Her face was bruised and her eyes were almost swollen shut but she opened them enough to see through slits. She had been beaten with a fist and a riding crop, and there were marks where a hot knife blade was stuck to her skin, but nothing worse. Dalton lifted Lois so that Cole could cut the ropes that held her hanging from the beams.

Dalton sat her in a chair and then both men became very conscious that she'd been stripped from the waist up. Cole walked down the hall to a bedroom and yanked a blanket off a bed. He used his dagger to slit a hole about halfway in the blanket that was big enough for Lois's head to fit through.

"Put this on," Cole said. "Your back is pretty bad. Anything else that you put on would probably be too tight." She nodded but didn't speak. Her lips were battered and bruised, so it probably hurt too much to speak.

Dalton was kneeling beside Henri. The nails had been ripped from his fingers and then they'd started on his teeth. He had the imprint of a knife point burned into his skin near each of his eyes. The knife was still laying on the stove, and the end of it was a glowing red. A potholder was around the handle. Cole handed Dalton a glass of water to pour over Henry to try to revive him. They needed to be going.

When Cole leaned over to give Dalton the glass of water, the French agent must have come around. The agent, seeing the opportunity, shoved Cole into Dalton. Thinking that he could escape, he turned to run out the back door. Only he ran into the red hot knife that Lois had in her hand. The glowing tip set the man's coat on fire as Lois shoved it deep into the man's bowels.

"Feel the heat. Isn't that what you said, you snail eating swine. Feel the fire in your gut." Lois, saying that and using both hands, ripped up. "Scream damn you. There's no one who cares."

The man's hand sizzled as he tried to pull the knife from his body. He collapsed to the floor dead.

"Damn, Lois," Cole said. "I hope I never make you mad."

The sentry that Cole had slugged at the door, hissed, "Run... DuFort is back." He then fell to the floor as if still out.

"Merci," Lois said.

Dalton translated for Cole, "He said to run, DuFort is back."

Lois paused, looking down at the sentry. "He has been very kind."

"The horses are out back," Cole said. "Go, Lois, we'll bring Henri."

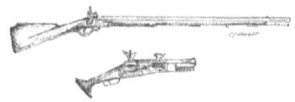

CHAPTER THIRTY SIX

L OIS HAD THE HORSES UNTIED and was leading them down a narrow path towards the back side of the property when Cole and Dalton came out with Henri. Once they left the trees and the shrubbery, the area opened up. Taking the time to tighten up the cinches on the saddles, they could hear shouts back at the house. Someone was cursing at the top of his lungs.

"That's DuFort," Lois said.

A glow was visible through the trees and brush, as torches were lit. Another shout came when they found the dead sentry in the back. DuFort shouted out more orders and men on horseback galloped off in the direction of Calais.

"They are going to get more soldiers," Dalton said.

"They haven't noticed yet that these horses are gone," Lois said.

"Let's move out of here before they do," Cole replied.

They moved out in single file. Lois led the way, even though she was hurting as she was. When they'd heard the news of the agents being caught and killed, she and Henri devised several plans to escape. Routes in every direction were scouted. Their plan had been a good one, only they were taken before they expected it.

"There is only one problem that I can see with the route we are taking," Cole said.

"What's that?" Lois asked.

"We are heading away from the sea and our rendezvous," Cole replied.

"There's that," Dalton agreed.

Cole stopped his horse after going inland for another mile. "We need to find food, water, and some bandages," he said. "Are we near any farms or villages?"

"We didn't go that far," Lois said.

Cole looked up at the sky, and saw that it was nearly dawn. Farmers would be getting up soon. "Let's ride to the top of that hill and see if we see any windows lit up."

Cole stood in the saddle, at the top of the hill, while Dalton held the horse still. He was able to reach a limb and climbed up in the tree. After a few minutes he came down, and said, "We are not far from a road. There's a house off to the left, and a bit further on are several lights that might be a village."

Remembering the man and woman that the soldiers were abusing on his last trip, Cole presented a plan. "Dalton, you and Lois ride to the second set of lights. Go to one of the places and ask to buy the things we need. Tell them the soldiers broke into your house, raped and beat your wife and now you are going to visit... make up somebody at a place you are comfortable with. Do you have coins?"

"Yes," Dalton said.

"Make sure that you rub them in the dirt to look like they'd been hidden. We'll ride along until we get near, then you walk and lead Lois's horse. They don't have any army markings, do they?"

Lois answered, "Not the two of them, they were Henri's."

Cole took the neckerchief from around his neck as an idea came to him. "Put the coins that you'll use in the neckerchief and tie it up."

Dalton did so, after rubbing dirt onto the coins.

"Damn," Cole said. "Your hands are too clean. Rub them in the dirt. If you see any mud put your hands in it to get dirt under and around your nails."

***

COLE FOUND A PLACE OUTSIDE the little settlement where he could await their return and still be mostly out of sight. Before long, Dalton came up the rise outside of town. Cole watched as he kept looking back. Once over the rise, it was not long before Cole saw two men following them.

"Henri...are you awake?" Cole asked.

"Oui," was Henry's reply.

"I have to leave you for a few minutes to go help Lois. You understand?"

"Oui."

Cole had tied the horses just back of the tree that Henri was sitting under. They all should be out of sight. Keeping as low to the ground as he could, Cole made his way down to the road. The men were walking fast now, since they were out of town. It would not take them long to catch up to Dalton and Lois.

When Dalton made it to the top of the next rise, he stopped. He could see both ways from that point. Seeing the men walking towards him, he turned to face them. That they would ask for money, there was no doubt. Dalton made a show of having none. The men were only a few feet away when one pulled a pistol. Cole had not anticipated this. If he fired from where he was, he might hit the horse or worse, Lois.

Damn it all, he thought. He stood up and waved his hand, hoping that Lois would understand. She did and backed the horse up. Cole now had a clean shot; only now one of the rogues had pulled a pistol and was speaking to Lois. *Hell*, he thought, pulling a second pistol from his waistband and cocking it. Did the sound travel that far or did the man see something in Lois's eyes? Whatever made him turn was the last thing to ever enter his mind. Cole's ball hit him in the chest, driving a button into his chest cavity. The thief's partner turned his back to see what had happened. Cole was aiming when Dalton's hand went around the thief's throat and jerked him backwards while plunging his knife into the thief's kidney.

Lois asked as Cole walked up, "What should we do with them?"

"Leave them where they lay. I'm sure the village people know they are a pair of rogues and feel that they picked on the wrong man and his wife. Leave their pistols where they lay. I haven't stepped on the road so the only tracks are yours and theirs. Keep going straight. There's a stream up ahead. Walk into the stream and then turn right and walk down it. I'll meet you there."

Once at the stream, they followed it until they came to a spot that looked like it would make a good camp. Cole climbed another tree but didn't see any signs of people as far as he could see. They had been able to get bread, two bottles of wine, meat, cheese, a pan, and some ointment and bandage material. While Dalton went to work on Henri's fingers, Cole walked a few feet down to the stream. Lois had walked down to the water as well. He stood behind her and helped lift the blanket off her head. As he stood behind her, she bathed her front, trying not to cry out in pain. She used a little bit of the ointment on a couple of places. When she had finished, Cole cleaned the caked and dried blood from her back. He bathed her wounds as gently as he could, knowing it still hurt. He liberally applied the ointment. He then took off his coat for Lois to hold to her front and then he dipped the blanket into the stream, washing the blood from it where some of the wounds had oozed.

"I don't think that we should build a fire," Cole said. "The glow, even from a small fire, could give us away."

"It's not near sundown yet," Lois said. "But you're right, the smell of wood smoke travels."

Dalton agreed in regards to the fire. He then spoke to Cole, "Your story worked like a charm," he volunteered. "A man who runs a small tavern gave us the wine. When I said that I had but a little money and pulled out the knotted rag to open and give them money, a man told me to put it away."

"The soldiers are all swine," the tavern man said.

It was nearly sundown when Cole checked the blanket. It was almost dry so he helped Lois into it again. He'd taken his coat and was putting it on when he saw one of the horses look up, its ears tucked forward.

"Shh!" Cole hissed. He ducked behind a tree and in some bushes. It wasn't a minute later that a man called out. Cole understood two words...Henri and Lois. The man walked into the camp.

"Jean," Lois and Henri both said.

"It is good that I found you," Jean said. "The entire country-side is up in arms. No one expected you to be this far inland. I saw the horse prints, however, so I followed them. You have done well. When I got to the village and heard of the man whose wife had been abused by the soldiers, I was impressed. Of course, I saw where your friend had taken Henri and the other horses around the village. You can tell your friend that he can come out now. I know he is there with his pistol and knife."

Jean kept talking but Cole didn't come out right away. He'd been betrayed once, that was enough.

Jean said, "I took the dead men off the road. It would do no good to have the authorities involved any sooner than necessary."

Hearing this, Cole swore to himself. He hadn't thought of that.

Dalton spoke to Jean, "How were you able to catch us so fast?"

"Once I could see the way you were headed, it was easy. When you went around places, I went through them. At the stream you went in, but you didn't come out. The water was a bit murky this way while it was not the other way. You washed in the stream," Jean said. "I saw the water and went that way." He had been speaking in English so Cole understood most of what was said.

Cole was just glad that it was someone he'd met previously. "Hello, Jean," Cole said walking out.

"Bonjour, Monsieur," Jean replied.

"Jean used to be a poacher before Madame Guillotine took away all the aristocrats," Cole told Dalton.

"Monsieur surprises me," Jean said.

"You forget that you guided Lee Bergevin and me once. He mentioned once when we paused to rest that you had been a poacher. 'That old poacher could run a horse into the ground,' were his words, I believe."

"In his day so could Lee," Jean said. "It will soon be time to leave, so if you need some sleep get it now."

When everything had gotten still and quiet, Jean sidled up close to Cole. "DuFort is beside himself. He has promised a large reward for the man who brings you in. He doesn't know your name, thankfully, but he plans to torture you and do what you did to his protégé."

"Protégé," Cole repeated.

"Hugo, the man that you gutted with a hot knife," Jean responded.

Cole started to say that it hadn't been him, that Lois had done it. Yet...he'd rather DuFort be after him than Lois.

"It was Pierre, in Calais, who turned Lois in. He was being watched, and once they saw that he'd passed a note to Nunnelly, the *Dorset's* captain, so they had him. When he wouldn't talk they started on his son, so he talked. They still killed his son, then Pierre. When DuFort found out Lois was involved, he was enraged. He'd planned on taking her to Paris to be his mistress. It was DuFort who hit her about the face. He was called away, and when he was leaving he told Hugo to have her ready to talk when he returned."

"You seem well informed," Cole said.

Jean smiled, "The sentry that you let live is one of us. He wanted to stop Hugo but he'd have been killed and we would have lost a valuable man."

"True," Cole replied.

"When we leave, we will go the way you are headed," Jean said. "Not too far away is a place with many horses. We will turn these loose there, and then head toward Dunkirk along the river. It will be easier travel, for both Henri and Lois."

Cole liked the idea, but as he'd been nearly captured once, he'd not let his guard down with anyone. It seemed as if Cole had just closed his eyes when Dalton shook him.

"Time to go, Cole," Dalton said.

Cole thought while getting up, *This is the first rendezvous we've missed*. He wondered what Phillip would be thinking.

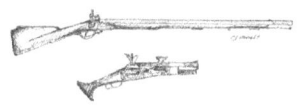

CHAPTER THIRTY SEVEN

T HEY MADE IT TO THE river, with Jean leading the way, a lot sooner than Cole thought they would. Traveling at night, as they did, lessened the danger of them getting caught. Cole had learned a long time ago to watch his horse for signs of danger. However, Jean taught him the ways of the forest. It all became much more obvious after they turned the horses loose in the pasture that Jean had spoken of. Before they got to the pasture, the saddles were hidden in a place where it would be some time before they were found, if ever. Dalton, Henri and Lois remained with the saddles while Cole and Jean went to release the horses.

"Use the time to rest and sleep if you can," Jean recommended. "When we return, we have several miles to go before we reach the river and a hideout."

"When do we eat?" Dalton asked.

"You eat while we walk. There are no taverns for a sit down meal." Jean had been very frank.

Cole thought that Jean was not as relaxed as he wanted everyone to think he was. At one point, they took a short break, as Henri's endurance was limited. Cole wished that they'd kept at least one horse, but that did no good now.

"It's quiet," Lois said.

Jean smiled, "Non, Madame, the forest is alive with sounds. You hear chirping, clicks, buzzes, hums, and wind rustling through the trees and brush. You can hear the scurries of small animals when a predator comes close. When the forest is truly silent, be still and watch closely. In the forest, nothing moves when danger is about. The animals have seen us. They see that we make our way, but we don't stalk."

Everyone was quiet for a bit and then you could hear something walking through the woods, stopping every few seconds. Lois gave Jean a questioning look.

"Deer," he said.

After five more minutes, they moved out. Henri's hands were swollen and red. Cole shuddered when he thought of Hugo, that villain, yanking out Henri's fingernails before starting on his teeth. Hugo was dead, thanks to Lois, but DuFort was still out there. Cole would not rest until they were aboard his brother's ship. Would DuFort send assassins? He had for Josephine. The woman had been very lucky. He hoped that Lois proved to be just as lucky.

It was coming on to dawn. The wind had picked up a bit and Henri was worn out. Cole and Dalton had basically carried him the last thirty minutes.

"Let's stop here so that I can get my bearing," Jean said. There were a couple of deadfalls over to the left. "Take Henri over there," he said. "It will offer some concealment."

Lois walked ahead, moving some down limbs so the path to the area would be easier. Once there, Dalton gave Henri a sip of wine, which was the last that they had. Cole sat down on a log, and Lois sat next to him. The trip had worked up a sweat, especially the last half hour. Lois fanned the blanket and the cool air felt good against her skin. It felt good to Cole as well. He scooted over a bit.

Lois, misunderstanding Cole stopped and said, "I'm sorry."

Cole looked at her, "Don't stop, it felt good." She smiled and started fanning again.

Cole, like any other man, had noticed at times, when climbing over downed trees, rocks, and such that Lois's makeshift tunic would open slightly, revealing the side of her breast. He wished that he'd thought and kept the reins from the bridle so that she could have tied the blanket tunic. If she'd seen him looking, she made no mention or tried to prevent it. *Because she is a lady,* Cole thought. *She knows we are trying to survive, and all else was secondary.* He'd do his best to be a gentleman.

"Let me look at your back when it gets light enough," Cole said. "If your wounds are better, you can wear my coat."

Lois smiled mischievously, "Is there another reason?"

Cole said, "Other than to give you greater freedom of movement, no." He smiled to himself then. "However, if there were a reason I'm sure you are already aware of whatever it might be, so there's no need asking me what is evident to you."

"Touché," Lois said still smiling. She had noticed him looking her way a few times and realized why. She did what she could to prevent exposing herself, but thinking back to the trip to France, lying in the fishing boat, their bodies entwined, he showed no signs of being bothered by their closeness. She now had the satisfaction of knowing. Yes! He was a man and was interested enough to look every chance he got. With the satisfaction of knowing for certain he found her inviting, was also the knowledge that he was a gentleman and that he'd protect her with his life. He was everything that

Linda had said he was. Unlike Linda, however, she had no desire for an intimate relationship with Cole. The memory of her husband was still very strong within her. She had said that to Linda, who had replied, "I was married at one time as well, but when I was in Cole's arms nothing else on earth mattered. He was not just some young stud. He truly made love to me in a way I'd never thought possible. When I dream, it's not of Matt, I'm ashamed to say. Maybe it's because Cole risked everything to uphold my honor."

Lois had listened and realized that Linda had been and still was in love with Cole Buckley. But like she said, it had been a dream, a dream that would never be realized.

Cole stood suddenly and put his fingers to his lips. "Shhh!"

Dalton saw Cole's movement and like his friend, he pulled a pistol. Lois got down behind the log, wishing that she had a weapon.

Jean walked up, not more than a minute later, "It's only me. We are very close to the river. At some point, I will go get some food, but for now I've located a couple of boats. Rest and when I get back we will eat and rest until its full dark. We will then take the river for a while."

Cole was glad for Henri's sake. Cole sat thinking of how good a cup of coffee would be. He then dozed off with Lois next to him and then Henri. They slept long and hard. The previous day had worn them out. Cole woke up, at one point, and saw Jean was asleep and he drifted off again.

Cole next woke up with Jean shaking him and saying, "Time to go."

**

THE BOAT TRIP WAS A blessing for everyone. Jean had distributed the food that he'd gotten, which was only bread and cheese but it filled their bellies. He'd found a boat that was suitable to carry five people...but just barely. The water was nearly up to the top of the sides of the boat.

Jean cautioned, "No sudden movement."

The flow was to the sea, so there was very little paddling needed. At times, sitting in the back of the boat, Jean would use his oar as a tiller and guide the boat. Cole took in as much as he could, never knowing when the experience might come in handy. At one point, they could see a fire on the riverbank.

"Duck down as far as you can," Jean had told everyone. Using the oar as a tiller he moved the boat over near the opposite bank.

Cole looked at the fire. *It was much bigger than needed*, he thought. Walking around the fire he saw soldiers. Jean laughed, a smirk actually.

When they were down the river from the soldiers, Jean said, "Soldiers from the city, who are afraid of the dark. They always build bonfires. They think that it will keep all the maneaters away." Jean chuckled when he said this.

The river had definitely been a blessing for Henri. Doing what little they could for his fingers had helped, but not having to use his hands to ride a horse cut down on the pain in his hands. His face was still very swollen, though. Hugo had not just pulled a few teeth; he'd broken off several trying to pull more. Henri kept his mouth closed as much as possible; saying the air made his teeth hurt more. His bread was soaked in the wine to make it soft and mushy so that he could eat it.

Cole had looked at Lois's back that morning. He'd cleaned away the drying blood. A few of the lashes were still oozing slightly. "I wonder what's in that ointment," he said.

Jean looked over and replied, "Usually it is lard, aloe, and honey. Sometimes if a woman or physician is knowledgeable enough of plants, they add more to it. They will sometimes add turmeric, which helps with pain."

The night sky was cloudy but the wind was nothing more than a breeze. Up ahead was the glow of another fire. This one was much smaller. Jean guided the boat toward the opposite bank where the trees created dark shadows hanging over the river, making the boat hard to pick out. Men were stirring around this fire, as well, and two boats were pulled up on the bank. One man walked to the water's edge and relieved himself.

Jean said, once they were past the fire, "Night fishermen, they are setting out a line of hooks."

Cole was thinking we've missed another rendezvous but, at least, we are traveling in the right direction and things were starting to look like they might actually escape.

It grew darker then and the wind picked up and it started to rain. *Damn*, Cole thought, *every time I think positive thoughts, things turn bad.* A half hour later the rain picked up and the boat was acting different.

"Too much water in the boat," Jean said.

Cole had watched as Jean tried to steer the boat towards the shore without letting the current capsize it. They were almost to the bank when Jean handed Cole a rope.

"Can you swim?" Jean asked.

"Yes," Cole replied.

"Try to swim ashore and help pull the boat in. It's a long rope but it will be a close thing. Wrap the end around a tree; otherwise, it will pull you in the river."

Cole handed his pistols to Lois and Dalton and then dove over the bow. With his weight gone the boat rose up from the water a little bit. Cole made it to the bank, waded ashore and snubbed off the rope to the first good size tree. For a moment, the boat turned sideways in the current, and then the stern turned and the bow was pointed towards the shore. He set to work pulling the boat ashore. Once they were close, Dalton jumped out and helped drag the boat up on the bank. Everyone else got out of the boat then.

Jean spoke, "Let's drag it into the trees, out of sight of anyone."

Once the boat was hidden, they looked for a place for themselves to hide. Cole touched Henri, and it startled him. The man was burning up with a fever. Leading the way, Jean walked into the woods. They'd walked no more than fifty yards when Jean stopped and pointed to their left.

"Stay here," he said.

Cole waited and watched. Fifteen minutes later, Jean was back. "I saw an old fishermen's shack. It's about to fall in but it will give some shelter."

Dalton and Cole helped Henri move and they finally made it to the shack. It was leaning badly and Cole thought if the wind got up it might blow over. Instead of using the door, they followed Jean around to a window with a hanging shutter. The floor was dirt and, at places, there were holes in the roof. It was better than nothing, though.

"How did you know it was here?" Cole asked.

"I didn't. I just saw where fires had been on the beach, so I looked and prayed."

"I hope that there are no vipers in here," Lois said.

Everyone turned to stare at her. Cole hissed, "You did have to say that."

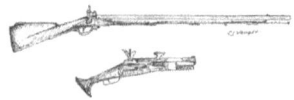

CHAPTER THIRTY EIGHT

THEY LOOKED AROUND AND FOUND a rat's nest complete with the rat. Running it out, Cole put it on the ground not far from the window. He put a small amount on gunpowder in the nest and used his pistol to create a spark to set the nest on fire.

They quickly added a few dry sticks to the small fire and it grew, with the smoke drifting out the open window. The rat knew where to build its nest as that was the driest corner. The fire was needed, especially for Henri, who was shivering so much that it caused his few teeth to click. A bit of canvas was in the corner so Dalton picked it up, running out another rat. He went over close to the window and shook it off. He laid the canvas on the ground near the fire.

"Lay here, Henri, it will be warmer," Dalton said.

"We should all try to sleep," Jean said. "We will take turns watching the fire."

"There's not that much fuel," Cole said. "I'll go get some wood. We can stack it by the fire and maybe when we need it, it will be dry enough to burn."

Cole, stepping out of the window, saw that the shutter was held in place by a leather hinge. He yanked it down causing the entire shack to groan. Lois gave a little shriek causing him to smile. Fifteen minutes later, he was back with an arm load of broken planks.

"There's an old boat out there," Cole said. "The planks will dry quicker than the limbs in the forest." Dalton went with Cole and they returned with their arms loaded down with wood.

"There's another bit of canvas that I can get," Dalton said. "It covered some of the boat so this wood is nearly dry." After bringing the canvas back, Dalton laid it down for Lois to lie on.

The morning sky awakened the group. The rain was now only a slight drizzle.

"We have to have food," Jean said. He'd gotten up and was looking out the window. "As long as the rain is here, we will burn the fire, but once it's gone people will be out and it will draw attention. I'll be back soon."

Cole went over to the window as Jean disappeared in the woods. There was a decided temperature difference away from the fire. "I'll hunt up some more wood," he said, speaking over his shoulder as he stepped out the window.

During the night, the heat in the small shack had dried their clothes, but they felt stiff this morning. The sky was overcast and the rain continued. Cole tore the rest of the abandoned boat apart and was headed back towards the shack when he heard voices. He rushed around the window.

"Dalton! Dalton," Cole hissed. The man looked up. "Voices! Recharge the pistols," Cole told him.

Dalton and Lois both set to work. *Something we should have done before now*, Cole thought. He turned and skirted towards the river, towards the voices. Soldiers!! He saw the uniforms. A boat was pulled up on the bank and several of them were looking along the bank for tracks or signs that someone had come ashore. Cole knew that the rain had washed away any tracks that they had made. If only they don't venture into the woods.

He glanced over at their boat. They had turned it over so that it wouldn't catch water. The wind and rain had caused a few small branches and leaves to fall and several lay atop their boat. A person would have to look hard to see it.

As the soldiers got back in their own boat, Cole felt uneasy. What had caused the soldiers to be on the river? He didn't believe it was a coincidence, not at a time like this.

Jean was at the shack when Cole got back. He was cleaning two woodcocks.

"I see that you got us a meal," Cole said. Jean smiled at him and kept cleaning the ducks.

Cole told him about the soldiers. "What are they looking for?" Cole asked.

"Who knows, maybe us, maybe someone else. No one knows which way we went," Jean replied.

Cole thought about that for a bit. "The boat," he said, "where did you get it?"

Jean looked as if he was in thought. "I took it from a place where many boats were along the river bank. Maybe it was missed and someone reported it."

Cole thought that made sense.

✳✳✳

THE RAIN HAD STOPPED BY the afternoon. They had eaten the woodcocks. They had tasted a bit gamey, but it was the first hot meal that they'd had in days and they enjoyed it. They'd been on the river better than an hour when Jean guided the boat to shore.

When they got out, Jean asked Cole, "Do you recognize this place?" Cole thought that it did look familiar. "This is where you met Theresa. Is she doing well?"

"I don't know," Cole lied. "I haven't heard from her since we got back to England."

"I'm sure that Lord Skalla has her and Lee hid somewhere," Jean replied.

No, she's not even in England, Cole thought. Why had he lied to Jean? The question had been simple enough. *Damn*, he thought. *I'm starting to act like a spy.* Jean and Theresa had been friends. Why shouldn't he ask about her?

Looking up, Cole judged it to be almost midnight or a little after. In less than two hours, they'd be at the trail that led down to the beach to where he was to signal the ship. No one knew that but him. Dalton was not familiar with the countryside. The rest of them, including Lois, only knew of the old place. Cole, for some reason, was glad that they were not going that far. Henri was about done in after an hour.

"We can rest for only a moment," Jean said. "We still have far to go."

"We may have to rest and layover another day," Cole replied. "How far is it to that den in the undergrowth?"

"An hour maybe, but we need to go past that," Jean said. "There's a place before the road to Calais."

"I'm not sure that Henri can make it that far," Cole responded.

"He must," Jean snapped.

Everyone turned to stare at Jean. "I'm sorry," he said. "We are close to where my friends got caught and it's been over a week since I saw my family."

Cole touched Jean's arm. "You have done well, Jean." The man smiled and nodded but didn't say anything.

When Henri looked up and said that he was ready, Cole slapped the side of his leg. "Damme, we need a lantern to signal the ship."

"Ship?" Jean said.

"Yes, they have decided not to use smugglers anymore but Navy ships," Cole replied.

Jean turned, "We should go."

Cole asked, "What about a lantern?"

"I will get us one," Jean responded.

They had walked another hour when Cole picked out the glow of a fire ahead. They should have already made it to this point, but travel with Henri was slow.

"Go on without me," Henri said.

"Never," Lois responded.

Cole was proud of the way she responded. She had spent too much time with the Frenchman to desert him now. They had quietly come abreast the fire down on the beach. Cole caught Dalton looking at him. He'd recognized the place. Cole shook his head no, so the words died on Dalton's lips. They continued on when they reached the point where they needed to go down to the beach.

"This is as far as we go," Cole said.

Jean heard Cole and turned. "Stop here?" he questioned. "We are not there yet."

"Yes, we are," Cole replied.

"They will be waiting at the other place," Jean said.

"Who, Jean? Who will be waiting?" Cole asked. "DuFort? Did you arrange it with him to be waiting for us there? Did you leave a note when you took the boat, Jean? Was that why the soldiers came down the river? You never did say where you got the woodcocks. We didn't hear any shots."

"I killed them with a stick," Jean responded.

"Maybe you did or maybe somebody gave them to you. Why, Jean? Why did you betray us?"

The man hung his head. "They have my family, Monsieur. They have already raped my wife while I was made to watch. My daughter, she will be next. She's only twelve years old. DuFort will turn her over to his men. My son will die."

"Where are they?" Cole asked.

"At Henri's house," Jean said.

Cole was torn as to what to do. "Wait here," Cole said. "I will arrange for the boat to come get Lois and Henri. We will then go get your family."

"No," Lois said. "I'm going with you."

"No," Cole said. "You must stay and help Henri."

Cole made the signal…Nothing. He made the signal again and got the reply. Without speaking, Cole, Dalton, and Jean started back down the path. *Is this a one way trip*? Cole wondered.

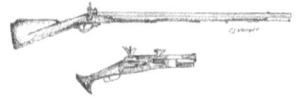

CHAPTER THIRTY NINE

T HE TRIP TO HENRI'S HOUSE didn't take as long since they were not burdened with the wounded man. Jean was not sure if DuFort would be at the house or just his wife and children. They went to the back of the house first. A man was sitting on the back steps smoking a pipe. Jean eased to the front but saw no one.

He came back to Cole and whispered, "No one in the front."

Cole looked at Dalton, "Think we can make it work again?"

"We can try," was Dalton's response.

"Wait," Jean said. "I know the man. Let me walk up to him."

Jean stepped out of the shadows. "Paul," he called. He spoke a few words but Cole only understood DuFort.

Jean went to go in the door and Paul turned with him. Cole threw his knife and the man grabbed at his back as Jean clamped his hand over the man's mouth.

"DuFort is here," Jean said.

Taking the man's weapons, they eased into the back of the house. The house seemed too quiet to Cole. He motioned the men back.

"Call to DuFort, Jean, tell him that Paul said he was here."

Cole took up a position across to the front room where Dalton had jumped through the window the other night. Dalton stood to the side of the kitchen where he'd be hard to see.

"Monsieur DuFort," Jean called out, and then he called again.

DuFort opened the door and shoved Jean's wife out and then had his daughter by the arm and he held his son by the hair. A man stepped out behind the group. He was still fastening his britches. Behind him were another man and another man behind him. Jean's wife and daughter were crying and the girl had blood on the front of her dress.

"The spies," Jean started and then realized what his family had just gone through.

DuFort laughed, seeing Jean's face. "We grew bored and decided to pass a little time away. What about the spies?"

"They're here," Cole said and stepped around the corner.

Just as he shot the man, the girl tried to pull free. The ball that was meant to blow his head apart didn't go where Cole had planned. It caught the corner of DuFort's left eye socket and took a large piece of bone with it. DuFort went down as Jean pulled a pistol and fired. His ball hit DuFort in the upper arm as the man was falling back. Cole raised his second pistol and shot the man behind DuFort. This time his aim was true. The last man grabbed the boy and pulled him out the window.

"Dalton, I think there's a window off that bedroom," Cole said. He knew there was from the time he'd slept in there.

Dalton eased out the back. Jean took his wife and daughter in his arms. Cole walked past them to the bedroom door. It was still open.

"One more step and the boy dies," the agent said in English.

"That boy is the only thing keeping you alive," Cole said. "Let him go and you can go free."

The man held a pistol in his hand but he was gesturing with it as he talked.

"Let the boy go. You can keep your pistol," Cole said.

"I don't believe you," he said.

Glass shattered at the same instant. The man's head turned into pulp as Cole heard the BANG of Dalton's pistol. The man was dead but Cole took the pistol from him anyway. Holding the boy's hand, they walked past DuFort. Cole couldn't believe it when he saw the man's chest rise and fall. The man was still alive. Cole pointed his pistol at the man.

"Let me," Jean's daughter said. She took the pistol and, holding it against DuFort's chest, pulled the trigger. The man's body jumped upward and then fell back.

Dalton came running back in. "Soldiers," he shouted.

Cole lifted the boy up in his arms and followed the others out the back door. As he neared the dead sentry, he rolled the body over and pulled out his knife. He wiped it on the dead man and hurried to catch up with the rest of the group. They stopped and watched the soldiers turn in the drive and then hurried across the road. They walked as fast as the girl could go and then they heard shots behind them.

"They saw where we crossed the road. Give me your pistols," Jean said. "I will try to hold them off."

Dalton laughed, "One man against men on horses." He then reached down and picked up the girl. "Did you play horse with your father?"

"Oui," the girl replied.

"I'm your horse now," Dalton said. "Hold on."

It only took a few minutes for the blood between the girl's legs to soak through Dalton's coat. He realized it for what it was, causing the anger in him to rise. He quickened his pace, determined to get the girl to safety. They were near the path down to the beach when shots were fired at them.

"Dalton," Cole called. "Take Jean's family down to the boat landing."

Dalton set the girl down, "You know the way better than me. You go with them."

Cole knew Dalton had spoken truthfully. He took out his pistols and gave Dalton the four that hadn't been fired. "Get behind the rocks."

Cole made his way down the path, with Jean's family behind him. The shots would probably alert the soldiers with the fishermen down the beach but he couldn't worry about that now. They were at the bottom of the hill when he saw someone running towards them.

Damn, he thought, *I don't even have a pistol ready to fire.* "Down," he hissed to Jean Paul's family.

He took out his knife and was about to throw it when he drew up. "Lois!"

"Yes," Lois said. Phillip was behind her with the sailors from the ship's boats.

"Take Jean's family to the boat. We've got to go help Dalton and Jean," Cole said.

Phillip and two of his men fell in behind Cole. He had heard several shots. He knew that Dalton had four pistols of his own and the four that Cole gave him. But what did Jean have? They made it to the top with Cole's breathing ragged, but Phillip's was worse.

"Dalton," Cole called.

"Yes," was Dalton's reply.

"Fall back, Phillip's here," Cole responded.

There were more shots heard, one ricocheting off a rock by Cole, the fragment stinging his face. As Dalton and Jean fell back, Cole saw Dalton trying to load his pistols. Cole took two and was reloading them when the soldiers started forward again.

"Pick out your targets," Phillip said. "Any man that misses gives me his rum ration for a month." This brought a chuckle, and Cole even smiled.

The soldiers were feeling brave since there'd been no more shots.

"Now," Phillip hissed, and everyone let loose.

Pistol balls buzzed into the rushing soldiers dropping several.

"Fuyons, fuyons!" someone called.

"They're retreating," Jean said.

They waited a bit and then started down the hill.

"Anyone wounded?" Phillip asked.

"No sir."

"Anyone dead?" Phillip asked.

"Only Frogs, sir."

Phillip took a few more steps and then spoke again, "Well damme. I guess I'll have to buy my own damn rum."

The seamen laughed again.

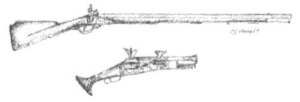

EPILOGUE

COLE, ANNE, CATHERINE, AND SAM sat at the table at Belcastle Manor. Phillip was due in that day for a week's leave. They were undergoing a quick overhaul and Captain Atwater had surprised him with the leave. Lord Bickford was a bit late coming to the table, as were Cole's parents.

Catherine spoke, "It's not like them to keep us waiting at the table like this. Father is always so strict about meal time."

The side door of the dining room opened. Lord Bickford came in with his arm over Kin Chantry's shoulder. Cole's parents were behind them and bringing up the rear was Phillip with Chloe. Lord Bickford called for some more place settings.

"Samuel, this is my good friend, Kin Chantry," Lord Bickford said. "I hope that you never stand against him in a court of law. He never loses. This young lady that Phillip has attached himself to is Kin's ward, Chloe."

Cole looked at his father, who gave him a wink.

During the meal, Lord Bickford said, "I didn't realize you had a ward, Kin."

"Yes, Charles," Kin replied.

Cole tensed. He'd never heard the earl addressed as Charles, other than by his parents.

"I'm sure you recall Chloe's father. He was a premiere silver-smith. I believe that he made the goblets with the Belcastle Coat of Arms. After Chloe's parents died, she lived with her relatives, but I felt she deserved more than she was getting. She's been with me a while now," Kin said.

A damned short while, Cole thought as he felt Anne squeeze his leg. The subject was dropped and the meal was served.

It came up that Sam had been promoted to lieutenant colonel, along with the fact that he was now in charge of the Regiment, even though on paper he was the third man down on the chain of command.

"Now that Cole is back with us, hopefully, we will have some mounts ready to go to battle," Sam said.

The conversation then went to Cole's promotion. Cole brought up that he'd had the chance to go on board Phillip's ship and how he had watched, in awe, as Phillip commanded the ship.

"You were the captain?" Kin asked.

"No, sir. Cole was speaking of getting the ship underway and ready for sea. A captain rarely does that. If he does, he has a very deficient first lieutenant," Phillip replied.

"Where does the first lieutenant rank on board the ship?" Kin inquired.

Cole was quick to answer, doing so with a smile and quoting something the new Lieutenant Ledoux had told him. "In the Navy, sir, the captain of a ship at sea is second only to God. Phillip, there-fore, is just one rank below."

The guests all laughed and Cole saw Chloe touch Phillip's hand. Cole asked if Chantry and his ward would be in Canterbury long.

"It depends. I am looking for the right mare for Chloe," Kin replied.

"We have some," Phillip said. "I believe that I have just the right one for her."

Later, after the meal, Lord Bickford let the others walk out ahead of him. Cole went to walk out the door, and Lord Bickford said, "Walk with me, Cole."

Cole slowed down and fell in with Lord Bickford. Anne looked back but walked on.

"Tell me, Cole, is this business with the Foreign Office over?" Lord Bickford asked.

"Yes, sir, I'm told it is," Cole said.

"It's my understanding that you've been used most unmercifully," Lord Bickford said. Cole looked at the earl but didn't speak. Lord Bickford continued, "I understand that were it not for your abilities, we would have lost more agents than we have." Cole didn't agree or disagree with the statement. "I have sources," the earl said. "I know you've had some close calls. Have a care, Cole. Neither your parents nor I want to be told that you've bee n killed or captured."

"I'll do my best, sir," Cole replied.

Lord Bickford responded, "I know that you will, son. You know, the last time that I saw Angus, he told me of this beautiful barmaid. It seems she turned every head in Deal."

"Yes, sir."

"You've spent a lot of time in London, Cole. Did you by chance run up on Kin?" the earl inquired.

Cole knew that he couldn't lie, "I did, sir."

"How did you find out who Chloe's family was?"

"She and Anne became friends, so she told Anne. When I heard how badly she said she'd been treated, I had it investigated. I found out that her uncle had tried to bed her so she was sent away while they collected her allowance," Cole said. Lord Bickford nodded his head. Cole continued his story, "We dined with Mr. Chantry. He'd known Chloe's father. Out of the blue, he asked Chloe to become his ward."

Lord Bickford smiled, "That was a while ago, right?"

Cole chuckled and said, "Yes, sir."

"So Phillip is in love with the girl," Lord Bickford commented.

"More than you know, sir, and in truth, for a couple of years now," Cole replied.

"He never mentioned it to me," Lord Bickford said.

Cole stopped and thought, choosing his words, "How does the future earl tell his father that he's in love with a barmaid?"

"I see," the earl said.

"Her father was the illegitimate son of Lord Chatham," Cole went on. "He provided for his son and thereby recognized the birth."

Lord Bickford looked at Cole, "Was Phillip going to present his case to me?"

Cole answered the earl, "I believe so, my Lord. He told me that if you didn't approve of him marrying Chloe, I'd be the Earl of Bickford."

"I see," the earl said.

"Look, he's showing Chloe his favorite mare," Cole said.

"He must love the girl," the earl said.

"Yes sir."

"Two years ago, you say?" the earl asked.

"Yes sir."

"Cole, I admire your friendship to my son, your brother. Remember this, Phillip's happiness, like yours, means more to me than titles," Lord Bickford said.

"Yes, sir."

"I would not have denied my son the right to marry the woman of his choosing."

"Yes, sir," Cole replied.

"Let's go on down with the rest of the people," Lord Bickford said.

"Yes, sir," Cole responded.

***

ANNE LET THE NIGHTGOWN SLIP off her shoulders to form a circle on the floor. Cole watched her every move as she walked to the bed. The sheets were cold so she snuggled up close to her husband.

"Will we live here in this suite, Cole?" Anne asked her husband.

"It was given to us for that purpose," he replied.

"There's more room here than at either the tavern or my parents," Anne said.

"We'll not be living at either of those places," Cole responded.

"So it will be here, after the war, I mean. This would be a good place to raise a child," she said.

"It's raised the three of us," Cole said, including Catherine and Phillip.

Suddenly, he rose up and asked, "Are you trying to tell me something?"

Anne smiled, "No, I was just planning for the future."

Cole put his arm around her, grabbing a breast and pulling her to him.

"You are through with the foreign business, aren't you?" Anne asked.

"Yes," Cole replied.

"No more saving damsels in distress." Cole rose up. "I have contacts," Anne said.

"Belinda," Cole said. Anne nodded.

Dalton had invited Lois to spend a few days at their place to fully recover. Henri went to Sir George's house to spend time with his sister and mother. Cole didn't think that Henri would ever fully recover.

"Cole, when do you think your regiment will go to France?" Anne asked.

"Next year, either late spring or early summer," was his reply.

Anne wiggled her little butt up to Cole, it was warm. "Cole!"

"Yes!"

"Make love to me," Anne said.

"I thought that you'd never ask," he said, as his lips met hers.

The hall clock struck midnight. Cole tried to put the thoughts of the recent weeks behind him. He hoped that Lord Skalla would take care of Jean and his family.

❖❖❖

A BOAT LOADED WITH ITS cargo came grinding into the beach's soft sand, back in Deal. The batman called out and the tubmen quickly loaded them up, front and back. Joe Lando stood watch with a batman at the top of the cliffs. He directed the supplies to waiting pack horses and wagons. As each wagon was loaded, they headed off taking their loads to pre-assigned places.

Up the road a bit, Major Letchworth sat with Sergeant Duncannon. They were there to make sure that nobody interfered with the smuggling operation below.

"It's a crying shame," Sergeant Duncannon said.

"Why is that, Sean?" Major Letchworth asked.

"We used to work our arses off to stop the smugglers. Now, we're watching to make sure no one interferes with the sods," the sergeant replied.

Looking up, both men heard the sound of a wagon approaching. "Unless I miss my guess, here comes the reason now," Major Letchworth said.

A wagon pulled up. The blonde hair of the widow, Linda, was recognizable right off. The other two people who got out were not known to the men.

"That's the reason," Major Letchworth said. "France welcomes the gold that our smugglers bring to the country. So we let them continue as long as they transport our spies."

"Some of them didn't do so well."

"Yes, but with DuFort no longer in charge, they'll flourish again."

"Aye," the sergeant said. "As long as they carries the Foreign Services spies."

"Stay here, Sergeant. I'm going to ride down and speak to Linda. If I'm not back when the spies shove off, go on back to the castle," the major said.

"Aye, Major, I'll do that."

"You have a good evening of it," the major said.

As Letchworth rode up, he greeted the widow. "Evening, Linda."

"Major."

"It seems like they're done here," Major Letchworth said.

"They are," Linda replied, and then she looked at the man a moment. "Want a nightcap, Major?"

"I'd love one," he said.

He got off his horse and tied it to the back of the wagon and climbed into the seat as they drove off. Joe Lando watched. *He'll not be Cole,* he thought. *But again, he wasn't a bad sort.*

Coming in 2024

Devil Boats, a novel of the officers and men in wooden PT boats, who braved the elements and the fury of the Japanese Navy, in the South Pacific during World War II.